"We should go," Alistair said finally.

"Yes, we really should."

Neither of them made any move to leave, even though the thunder issued another warning. The intruding people rushed past, in a hurry to find shelter.

"This is improper."

"An egregious violation of propriety," Amelia agreed.

"You are trouble."

"And you like it," she blurted out. But she meant *And you like me*.

He was serious for a moment—agonies—and then his lips drew up into a seductive smile.

"Yes, yes I do," he said. She knew he really meant that he liked her. *He liked her!* The truth of it made her warm up from the inside out. Not many gentlemen liked her—she was too imprudent, impudent, improper, just too much.

But this man liked her.

Gad, she was surely starting to fall for him now.

By Maya Rodale

Keeping Up with the Cavendishes
CHASING LADY AMELIA
LADY BRIDGET'S DIARY

Bad Boys and Wallflowers Series
WHAT A WALLFLOWER WANTS
THE BAD BOY BILLIONAIRE: WHAT A GIRL WANTS
THE BAD BOY BILLIONAIRE'S GIRL GONE WILD
WALLFLOWER GONE WILD
THE BAD BOY BILLIONAIRE'S WICKED ARRANGEMENT
THE WICKED WALLFLOWER

The Writing Girl Romance Series
SEDUCING MR. KNIGHTLY
THE TATTOOED DUKE
A TALE OF TWO LOVERS
A GROOM OF ONE'S OWN
THREE SCHEMES AND A SCANDAL

MAYA RODALE

Chasing Lady Amelia

KEEPING UP WITH THE CAVENDISHES

AVONBOOKS

An Imprint of HarperCollinsPublishers

Excerpt from *Lady Claire Is All That* copyright © 2017 by Maya Rodale.

CHASING LADY AMELIA. Copyright © 2016 by Maya Rodale. All rights reserved. Printed in the United States of America. No part of this book may be used or reproduced in any manner whatsoever without written permission except in the case of brief quotations embodied in critical articles and reviews. For information, address HarperCollins Publishers, 195 Broadway, New York, NY 10007.

First Avon Books mass market printing: July 2016

ISBN 978-0-06238676-2

Avon Trademark Reg. U.S. Pat. Off. and in Other Countries, Marca Registrada, Hecho en U.S.A.
Avon, Avon Books, and the Avon logo are trademarks of Harper-Collins Publishers.
HarperCollins® is a registered trademark of HarperCollins Publishers.

16 17 18 19 20   OPM   10 9 8 7 6 5 4 3 2 1

For my family.

Acknowledgments

Thank you to everyone at Avon for all their work to get my books out in the world! Thanks to Tony for help scheming and plotting.

Chasing
Lady Amelia

FASHIONABLE INTELLIGENCE
BY A LADY OF DISTINCTION

This is certainly the most exciting season in recent memory, thanks to the arrival of the Cavendish family.

If you haven't heard all about them— perhaps because you have been rusticating in the country, or gallivanting around the Continent—this author shall fill you in on the most shocking turn of events. The new Duke of Durham is *American*. Even more scandalous— yes, do fetch your smelling salts—this American is a horse-thieving horse breeder. Or shall we say *was*; he is a duke now.

How, you must be wondering, could such a thing occur? Once upon a time—a few decades ago—the fifth duke's younger brother absconded with the family's prize stallion, married an American and set up a farm in Maryland, where he proceeded to raise horses . . . and four children.

His son is now the seventh duke. His three sisters are of marriageable age. All of them are prone to trouble, but one more so than any other . . .

Chapter 1

In which our heroine causes a scandal. Again.

Almack's Assembly Rooms
London, 1824
Shortly after midnight

*I*t was in the illustrious and exclusive Almack's assembly rooms that Lady Amelia Cavendish, previously of America and presently of England, officially confirmed that having one's brother inherit a dukedom was not all it was cracked up to be, in part because she was not permitted to use phrases such as *cracked up*.

In fact, there was very little for a duke's sister to do, other than look pretty, speak about the weather, or get herself married.

These things held no appeal for Lady Amelia, beloved younger sister to the new duke of Durham.

After weeks, and days and hours of biting her tongue and minding her manners, she had officially reached her very last nerve, the end of her rope, her wit's end.

It was yet another evening in which she and her two sisters, one brother and their aunt, the Duchess of Durham, had spent their time circling the room speaking with Lady This or Lord That—Amelia couldn't be bothered to learn all the names and titles of the British aristocracy, as it went against her independent American nature.

Of all the balls, routs, soirees she and her siblings had attended, this one had reached unparalleled levels of tedium.

The duchess made a point of introducing the sisters to eligible gentlemen. She had made it her life's mission to see them all wed sooner rather than later, and to Englishmen deemed "suitable," which more often than not meant "horrible" in Amelia's book.

She rather thought that sticking forks in her eye would be a vastly preferable activity. Not that sisters of dukes ever committed such acts, but if they did, they would *surely* use the good silver.

As Amelia loitered along the perimeter of the ballroom, trailing behind the duchess, who was on the prowl for potential husbands, she amused herself (barely) by debating what, exactly, had pushed her toward the edge this evening.

There was the fact that they now spent *every* evening attending at least one or two balls, dinners, soirees, musicales, and the like. The fact that she'd had to spend the day diligently being taught the finer points of etiquette, forms of address, and steps to country dances. There was the fact that this evening alone she had been introduced to no fewer than six gentlemen who wished only to talk about the weather and look down her bodice.

It was enough to make any girl mad with boredom. Or just plain mad.

And now her satin slippers pinched her toes, the whalebone of her corset dug into her skin, and her maid had certainly used an excess of hairpins, all of which seemed to be poking sharply into her scalp. In an advanced state of physical discomfort, she was in no mood to endure the same conversation, *again*, about the weather (it was clement), the social season (it was tedious), her prospective suitors (or lack thereof) and the frequency of attacks from native tribes in America (not nearly as much as the English imagined), and "sly" digs at her brother's former occupation as a horse breeder and trainer.

Never mind the fact that she and her siblings had been in England for weeks, days, and hours and she had yet to visit the British Museum, stroll through the gardens at Vauxhall, or attend a show at Astley's Amphitheatre.

But she'd had a *marvelously* thorough tour of the ballrooms and drawing rooms of London.

"Smile, Lady Amelia," the duchess murmured in her polite do-as-I-say voice. One of her sisters would have punctuated the command with a pointy elbow to the ribs, but the duchess would never do something so crass.

Her Grace, the Duchess of Durham, Amelia had quickly discovered, was Something Else. She was one of those small, frail, wispy, and pale ladies of middle age who seemed like they might be blown away and be dashed to bits against the cobblestones.

And yet.

Josephine Marie Cavendish, Her Grace, the Duchess of Durham, was made of strong stuff, like steel or granite or glaciers. Her gaze was sharp and missed nothing. Her wits were sharper. She was also graceful, elegant, and unfailing polite and proper at every hour of the day. The duchess knew every person one needed to know, and everyone in London seemed to fear her.

One did *not* call her Josie. Amelia had asked and was treated to a frosty "One does not."

The duchess also had the sort of indomitable will that could command armies. Amelia would have adored her if she weren't so vexed by her most of the time.

The Cavendish siblings—James, Claire, Bridget,

and Amelia, newly arrived from America—were Josephine's army.

Her mission: to find husbands for each of the girls and to ensure that James, the new duke, settled into his role, wed, and had an heir, thus securing the dukedom for another generation.

Her one impossibly insubordinate foot solider: Amelia.

The duchess had a sharp mind, but so did Amelia. The duchess had very firm opinions, and by God so did Amelia. The duchess was accustomed to having her way. And as the youngest sibling, so was Amelia.

In order to potentially find a fleeting moment of amusement, Amelia decided to obey the duchess's command to smile.

She stretched her features into a grin designed to be more comedic than pleasant. It only deepened with genuine amusement when some poncey, overstuffed lord caught a glimpse, dropped his jaw, and turned away. Ha!

"You look like a gargoyle," James said, laughing.

With merely a glance, the duchess conveyed that dukes did not intimate a resemblance between young ladies and hideous creatures.

"Perhaps try smiling a bit less, Lady Amelia."

Amelia did her best impression of a simpering English lady. She'd had plenty of occasions to practice the vacant smile, letting her eyes cross ever so slightly while swaying delicately on her feet, which were presently tormented by these tremendously uncomfortable slippers.

Perhaps she could slip them off under her dress and no one would notice?

She carefully slid one foot out, then the other, and smiled at the relief of being able to wiggle her toes and feel her feet flat on the floor.

"Much better," the duchess murmured. "Now let us take another turn about the room."

"Ah, Lady Nansen. Lord Nansen!" The duchess and her charges paused before a couple that looked just like all the others Amelia had been introduced to: they were of an indeterminate middle age, decked in an array of brightly colored silks and satins, and honestly, a bit jowly and gray.

"I haven't yet introduced you to my nephew and nieces."

"And we have been dying to make their acquaintance," Lady Nansen said, fanning herself furiously. "The ton has spoken of nothing else."

The duchess performed the introductions. Upon meeting James, the new duke, fawning ensued.

Everyone fawned over James these days—but then when his back was turned they whispered about how his father was a horse thief and that James had been raised in the stables and how tragic it was that Durham was now in his hands.

"And Lady Claire."

Amelia watched as they took in Claire's spectacles and her distracted, impatient demeanor. She had *not* mastered the slightly vacant look of a simpering miss and with a brain as sharp as hers, never would. Amelia watched as Lady Nansen decided that Claire would never be an "incomparable," or whatever they called the popular girls of the ton, and flitted her attention to the next sister.

"Lady Bridget."

Amelia watched as her middle sister glided into an elegant curtsy. The duchess beamed. Lady Nansen judged.

"Your practicing is paying off," Amelia murmured. She'd caught Bridget curtsying in front of the mirror in the ballroom for an hour last Thursday.

"Do shut up, Amelia," Bridget said through gritted teeth. Unlike the other Cavendish siblings, Bridget actually cared about fitting in here. She was obsessed with learning and following the rules.

"And Lady Amelia."

She gave a smile somewhere between gargoyle and simpering miss, but perhaps more on the gargoyle side of the spectrum.

"You must have your hands full, Duchess, trying to make so many matches."

"It does give one something to do all day," the

duchess replied, with a tight-lipped smile that Amelia dubbed the One Where I Am Smiling Even Though I Hate What You Just Said. "But I do have every confidence that they will make splendid matches. In fact, I have someone special in mind for Lady Amelia this evening."

The duchess beamed at her charges, as if they hadn't been foiling her every effort to marry them off. Amelia began to dread meeting "someone special."

"I say, Duke," Lord Nonesuch or whatever began, "do you have an opinion on any of the horses running Ascot?"

The lords always asked James for his opinion on which horse would win a race, so they might win a wager. And then they turned around and made snide remarks about his experience raising and training horses—as if he were beneath them because of this knowledge. Even though he now outranked them.

"I do," James said, smiling easily.

"Don't suppose you'd tell a friend who you think will be the winner?" Lord Nansen or Nancy said jovially, with a wink and a nudge.

"I might," James replied.

This was a conversation he'd had before and Amelia had begged him to do something nefarious, like deliberately suggest a losing horse. But James refused and just smiled like he knew the winner and never said a word.

"I suppose you're going to build up Durham's stables," his lordship said.

"Nansen, he doesn't have time for horses," his wife said in that exasperated way of wives. "He must find a bride first."

The duchess beamed, an I-told-you-so smile.

Then Lady Nansen turned and fixed her attentions on Amelia. Her fan was beating at a furious pace.

"And Lady Amelia, have you found any suitors you care for?"

"After having met nearly all of England's finest young gentlemen, I can honestly say that no, I have not found any suitors that I could care for," Amelia said. "But I do have a new appreciation for spinsterhood. In fact, I think it sounds like just the thing."

Just the thing was a bit of slang she had picked up. Sticking forks in her eye was *just the thing* (but only with the good silver!). Flustering old matrons with an honest and direct statement was *just the thing*.

Lady Nansen stared at her a moment, blinking rapidly as she tried to process what Amelia had just said.

"Well your sister seems to have snared the attentions of Darcy's younger brother," she said, evidently disregarding Amelia and focusing on Bridget, the one who cared about fitting in and finding suitors.

"Are Lord Darcy and Mr. Wright here to-night?" Bridge asked eagerly. Too eagerly. "I haven't seen them."

"It's not a party without Darcy," Amelia quipped.

Darcy spent the majority of every social engagement standing against the wall, glowering at the company, refusing to dance, and begging the question of why he even bothered to attend.

But that was neither here nor there and no one deigned to reply to Amelia, so she sighed and lamented her choice in footwear quietly to herself. When Lord and Lady Nansen took their leave and sauntered off, the duchess turned and fixed her cool, blue eyes on Amelia.

"You might endeavor to be a touch more gracious, Lady Amelia."

The Duchess always said everything in perfectly worded, excruciatingly polite phrases. Translation: *Lord above, Amelia, stop acting like a brat.*

"I'm just . . . bored."

And homesick. And unhappy. And dreading the future you have planned for me. And a dozen other feelings one does not mention when one is at a ball.

"Bored?" The duchess arched her brows. "How on earth can you be bored by all this?" She waved her hand elegantly, to indicate everything surrounding them. "Is all the splendor, music, and the company of the best families in the best country not enough for you? I cannot imagine that you had such elegance and luxuries in the provinces."

Everyone here still referred to her home country as the provinces, or the colonies, or as the remote American backwater plagued by heathens, when Amelia knew that it was a beautiful country full of forthright, spirited people. It was her true home.

They operated under the impression that there was no greater fun to be had than getting overdressed and gossiping with the same old people each night, in crowded ballrooms in a crowded city.

She missed summer nights back home on their farm in Maryland, when she would slip outside at night with a blanket, to look up at the vast, endless expanse of stars.

This, no matter what the duchess said, just did not compare.

Amelia shrugged.

"We already met half these people at the six other balls we have attended this week," she said. "The other half are crashing bores."

Crashing bores was a phrase Amelia had read in the gossip columns. The violence of it appealed to her.

"I suppose it would be too much to ask you to pretend to act like an interested and engaging young lady." Then, turning to Lady Bridget, the duchess said, "I daresay she couldn't."

With that, the duchess turned away.

She *turned away*, leaving the words hanging in the air, floating to the ground, just waiting for Amelia to pounce on them.

"Well that was a challenge," Claire said.

"I'm not certain she could manage it." Bridget sniffed.

Really? *Really?*

"Is that a dare?" Amelia asked, straightening up. Oh, she would pretend all right. She would pretend so well they'd all be shocked. It would give her something to do at least. "Because I will take that dare."

"I'd like to see you try," Bridget replied. Then, muttering under her breath she added, "For once."

Amelia reddened. Admittedly she hadn't been taking this whole sister-of-the-duke business seriously. But she would show them. So instead of sticking her tongue out and scowling at Bridget, Amelia stuck her nose right up in the air and turned away.

"I am delighted to make your acquaintance," she said ever so politely to Lord Billingsworth when they were introduced.

And to Lord Diamond she said, "I am *so very delighted* to meet you," while sweeping into a low curtsy that rivaled Bridget's, even though she certainly hadn't spent her time practicing.

"It is a pleasure to meet you," Lord Diamond said with his gaze fixed firmly on the contents of her bodice. *That* was why she hated curtsying.

"No, the pleasure is *all mine*," Amelia replied grandly. So grandly that he seemed slightly taken aback by her enthusiasm.

And when Lord Babcock asked her to dance, she replied, "I cannot imagine a greater joy than waltzing with you, Lord Babcock. Why, I should like it more than anything in the world, including a new bonnet, or world peace."

"It's Lord Babson, actually."

"Is that so?" She did her best "simpering miss" laugh.

After an hour her feet were killing her. Slowly. These shoes were devious, cruel instruments of torture, clearly designed and crafted by someone who hated women. Especially women who wished to stand and move about the room without suffering extreme agonies. These cursed shoes had turned her, a woman who did love to dance and move, into a creature who wished for nothing more than to lie down and never get up again.

It was the way they pinched her toes. And the way they failed to offer desperately needed support after being on her feet for hours. And the way the leather bottoms were so slippery on the waxed parquet floors, forcing her to keep her movements delicate, slow, and restrained lest she find herself flat on her back. And even the satin had a way of rubbing against her skin, leaving it raw.

But they were bejeweled. She was supposed to tolerate this pain because the shoes were pretty and sparkled in the candlelight. Not that anyone even saw them, because her long skirts covered them.

Amelia suspected that said hideously uncomfortable shoes were not purchased at a shop on Bond Street but had actually been stolen from the Tower of London after being used to wring out confessions from prisoners of war. Or perhaps they were part of a massive conspiracy to ensure the lady population of London was so distracted by the pain in their feet that they didn't think of anything else, such as all the boorish, unappealing gentlemen who had things like "titles" and "estates" that were supposed to make a girl overlook things like personality or respect for women.

Amelia began to debate what would be worse: marriage to one of these dolts or having to wear these shoes for the rest of her life. Honestly, at the moment, it was a vexing decision. She was mulling these things over when the duchess had another introduction to perform.

"Lady Amelia, may I present Lord Eversleigh."

"I am *so delighted* to make your acquaintance, my lord," Amelia said. "It is truly an honor. I considered myself blessed. In fact, my life was lacking in meaning until this moment."

"Laying it on a bit thick, are you?" Bridget asked. The duchess was in conversation with someone nearby, they had lost Claire in the crowd, and James was dancing and not looking happy about it.

"Oh hush."

"Otherwise your performance is commendable," Bridget said. "You almost have the duchess fooled."

"Do you, perchance, have a knife?"

"I'm not in the habit of carrying weaponry in my reticule, no. Why do you ask?"

"Because I think I need to cut my feet off. These shoes are evil torture devices and I wish to be free of them. If I have to remove limbs, I will do it."

"I shall not even dignify that with a comment."

"You're right. Divesting myself of limbs would be messy business for a ballroom. Removing these shoes, on the other hand . . ."

"No."

"I'm sure no one will notice. These skirts are long and will cover my feet."

"No. Amelia, do not do this."

Amelia ignored her and glanced around her, trying to solve the problem of where to stash her shoes if not on her feet. Her gaze fell on a potted palm nearby and her heart skipped a beat. She

could slip off these torture slippers, tucked them
there, and return for them before they left.

"Ladies do not remove their shoes and stash
them in potted palms," Bridget lectured, as
if Amelia didn't already know this. As if that
wasn't the most basic common sense.

But she had reached her last nerve, the end of
her rope, her wit's end.

"I am aware," Amelia said, sighing with delight as she slipped off her right devil shoe.

"Amelia, stop that!"

"Oh no, there is no stopping me now," Amelia
said. The left shoe, a spawn of Satan, was removed and Amelia thought she would die with
pleasure.

"You'll embarrass us if anyone finds out!"

"No one will find out."

"Yes, they will! Amelia, the ton already says
enough horrible things about us without you gallivanting about the ballroom in your stocking feet!"

"At the moment, I couldn't care less what the
ton will think. And admit it, Bridget, you only
care what Lady Francesca thinks of you."

Lady Francesca was the most popular unmarried girl in the haute ton and Bridget had aspi-
rations of friendship with her, though Amelia
doubted Francesca felt the same way.

"That's not true."

"You're right. You only care what Loooord
Darcy thinks of you."

Bridget blanched.

"Please stop talking and put your shoes on. I beg of you."

Bridget's cheeks were turning pink now. Amelia didn't mean to taunt or embarrass her sister; this wasn't about Bridget at all. It was simply a matter of self-preservation.

"I feel as if I am speaking to a toddler," Bridget lamented in the way that only an older sister could.

"If I were a toddler, I wouldn't stop at the shoes. This blasted corset . . ."

"Amelia!"

"It's *Lady* Amelia."

And with that she shuffled a few steps closer to the potted palm and "accidentally" dropped her fan, providing an excuse for Amelia to bend over, stash her shoes in the palm fronds, and then pick up the fan and stand, fanning herself, as if nothing were amiss.

Bridget closed her eyes and groaned.

Amelia smiled. Truly smiled.

The duchess seemed to materialize before them, with yet another potential suitor by her side. Amelia took one look at the spotted beanpole of a boy and wondered if he was even old enough to attend Almack's and court women. Though he had to be at least eighteen, she wouldn't put him past fourteen or fifteen.

"Ah, there you are. I wanted to introduce Lord Matthew, Brookdale's heir. This is the special gentleman I was telling you about, Amelia."

Faced with the prospect of three sisters, Lord Matthew looked like he was dying a slow death of mortification.

Frankly, the feeling was mutual. *He* was the "special someone" the duchess thought would be an excellent match for her? Amelia supposed he was better than the other Lord Something the duchess had pushed her in path, the one who said, "I have fond memories of attending Eton with your father."

Not. Suitable. At. All.

"And I, uh, ahem, I was hoping one of you would, uh, ahem, er, favor me with a dance," Lord Matthew mumbled. He glanced nervously around the three sisters and his gaze settled on Amelia, as the closest in age to himself. "Lady Amelia?"

"You can't say no," Bridget said in a horrified whisper. She was right. Not only was it Not Done to refuse a dance, Amelia felt for the boy. He was so young and so awkward that even the slightest embarrassment would probably traumatize him for a lifetime.

"I can't very well go do a quadrille or reel or whatever in my stocking feet," Amelia whispered back, slightly panicked.

Amelia's mind churned at a furious pace.

She could not refuse this sweet, awkward boy, because it would be rude and, she sensed, potentially humiliating and damaging to him. But there was no way to hide her stocking feet during a dance—which she hadn't expected—and if she were seen, it would only fuel the rumors her family was doggedly trying to stifle. Contrary to what she told Bridget, she did care about her family's reputation.

Lord Matthew started to turn a rather unsettling, mottled shade of red as the seconds ticked by in which Amelia did not reply.

There was only one way out. She gave him a genuine smile, held out her hand and said loudly, "I would be honored to dance with you, Lord Matthew."

Then she fainted.

Chapter 2

In which our hero has arrived.

White's Gentleman's Club
A little after midnight

It'd been six years, five months, and fourteen days since Alistair Finlay-Jones had last set foot on English soil. As far as anyone knew, he'd had a capital time gallivanting around the Continent and living the life of a debauched aristocrat and idle heir to Baron Wrotham. He had done his utmost to live down to the baron's expectations of him.

"It's been an age, Alistair," his old friend Rupert Wright said over a game of cards and brandy. "What brings you home?"

That was the question, was it not?

He paused for a moment, dramatically. Shuffled the cards in his hands, debating which lie to tell. But then he glanced at the faces of his old friends—Darcy, Rupert, Fox—and decided to speak the truth.

"I have been summoned."

There was no need to say who had summoned him. There was only one possible person who had any reason or motive to take an interest in his whereabouts: his uncle and sole remaining relation, Baron Wrotham. There was also only one possible reason why the baron would care to have his distasteful nephew back in the same country.

"Any idea why?" Fox asked.

"Come on, Fox. There is only one possible reason," Rupert said with a laugh. Fox was fast with his fists but a bit slower with his wits.

"Marriage," Darcy said dryly. "And duty to one's station."

"Those are two things," Fox said, appearing confused.

"They are one and the same," Darcy said in that Darcy-ish way of his.

"At any rate, we can be certain it's not for my company," Alistair said. It was well known that the baron was embarrassed by his nephew, for reasons that could not be helped, and enraged at his nephew for something that was very much Alistair's fault. "I have an interview with him to-morrow. Bloody early, in fact."

"Don't suppose you'll want to call it a night so that you are well rested?" Rupert asked with a grin.

Alistair's only reply was to signal to the waiter to refill his glass of brandy. Then he lit another cheroot and settled in. After six years abroad, it was strange to hear English voices around him—wealthy, male, English voices. In his years abroad, he'd heard all kinds of languages— French, German, Italian, Hindi—and he'd learned enough to get by and not be so lonely, but not enough to develop a deep friendship or share his secrets.

Not that he wanted to talk about those. How very English of him.

But he, Darcy, Fox, and Rupert had survived Eton together, then Oxford. They knew his past, and even after six years apart they settled into a comfortable routine of wagers and games— Rupert won frequently, though Alistair did enjoy raking in a small fortune from Darcy, who seemed unusually distracted.

"What have I missed while I was away?" Alistair asked. Then, grinning, he referenced the conversation earlier in the evening. "Besides Darcy in the lake?"

It seemed the relentless proper Lord Darcy had found himself soaking wet in a lake at a garden party. Women had swooned.

"Fox has women troubles," Rupert remarked.

"Fox is not speaking of his women troubles," Fox replied sharply.

"So you admit you have them?" Rupert needled.

"What did I say about gossiping like schoolgirls?" Darcy grumbled.

"The only thing anyone is talking about is the new duke of Durham and his sisters," Rupert said.

"Enough about the Americans," Fox grumbled. "We've discussed them enough this evening."

The conversation shifted to other gossip and Alistair listened, hoping for a clue as to *why*.

Why, after all these years, had the baron finally deigned to remember him? *Why*, after that unflinching fight in which the baron said he never wanted to see his nephew again, did he summon Alistair back to England?

And *why* did Alistair come running?

He knew why and he didn't like the reason. But he also didn't know what to do about it. Other than come running when the baron called.

Alistair loosened his cravat. It'd gotten awfully tight.

"But never mind us," Darcy said. "What have you been doing these past few years?"

Searching for . . . something.

"You know . . . this. That." Alistair sipped his drink. Played a card.

"Illuminating," Darcy replied dryly.

"You should write a book," Rupert suggested.

"Sell your story to the gossip rags," Fox added.

The truth was he hadn't done more than this and that in a variety of foreign locales. This and that being trying to forget the reason he left England in the first place. And, he supposed, waiting for this very moment when the baron called him back.

"I'm afraid there isn't much to say. At least, nothing of interest to the newspapers," Alistair said with a shrug. And then, because they were men and not schoolgirls prone to gossip, the conversation turned to the card game at hand.

Long after midnight, they stepped out of the club onto a desolate St. James's Street. Alistair refused Darcy's offer for a ride home in his carriage, preferring to walk home through the streets of Mayfair instead.

In which our heroine is . . . distraught.

Half past midnight

The carriage ride from Almack's, scene of the scandal, back to Durham House was fraught with tension. The duchess, of course, did not do anything so pedestrian as yell or even scold. Oh no, Her Grace had a particular gift for radiating fury that one was helpless to ignore.

Amelia was not accustomed to it. Memories of Amelia's own mother were dim, having lost her at a young age; Amelia had been raised with Claire's absentminded scoldings and James's pleas to just not get into *too* much trouble.

Without even saying a word, the duchess had Amelia shrinking back against the squabs in the carriage. Beside her, Bridget was sulking terribly, as if Amelia's little scene was a deliberate affront to her own personal happiness.

Perhaps it hadn't been a *little* scene. Despite her best efforts, she hadn't managed to conceal her stocking feet when she "fainted" and fell to the floor. Lord Matthew, being young, embarrassed, and terribly awkward, turned and ran; in the process of fleeing the scene he barreled into the Dowager Countess of Pelham, who fell into the arms of Lord Babson. As she was not a petite woman and he was the sort of man for whom physical exertion meant pouring his own brandy rather than cross the room to ring for a footman, he was unable to support her and they both tumbled back into a footman with a tray laden with champagne glasses. There was a terrific clatter followed by a horrible hush.

Everyone saw everything: the fleeing suitor, the tangled lord and lady, the shards of broken champagne glasses, and the stocking-footed American girl sprawled on the floor.

No one had caught her when she "fainted."

"If you think about it, it's quite humorous," she said in a small voice, daring to interrupt the silence.

Or not.

It was a long moment before anyone even acknowledged she had spoken.

"Amelia, the last thing we needed is *more* rumors about our backward, heathen-ish, and savage American manners," Bridget said, sighing with tremendous despair. Amelia wanted to tell her to stop caring so much what the gossip rags said—she hated seeing how her sister's happiness had become dependent on it—but for once knew to hold her tongue. "You weren't wearing shoes! At a ball!"

"They hurt my feet," Amelia ground out. "And I don't see why I should suffer."

When they'd been at home in America, she wore comfortable boots or nothing at all. Never once had she been reprimanded for it. Of course, she understood that the rules were different here in London, amongst the aristocracy. She knew right and wrong (unless it was the order of precedence; she was still a bit shaky on that). She knew she was supposed to smile prettily and actually consider pledging her troth to one of the simple-minded, weak-chinned boys the duchess was forever thrusting in her direction.

The removal of shoes wasn't merely a matter of comfort.

It was rebellion.

She didn't feel she could say that. Instead, she mumbled, "I wasn't expecting an invitation to dance."

"I don't wonder why we don't receive many," Bridget said darkly. "We are the laughingstock of London."

"You don't really want to dance with any of these stuffy old bores, do you?"

Even in the dim light of the carriage, Amelia could see Bridget's cheeks redden. She did want to dance with at least some of those stuffy old bores. She wanted to impress stick-in-the-mud Lord Darcy and the snobby Lady Francesca DeVere and her vapid ~~minions~~ friends. Amelia knew this because she read Bridget's diary.

"Amelia, *some of us* are trying to fit in here."

Some of us = Bridget. She spent every waking moment trying to be the Perfect English Lady. James spent every free moment down at Tattersall's or riding in Hyde Park. He may have left their horse farm, but he still managed to find something like it here. And Claire snuck out to meetings of the Royal Society of Maths or something dull like that. They still got to be themselves, carve out a few hours each day to live like *before*.

Amelia had been allowed to run free at their farm in Maryland; James hadn't cared if she wore breeches to ride astride, Claire hadn't forced her to learn how to keep house and Bridget had been more prone to join her on adventures rather than practice curtsying in the mirror for hours on end.

But here she was always dressed up and perched in the drawing room or paraded around a ballroom. It wasn't in her nature to be so still, so trussed up, so *caged.* And she was supposed to do this so some man might decide he'd like to be her lord and master for the rest of her life.

She knew the feeling of wind in her hair and answering to no one; the idea of marrying someone—anyone, just because the duchess said she ought to—made Amelia sad in her soul. And rebellious in the ballroom.

"Some of us do not appreciate the reputation of the Cavendish name being sullied," the duchess said. "Especially when we have devoted our lives to upholding it."

Amelia glanced at the duchess in the dim light of the carriage. How did she do it; how did she behave herself for such a long time? Did she ever just long to take her shoes off if they hurt? Her Grace sat with her spine ramrod straight. Everything about her was immaculate, even at this late hour. No, Amelia concluded, she couldn't possibly have such longings like taking her shoes off or letting her hair down.

Hoping for sympathy, Amelia looked to her beloved brother James, who always came to her rescue. He would call her Scamp and wonder aloud what the devil he was going to do with her. The answer was that he wouldn't do anything, but love her and urge her to be more mindful next time.

"It could have been worse," was his meager, pitiful defense. Then he looked away, focusing intently on the darkness outside of the carriage.

It could have been worse. She could have removed her dress and run shrieking through the ballroom or set fire to the drapes.

It could have been worse. Ha.

The rest of the carriage ride was passed in excruciating silence. In which not one of her siblings came to her defense.

This was a first.

Also a first: not one of her *beloved siblings* gave her so much as a sympathetic glance and she truly would have loved a little indication that they knew she hadn't meant to cause a scene and embarrass them all. If only someone would understand that she wasn't ready for all this social whirling, all these potential future husbands, all this planning to settle into a new life.

Ever since that letter arrived informing James of his new station and summoning them to England, they'd been a strong family unit.

One for all and all for one.

Until tonight. She'd felt abandoned tonight.

Finally, they arrived at Durham House, a monumental and imposing stack of stones in the middle of London.

"Well Amelia, I hope you enjoyed yourself this evening," the duchess said crisply while she handed her satin cape and gloves to Pendleton, the butler.

"Immensely." Her voice veritably dripped with sarcasm, which was a disguise for hurt feelings.

"You needn't take such a tone," the duchess said sharply.

Amelia felt her heart starting to pump harder and her head started to pound.

Smile more. No, smile less. Suffer through the pain of your footwear. Let this old gentleman look down your bodice. Dance with whomever asks even if you do not wish to dance with him. Simper.

And now her *tone* wasn't right.

According to the duchess, she couldn't do *any-thing* right. And according to her siblings too, since they weren't coming to her defense as they usually did.

She felt lonely, and tired, and wronged. And in such a state, she hardly behaved at her best.

"Of course," she said wearily. "Sarcasm and taking such a tone are unbecoming of a lady. I'm so bloody bored of being A Lady. And don't tell me ladies don't say words like *bloody*, because I am well aware."

"Then why must you persist in using such in-delicate phrases?"

"Because I must have something to amuse myself." Then for good measure she added,

"When I am so bloody bored. All the bloody time. Sorry, Duchess, but husband hunting is not my preferred sport."

"Amelia . . ." Claire started, in her let's-be-reasonable voice.

"Oh, don't *Amelia* me," she said, stomping up the stairs. "Not tonight. I am no mood for more lectures on how exactly to smile, or the precise tone of my voice or whatever other stupid rules I happen to break because I am some ignorant and uncivilized girl. I won't bend over backwards trying to please people who are determined to laugh at me anyway."

She looked at Bridget as she said it. And that was just enough over the line.

"They aren't. . . ." Bridget's voice trailed off in her halfhearted defense of the ton. Her hands balled into fists, crumpling the satin and silk of her skirt. "You don't have to make it so easy for them to laugh. Or hard for me to succeed. And you don't have to be so childish, either, Amelia."

That got Amelia's blood boiling.

"Expecting that you not divest yourself of your footwear at a formal ball is not an outlandish request," the duchess said dryly. And then, echoing the sentiments of the ton, she added, "At least, not in England."

"You are lucky it was just my shoes, when I'd really like to remove this blasted corset, douse it in brandy and set it afire," Amelia muttered.

"Just don't use the good brandy," James said dryly.

"You're not helping," Claire, Bridget, and the duchess said to him in unison.

Amelia was halfway up the stairs, on her way to at last removing the offending garment.

"Between her language and the shoes, every-one will think you were raised in the stables," the duchess lamented.

"To be fair, we practically were," James re-marked from where he leaned idly against the wall. Not coming to stand beside her, either liter-ally or figuratively.

"And everyone already thinks so," Bridget muttered.

"Please do not remind me of that fact," the duchess said, closing her eyes. "I am trying very hard to forget it and very, *very* hard to ensure that the rest of the ton forgets it as well."

"You could always send me back if I'm such an embarrassment to you all," Amelia challenged.

She was very attached to her family. But to-night . . . tonight she felt it might be for the best if she did return home, on the other side of the world, where she couldn't embarrass them or ruin things.

"Amelia, we agreed . . ." Claire started. Again, with that calm and rational voice that oddly only served to make Amelia more frustrated.

Yes, they had agreed to come to England and

see what life was like here. Because opportunities to be dukes did not come along every day. But Amelia had seen enough. This life was not for her. And if she married an Englishman, then she could say goodbye to ever returning home.

"And you did say you wanted to see more of the world," Claire added. "Think of this as an adventure. A chance to explore."

"I do want to see *the world*," Amelia said. "Not every drawing room and ballroom in London. I mean, honestly, how much damask wallpaper, gold-framed portraits of dead aristocrats, and fancy tea sets does one girl need to see?"

Her voice was rising now, trembling a little. She couldn't help it. Amelia had a vision of her life as an endless stream of tea parties in damask wallpapered rooms, under the disapproving gaze of dead aristocrats, alone except for some stuffy old English bore.

"I want *more*," she said. The word *more* was ripped from her heart. There had to be *more* for her than constricting her thoughts, words, and movements so she fit into a place she didn't even want to be. There had to be more of the world for her to experience than ballrooms and drawing rooms.

The duchess pursed her lips. "Lady Amelia, you are hysterical."

The three not-hysterical Cavendish siblings winced.

"Hysterical?" Amelia turned and started descending the stairs in a fury.

"Duchess, never tell a hysterical woman that she's hysterical," James said. Then, to no one in particular, James added, "It's the sort of thing a man learns when he's responsible for three younger sisters."

"Well, if she would just calm down . . ." the duchess said. Logically. But then again, she hadn't any experience with children.

"Calm down?"

"Even worse," Claire said, shaking her head. "Never tell a woman, especially Amelia, to calm down."

"If you are such experts, then you handle the situation," she said, throwing her hands up.

"We have found . . ." Claire began as Amelia now muttered about the injustice of a woman being deemed hysterical for wanting more from her life than to marry some inbred Englishman.

". . . over the years . . ." Bridget added, while Amelia carried on about damask-papered prison walls and the interchangeability of corsets and straitjackets.

". . . that it is best to simply allow her to exhaust herself," James said.

Amelia had had enough. She started pulling the hairpins from the elaborate coiffure her maid had done earlier. An hour of her life spent forcing her wild curls into an unnatural arrangement.

Well, no more! She flung the hairpins one by one across the foyer. They skittered across the marble floor. They ricocheted off crystal sconces. They plunked against portraits and fell to the floor.

"Well," the duchess said. "There is only one thing to do, I suppose. I shall send up Miss Green with some laudanum."

A short while later, Amelia felt much calmer. She'd drunk a cool glass of water that Miss Green had brought to her. Her maid had helped remove her corset, gown, stockings, and stays and dressed her for bed. The others retired, leaving her alone.

But Amelia wasn't tired. She had a restless energy, always, even now. It was this feeling that there was always something more out there, just beyond her reach or her vision. The world over, people were having love affairs, conducting business, fighting duels, performing operas, trekking across deserts, making great works of art, or simply cooking dinner. Or kissing.

She longed to experience it. All of it. As a lady she was allowed none of it. Not love affairs and kissing, or fighting duels or simply cooking dinner. To say nothing of trekking across deserts. There was a whole world out there, pulsing with activity.

And Amelia was cut off from all of it.

Like some fairy-tale princess locked in a tower. She moved to the window and opened it. She looked out at the dark, silent night and looked up at the stars twinkling over the city.

And then she heard a man singing. The sound was too faint for her to make out the words, but there was no mistaking a lovely melody in a man's baritone ringing through the night.

She leaned forward, resting her weight on her elbows, staring out the window dreamily and hoping to catch a glimpse of him.

How lovely it must be to stroll along the quiet streets at night, singing a song, and not caring who heard. What freedom he possessed!

Why, if she were out on the streets at night, as a lady, which one should *never* do, she would have to take the utmost care to get right back inside immediately before Danger Befell Her. And it wasn't clear which kind of danger was worse for a woman: the sort that came from unrepentant and unscrupulous scoundrels devoid of a moral compass but brimming with nefarious intentions?

Or the danger that came from a single glance out the window by a woman prone to gossip about what she saw?

Amelia sighed, thinking how unfair it was that a man could go out at night, singing loudly in the streets, not fearing for his life or his reputation. He could enjoy a leisurely stroll on a beautiful summer night, not a fear or care in the world.

She would add it to her list of things she'd do if she were a boy. Such a list also included visiting a gaming hell, racing at Ascot, embarking on a Grand Tour, or simply getting out of calling hours. Or perhaps Not Getting Married Ever.

Amelia finally started to feel calm. She yawned.

But still she lingered at the open window. His singing was quite lovely. And she longed to know, just for a moment, what it was like to take a quick stroll on a dark summer night while singing a song.

She couldn't shake her curiosity. The idea swirled around her head, dreamily. And then wicked thoughts crossed her mind.

Everyone had gone to bed.

No one would notice if she slipped out for a moment.

Everyone was already mad at her, what was one more little indiscretion?

His voice was closer now, warm and low and tempting.

She yawned once more and could not, for the life of her, think of why she should not put on a dress and boots and slip outside to meet the man with the wonderful voice and have the freedom to stroll through the streets and sing in the dead of the night.

She did just that, donning the dress, stockings, boots, and a spencer. She slipped out of her bedroom, darted down the corridor and down the servants' stairs, skipping the creaky one (third from the bottom). And then she stepped outside and into the night.

Chapter 3

**In which our hero and heroine
should not be meeting like this.**

Very late at night

It was a warm summer night in Mayfair and
Alistair sang an old drinking song as he walked
back to his flat after a night pleasantly spent
drinking and wagering with his old friends at
White's.

At this late hour, the streets were empty.

Except for . . . a woman?

He slowed his pace and observed.

She strolled slowly and stumbled slightly. As
he drew closer, he heard something like singing,
but she was slurring her words and it was hard
to discern what she was saying. Or singing. But
she did have a lovely voice.

A lovely figure too, from what he could glimpse from behind. Women with lovely figures and voices oughtn't be strolling the streets of London, not even in Mayfair, at this late hour.

He caught up with her.

"Madam."

She whirled to face him, nearly falling flat on her face as she did so.

"Good *evening* sir. Or is it lord? Or mister or right honorable? I *do* apologize for not knowing." She tried to curtsy, which was a terrible idea, given her difficulty standing. He propped her up. "I am *delighted* to make your acquaintance. You must be the man with the song."

In the moonlight, he could see that she was young. Far too young and far too female to be out on the streets alone, never mind that she was out at night. Never mind that she was clearly three, possibly five sheets to the wind.

Given that this was Mayfair, a neighborhood populated by the marriage-minded mamas, the most dangerous subset of human for the common rake, Alistair had half a mind to rush away from her, in the event that this was some marriage trap.

But then he looked into the dark pools of her eyes fringed with dark lashes and thought, *It could be worse.*

He put the thought out of his mind.

Madness, that.

"I have been looking for you," she told him. At least, that's what it sounded like.

"May I escort you home?" Better him than, oh, anyone else she might encounter. Besides, it's not as if he needed to be up in a few hours for an interview so important he was summoned from another continent for it.

"No, thank you. But it is *so kind* of you to offer." She tried to dip into another curtsy and thought better of it. She swayed slightly, leaning in toward him.

"May I escort you elsewhere?"

"No, thank you. I prefer to walk."

"It is not safe for a lady on the streets alone, especially at night."

"It isn't safe for a lady anywhere, ever. But now I have you to protect me from the dangers." She nestled up to him, resting her cheek on his chest. Then she yawned. "You will, won't you?"

"Yes," he said softly. Because honestly, what else could he say when a lovely young woman pressed against him like that?

"Let us walk," she said, quickly stepping away from him and pitching forward. He quickly darted forward and linked arms. She leaned heavily against him and they took a few slow steps. "And do carry on with your song. It tempted me to come out. Like the sires."

"The sires?"

"You know, from the odessisseusness."

"I beg your pardon?"

"The Greek story."

"Ah," he said, comprehension dawning. "The sirens. From the *Odyssey*."

"That's the one! That's *you*."

"I can assure you, I'm not luring you to your death. Quite the contrary, I would like to see you home safely. Where do you live?"

"America."

Wrong. Impossible. Try again.

"Where do you live?"

"One of these big old drafty houses." She waved her hand in the general vicinity of the approximately twenty houses lining the street.

If he had stayed in England, he would know who she was, who she belonged to, and which house was hers. She was obviously a person of quality if she was referencing the *Odyssey* and lived in a drafty old Mayfair house. Or perhaps she was merely a governess. Either way, the last he checked, the young ladies of England of any social class were not encouraged to drink themselves into a stupor and wander the streets alone.

The girl was leaning more and more heavily upon him. Her footsteps were slowing. He probably had precious few moments before she blacked out entirely.

"Miss, where do you live?"

She slumped against him. Yawned loudly. She

rested her cheek against the wool of his jacket and her hands slid against his chest.

"Oh bloody hell," he muttered.

She mumbled something that sounded like, "Ladies mustn't use such language."

"Good thing I'm not a lady."

"Wish I wasn't."

She nestled even closer against him. He could feel that she was *very* much a lady.

He suddenly, keenly regretted not accepting Darcy's offer of a ride. At this very moment he could be back in his lodgings, loosening his cravat, removing his boots, and falling into bed to snatch a few precious hours' sleep before the baron told him why he'd been summoned back after six years abroad.

But no, he was on Bruton Street in the middle of the night, in a hellish predicament. Somehow, he was in possession of a drunk or drugged woman who probably had rich and powerful relatives who would make him pay for his role in this farce.

Alistair considered his options. He could knock on each door and make inquiries: *Does this girl belong to you? No? Do you know to whom she belongs?*

He couldn't just *leave* her on the street.

Perhaps he could leave her on a doorstep of one of these houses, ring the bell and run, thus making her someone else's problem. A butler would know what to do with her. Butlers always knew what to do.

But that would certainly ruin the girl.

And she seemed like such a sweet girl, with her dark eyes and tumble of curls and mentions of ancient Greek literature. Drunken, unchaperoned, slightly flirtatious antics notwithstanding. He wanted no part in her ruination.

But Alistair didn't exactly want the responsibility of *saving* her from such ruination either. He wanted to collapse in his own bed before what promised to be a life-altering interview with the baron. And to do that, he needed to get rid of this girl.

Alistair grabbed her warm, limp shoulders and shook her.

"Where do you live?"

Her head lolled to the side, dark curls tumbled out of her coiffure. She muttered something completely unintelligible. Oh, bloody hell.

Alistair glanced around at the dark night and desolate streets. There was only one possible course of action.

Chapter 4

**In which our hero is given a mission,
should he choose to accept it.**

Early morning—but not early enough

The next morning Alistair woke up with a start. Heart pounding. Panicked. He reached for his timepiece and swore when he saw that it was half past nine. He was due at the baron's at ten o'clock. He needed time to shave and dress—hopefully Jenkins was up and had tended to the clothes Alistair left on the floor last night.

There was also the matter of the girl.

He'd carried her home, reluctantly. The *last* thing he needed was to be saddled with an unconscious young woman. Especially one who likely came from a prestigious family. They would not take kindly to finding her thus, and especially with the likes of him.

He especially did not need an unconscious woman who nuzzled against his chest affectionately. She snored softly and it somehow managed to be adorable, which annoyed him, though not as much as having to carry a sleeping female, who seemed to become heavier with each step he took. Alistair wasn't some Hercules and she wasn't as light as a feather.

When they finally arrived at his flat, he left her sprawled on the settee in the small chamber that passed for the drawing room in his suite of rented rooms.

She was still there when he woke up in a panic. Heart pounding. Now he needed to get rid of her. Not in a nefarious way, just in a she's-not-my-responsibility way.

He dressed in breeches and a shirt—Jenkins had taken care of everything, good man—and peeked in on the girl. Beautiful pale skin. A dark mass of curls. Pink lips parted slightly.

"Good morning," he said.

There was no response.

He shook her shoulder. Nothing.

He paled, fearing her dead. The *last* thing he needed was a highborn and gently bred woman, dead. In his flat. He'd hang for sure.

He pressed his fingertips to her wrist and exhaled when he felt a pulse, confirming that she was indeed among the living. She was just sleeping off one hell of a bender.

"Jenkins," he called loudly. His valet slept in a room off the kitchen. He emerged a moment later. "I need my waistcoat and jacket. Something must be done with my cravat. Also, there is a woman on the settee."

"I have brushed your wool jacket, which I found on the floor, which is apparently a suitable place for it."

His disdain for Alistair's disregard for his clothing was apparent.

"Thank you. I am late for a meeting with the baron. An interview for which I have traveled all the way from Europe."

"I am aware. I was with you. If you'll recall."

Of course he recalled. Jenkins had been by his side on his first day at Oxford, when he'd been hired to serve as valet to both Alistair and Elliot whilst they were at school. He hadn't left Alistair's employ since.

"And if you'll recall, I mentioned a woman on the settee." He glanced down at her. She was quite pretty. He should probably move her to the bed, because eventually she would wake up and it wouldn't do for her to discover she'd been deposited on a rickety little scrap of furniture.

Reluctantly, he scooped her up. She was warm, curvy, and all kinds of luscious in his arms. He dropped her on his bed as if she were something dangerous from which he needed distance.

She smiled a lazy, sleepy, sweet-dream smile and curled up and kept sleeping. God, he wanted to strip off his clothes and join her. Bury his face in the crook of her neck and breathe her in. Then, more. But what man wouldn't?

"See that she gets home safely before I return," he told his valet.

"Where is her home?"

"You'll have to ask her. If—no, *when*—she wakes up."

Confident that his valet would manage to get rid of the girl by the time he returned, Alistair set off for his meeting with the Baron.

10:00 in the morning

Alistair knocked once, twice, thrice at number seventeen Curzon Street. Rutherford opened the heavy oak door. He stared, blankly, not showing any sign of recognition.

"I am here to see Wrotham," Alistair said. Obviously.

"Your card, please."

"Rutherford, we have been acquainted for over twenty years now, since I was sent to this very household to live with my uncle, the baron, as his ward, at the tender young age of eight. As a cruel twist of fate would have it, I am the heir to Baron Wrotham, this house, and *you*."

Rutherford sneered at the phrase *cruel twist of fate* and Alistair couldn't fault him for it.

"I will see if Lord Wrotham is at home to callers."

It was clear that Rutherford hadn't yet forgiven him for that stupid, tragic thing he'd done. Hell, no one had. Not even himself.

So Alistair cooled his heels in the foyer, willing to wait out the ridiculous charade. Of course Wrotham would be home to him; the man had summoned him from Europe for this interview. And finally, after precisely fifteen minutes had passed—fifteen minutes in which he wondered about the girl in his flat and not the mysterious reason for which he'd returned to England after six years—he was summoned to the baron's study.

The room hadn't changed at all; Alistair noted the same dark paneled walls, a faded forest green carpet, and white marble mantel with the same portrait hanging above. Alistair couldn't bring himself to look at it.

"Finlay-Jones." His uncle, and sole surviving relation in the world, greeted him formally. As if he did not wish to acknowledge their connection.

"Wrotham."

"I'm surprised to see you here," the baron said, glancing up from where he sat comfortably behind a large carved oak desk. He was a typical English lord: slightly pale and puffy from an excess of fine food and wines and a dearth of fresh air and exercise. In the intervening years, the lines around Wrotham's mouth had deepened. His hair had gone from black to gray.

"Well, you did request my presence in no uncertain terms," Alistair pointed out. The exact words of the letter were burned into his brain:

I have figured out a way for you to be useful. Call upon Wrotham house in London immediately.

"Well I didn't think you'd listen. You're not known for your sense of duty, responsibility, or discipline."

This was fair. He managed no estates, did not run a business or engage in trade; he had not entered the clergy or enlisted in the army, navy, or what have you. Why should he? In school, he thought he might pursue a profession, but then Elliot died and that changed everything.

Suddenly, Alistair was The Heir, a role he'd never been prepared for and a role he never wanted. It was a role Wrotham hadn't wanted him for either.

There was only one thing to do, as he saw it: live life to the fullest because it could end at any moment. So Alistair traveled around Europe, then even as far as India, living.

Perhaps, in the back of his mind he was searching for something, something impossible:

a sense of belonging. A feeling of home. Lord knows he wouldn't find it here, at number seventeen Curzon Street.

"And how is Lady Wrotham?" Alistair asked politely, changing the subject away from his failings to the baron's very young, pretty wife, whom he wed shortly after Elliot's funeral.

"Still barren," he said witheringly.

"Ah, I see."

And he did. Clearly. Wrotham hated having someone like *Alistair* as his ward, let alone as his heir. He never did forgive his brother's choice in a wife. Never forgave Alistair for his mother, either. The only way for him to oust Alistair was to have another son. Hence the young wife.

"Did you have a reason for summoning me?" *Or was it just to see if you could?*

"Yes, as a matter of fact, I do. If you must be my heir"—the word *must* hung in the air, heavy with regret, grief, and embarrassment—"then you might as well make yourself useful."

"Of course."

He meant it. Even though Wrotham detested him, Alistair still craved his acceptance. They were family after all. They shared blood.

Alistair craved his forgiveness, too. He would do anything, ANYTHING, to make up for what could never be made up. Wrotham had tolerated his nephew at best, but what had happened six years ago . . . that destroyed everything.

"There is a ball tonight. You will attend."

I traveled from Europe to attend a ball. Of course.

"And at this ball, you will make the acquaintance of the hostesses. The new duke of Durham is some horse-breeding hick from the colonies. It's an embarrassment. Almost as much as the three sisters he brought with him. The duchess has her work cut out for her with that lot. Needless to say, they are having a difficult time finding acceptance with society."

"I see?"

"Obviously you don't. You won't just make their acquaintance," the baron said, now smiling, presumably at his own genius and/or ability to manipulate Alistair, "but you will also marry one of the girls.

"Marry?"

"Eventually, the duchess will succeed in her efforts to launch them into society. And then it'll be too late for the likes of you to snare one."

There it was again: the likes of *you.* Not even a gentleman's education and his status as heir to a barony could erase the fact that he was born of an English man and Indian woman. He did not have a pedigree. He did not have enough wealth to make anyone overlook that lack of pedigree. And he was only the heir of a minor barony, due to happenstance and a tragic accident.

Mr. Alistair Finlay-Jones was no one's definition of a catch.

The likes of him would never have a chance with a duke's sister unless something was very wrong with her. But still, he did not reject Wrotham's order outright. And it rankled, slightly, what he would consider doing for someone's approval. Marry. Til Death Do They Part.

"I suppose it's their dowries you're after," Alistair remarked.

"It so happens that when one no longer cares for the future, he makes riskier bets on the future," Wrotham remarked wryly. "Sometimes these pay off tremendously. And sometimes they do not."

"You owe money."

"Try not to be so blunt. It's ungentlemanly." Wrotham gave him a withering glare. *Idiot.*

"Right. So I am to attend the ball and marry one of the American girls."

"I hope your courtship shows more subtlety than what you've just demonstrated. Otherwise we're sunk."

"You are sunk."

"That's what I said."

"No, you said *we.* I have nothing to lose. If you'll recall, you cut me off. Completely. Not a penny to my name."

Not that Alistair blamed him for it.

"Well here's your chance to land us a fortune," the baron said, showing no remorse. "Hopefully, even you can manage it. Given one of the chit's scandalous antics last night, you have a fighting chance."

Wrotham turned his attentions to some papers on his desk, clearly sending the message that this interview had concluded. Alistair had received his orders and would, of course, obey them.

"Best be off then," he said, rocking back on his heels. "I ought to stop at the tailor. I'll want to look my best when I go a-courting."

"Try not to ruin this, too."

It was then, and only then, that Alistair allowed himself to look over at the portrait of Elliot hanging above the fireplace. He'd been young, vibrant, and handsome then. The painter had somehow managed to capture that spark in his eye that made all the girls mad, or the smile that always got him out of trouble. He'd been Alistair's best friend. He'd been Alistair's family—the only family who cared for him, anyway, after his parents had died.

And Alistair had been responsible for his death.

On the way back to his flat, Alistair stopped to buy a newspaper. If he was going to reenter society, he would need to know all the latest gossip—who was this season's incomparable, who was rumored to be having affairs with whom, what wagers were in the works, and just what the ton was saying about the American girls and their scandalous antics from last night. He picked up an issue of *The London Weekly*, intending to have a leisurely read upon returning to his quiet and empty flat.

But he let out a low whistle when he saw the cartoon on the front cover.

It depicted a girl in the act of fainting, with her hand draped languorously over her forehead. Her bare feet and ankles were rudely exposed. Her gown was a clashing pattern of stars and stripes in an outdated style. She wore a chieftain's headdress, with beads and feathers. In her hand was a riding crop, which the accompanying text explained as a reference to decades-old gossip about Durham's younger brother absconding to America with his prized stallions.

The message couldn't be any clearer: She was the wild, uncivilized descendent of a horse thief. She was not to be trusted. She was not one of them.

Alistair saw just why his uncle had selected this girl, or one of her sisters: she was a laughing-stock. An ill-mannered, horse-stealing heathen of a girl, running barefoot and wild amongst the refined members of the haute ton. He imagined the worst.

But she was, presumably, in possession of a hefty dowry. And in time, perhaps, people would forget this incident and just remember the title.

Until then, a mixed-race, fortune-hunting scoundrel would have a chance with her.

Ah, romance.

"You going to buy that, or what?" The shop-keeper wanted to know; and it was clear there was only one correct answer to the question.

"Here." Alistair gave him a coin and started walking away, slowly, unable to look away from this cartoon girl because he also noticed a famil-iar mop of dark curls, a pert little nose, and a rosebud of a mouth.

"Well I'll be damned," he said softly. If he wasn't mistaken, the girl he was supposed to marry was currently in his bed.

Chapter 5

**In which our heroine wakes up
where she should not.**

10:37 in the morning

It was tremendously disconcerting to wake up in a strange bed and to have absolutely no recollection of falling asleep in it. No, tremendously disconcerting did not do the feeling justice. Terrifying came close, as did horrifying and baffling. This was, beyond a shadow of a doubt, something no true and proper lady ever did. It wasn't something even Amelia Cavendish, rebellious lady of two continents, had ever done.

Yet here she was.

In a strange bed.

In a strange room.

Without even the slightest memory of how she might have arrived here.

If there was ever a time for swearing, this was it.

"Bloody hell," Amelia whispered, because while the room seemed empty, one never knew who or what lay beyond the doors. She was not ready for discovery.

She had just woken up.

In a strange bed.

In a strange room.

Without even the foggiest notion of how she might have arrived here.

When *bloody hell* seemed insufficient, she added, "Holy mother of God."

As far as she knew, there was no one here to reprimand her for unladylike language. But that was the least of her concerns.

Take a deep breath when you are scared. James had taught her that.

Think logically. Claire had always advised her thusly.

Think of what a good story it will be in your diary later. That was Bridget, or how Amelia preferred to imagine her. In truth, Bridget would probably be taking this as a personal affront to her quest to be a True Lady.

Thinking logically, though. That seemed just the thing.

If she did not know where she was, she probably hadn't set out for here intentionally. If she did not recollect coming here, she must have been brought here.

She immediately proceeded to imagine the worst: some horrid thug with a few blackened teeth and even fewer brain cells, and who perhaps frothed at the mouth. He would have beady eyes and an air of malevolence.

This was bad. This was beyond bad. This was The Worst.

She didn't need Bridget or the duchess to tell her that.

This was quite possibly—nay, definitely, absolutely—the worst scrape she'd ever found herself in, and Amelia wasn't a stranger to terrible predicaments.

The first thing to do was take stock of the situation. And be logical. And be a deep breather.

She was still wearing her dress. That was something. She reached under the covers, under her skirt and . . . exhaled a sigh of relief. Her underthings were on, properly. Which didn't mean they hadn't been *off.* But she didn't feel different at all and she felt like she would feel different if something had happened.

Next, Amelia reached up and felt her hair—a tangled, knotted mop of curls that would require the dedicated attentions of at least two lady's maids to untangle. Whoever had kidnapped her had not the forethought or experience with a woman's curly hair to know that it would need to be braided before bed or else *this* would happen.

But hair troubles were the least of her worries.

Amelia slid out of bed, taking care not to make a sound just in case Someone Was Out There. She was not yet ready to face a person, or this day.

When standing, it became apparent that her dress was open in the back. She spun around a few times like a dog chasing his tail, trying, and failing, to do some buttons herself. Stupid fashionable dresses that require maids. She could not manage it on her own, which meant she could not leave. Walking down the street with her dress falling off was just not done.

But presumably she *had* walked down the street at some point, with her dress undone. That was terrible. She took a moment to pray, fervently, with her hands clasped at her heart, her gaze lifted to the heavens and her lips moving slightly, that she hadn't been seen.

She gave up after a moment. She may not have been seen, but getting back to Durham House, half attired, in daylight, without attracting attention, would require more than an act of God.

"Hell and damnation," she muttered.

She decided to explore, perhaps find a clue as to where she was.

The bedroom was small, neat. Sparse. It didn't even seem as if someone lived here, but there were sheets and a blanket on the bed. She pushed open the door, which opened into a small drawing room. It contained a tiny, rickety settee and not much else of note. Her spencer was thrown over it. Amelia picked it up, ready to put it on over her dress.

The next room was a very small kitchen, and there was another room just off that. It was empty, save for a cot and washstand.

She was alone.

Escape!

This was her opportunity.

She spied the door that surely led out of the flat, into the corridor then out onto the street and then . . . she did not know what then. Where was she? How was she to get back? Knowledge of how to get herself to Durham House required knowing where she was presently.

This was, she believed, a conundrum.

Take a deep breath.

Think logically.

Think of what a good story this will be in your diary later.

With a heavy, nervous heart, she made her way toward the door.

But it opened before she could reach it.

A man stepped over the threshold.

It was with some relief that she noticed he was handsome. As if that made him safe, which was ridiculous. But she had been expecting the very worst, straight out of a gothic novel. Missing teeth. Beady eyes.

And yet here was a handsome man gazing at her with warm brown eyes (that were not at all beady) and a kind smile (all teeth seemed to be present). He was breathing hard, as if he'd run here, and she noted the rise and fall of his broad, flat chest that tapered to a narrow waist and muscular legs and . . .

Oh God, was she really noticing such things?

Now?

Somebody ought to smack some sense into her.

"You're still here," he said, sounding relieved. "Good morning."

English. Of course he was English. And his accent sounded more like their oh-so proper neighbor Darcy, an earl, than the accent of the grooms in the stable. Which meant that he might move in the same circles as the duchess, which meant that he was more "acceptable" though it also meant that she was at greater risk of discovery and ruination.

"Good morning?"

Because honestly, what did one say at a time like this? Was it a good morning? In the space of a few heartbeats it had gone from certain to disaster to . . . intriguing. Who was this man? Why was she in his flat? Was this even his flat?

Either way *good* wasn't the right word for this morning.

"We have not been properly introduced." So he

was polite. And prone to vast understatements. "My name is Mr. Alistair Finlay-Jones, gentleman and rescuer of drunk ladies of Mayfair."

Ah, so he possessed something like a sense of humor. But he could still be a blackguard for all she knew.

"I wasn't drunk," she said adamantly. "Nor was I wandering the streets of Mayfair alone. That is absurd."

The duchess would kill her, for one thing. For another, she was barely able to use the necessary without a chaperone breathing down her neck. Wandering the streets of Mayfair. Drunk. Alone. In the dead of the night. The man was barking mad, clearly.

And yet, here she was. Alone with a gentleman to whom she had not been *properly* introduced. In his flat. With her dress partially undone. And no recollection of how any of these things came to be.

"Is it absurd?" He tilted his head. A lock of dark hair fell across his forehead.

"I think it is," she said with less conviction.

She remembered the events at Almack's, and winced. She remembered the horrid carriage ride home and had a vague recollection of shouting at everyone and flinging her hairpins around the foyer, which probably explained why her hair was a tangled, untamed mass of curls at the moment.

And after that—nothing.

Not. One. Thing.

She would have at least remembered starting in on James's bottle of brandy in the library, if not finishing it. But the only thing she drank was a glass of water that Miss Green had given her.

"I don't suppose you know how I've come to be here," she said.

"You were wandering the streets of Mayfair alone, after midnight, in an advanced state of intoxication. Admittedly I was as well, though I am far more adept at holding my liquor."

"Clearly I shall have to improve through practice. Though I wasn't drunk."

"Of course," he replied, agreeable even though she was certain he didn't believe her at all. "I couldn't very well leave you on the streets."

"You could have returned me to my home."

"And where would that be? You were not very forthcoming with the information last night. When I asked, you said America."

That is exactly what she would have said. Drat. Perhaps he was telling the truth.

"You brought me here instead."

"I couldn't very well leave you on the street."

Amelia looked at him and around the room. The sparse collection of rooms that barely looked lived in. He must have only just moved or have been impoverished. Or both. Her gaze landed on the settee, which would barely seat two, and then her gaze shifted back to him, all six feet of him.

"You must have been awfully uncomfortable sleeping on that little thing all night."

"Oh, it was nothing," he said and she was sure he was lying.

"Especially while I enjoyed your large, comfortable bed," she said, holding his gaze. She took a small delight in the way his cheeks pinkened slightly. "I'm not sure if you are a gentleman or a scoundrel."

"Whichever the lady prefers."

She took one look at those brown eyes and thought, *Scoundrel. Definitely scoundrel.*

"The lady prefers to return home. I have stayed long enough. In fact, I only waited because I needed to have my dress buttoned up. Would you mind helping me? I don't suppose there is a lady's maid about?"

"Would you believe that I've doubled as a lady's maid a time or two?"

She looked him over: tall, with a broad chest tapering to a narrow waist, olive skin and dark hair, not to mention the kind of face that made even a nun simper.

"Yes, I would absolutely believe it."

He burst out laughing. "Turn around then."

He proceeded to do up the buttons, slowly, fingertips brushing against the soft skin of her back. He wasn't rushing. She felt the warmth of him from standing so close. This was intimacy that was new to her.

And then he was done, quickly. Gently. Her skin was tingly and she was feeling . . . feelings. He definitely had practice as a lady's maid.

"Thank you," she said softly, turning to face him. Perhaps they would meet again. Or perhaps it was best if they didn't. So she enjoyed one long, last look at this handsome stranger. "I should go."

"Allow me to walk you home."

He smiled, and she was tempted, if only because she didn't know which way to go. But being seen with the likes of him would only make things worse. The only thing worse than a lady alone was a lady alone with a man.

"I am perfectly capable of finding my own way, thank you." She smiled to be polite and started for the door. Then the truth reared its head again: she didn't know where she was or how far from Durham House, though she knew better than to ask him or mention the name Durham. He seemed like he could use ransom funds. "If you could perhaps lend me a few coins for a hack? I will see that the money is returned to you."

"Of course." He pulled some money out of his pocket and handed it to her. His bare hand brushed against hers.

"Mr. Finlay-Jones, thank you for not leaving me on the streets to a dire fate."

"I could not do so and call myself a gentle-man," he said with a grin.

He stepped aside to let her go and after she stepped into the hall, she turned, and said, "If we should meet again—"

"I hope we do."

"—we must never speak of this."

He paused. "Speak of what?"

"Exactly," she said with a smile. "Goodbye, Mr. Finlay-Jones."

Chapter 6

In which the girl gets away.

11:07 in the morning

Alistair did not believe in luck. Anything that looked like luck in his life—like, say, being the son of a second son and yet finding himself heir to a title—came at too high a price to be called luck.

But finding that American girl had been lucky.

Finding that American girl and taking her home had been damned lucky. Leaving her alone in his flat and then returning to still find her there was even luckier still. He arrived, gasping for breath from sprinting, just as she was about to leave.

How. Damned. Lucky.

Especially after being ordered to marry her.

There was never any question that he was going to do his utmost to honor the baron's request. The baron was a stuffy, proud man obsessed with prestige, privilege, and his lineage. He cared more about the circumstances of a man's birth than a man's character. He had barely tolerated his nephew, the product of a union between an Englishman and an Indian woman. He certainly ceased trying after that horrible accident with Elliot.

The sad fact was that Alistair would do anything for his approval. He felt he owed the baron a debt he could never repay because he took Alistair in, and raised him as a gentleman. He owed the man a debt he could never repay because Alistair was the reason the baron's beloved son and heir died.

And so, if all the baron asked was that Alistair attend a ball and court a pretty girl, there was no question of saying no.

But there was also never any question that it would be easy to land one of these girls, even if they wore feathered headpieces, eschewed shoes at ton functions, and accessorized with riding crops.

He was just another impoverished, untitled fortune hunter who would be jockeying for attention with all the other impoverished, untitled fortune hunters, some of who stood to inherit loftier titles that his. At any given ball, there would be hundreds at least. He would have, at most, thirty seconds to make an impression during an evening that would probably consist of an endless stream of introductions.

He could not bet his redemption that a woman would look twice at him. He would not wager that he would come up with the perfect line to woo her and win her in the course of a polite introductory conversation. There was too much at stake to count on sparks flying.

So yes, finding that American girl last night had been lucky. Not that he'd realized what a treasure had stumbled into his arms—her words were so slurred it was impossible to understand what she was saying, let alone the accent with which she said it.

But this morning . . .

He came home to his sparsely furnished rented flat and there was a pretty girl there. Waiting for him.

That was when he realized that the moment of being welcomed home was everything he'd ever wanted. That was that indefinable feeling that had propelled him across continents, the fuel for his wandering. It was, simply, the feeling of having someone to come home to.

And then she opened her mouth to speak and there was no denying that she was American. Between the cartoon in the paper and the words she spoke, he was utterly, absolutely certain.

She. Was. The. One.

His heart had started to pound so hard it was a wonder she hadn't heard it and asked about the noise. Given that he'd found her in Mayfair, not far from Durham's place, meant that odds were high that she was one of *those* American girls. She could have been a servant brought over with them, but last he checked, servants in any country weren't in the habit of referencing the *Odyssey*.

She was the one.

And she had just walked out the door.

She had just walked down the corridor, descended the stairs, and out the door onto the street. And just like that, she was gone.

11:13 in the morning

Amelia ought to be in a rush. She ought to launch herself at the first hack she saw and direct the driver to take her to Durham House. She ought to do her best to sneak in via the servants' entrance and pretend that she'd slept late after the exhausting events of last night. She ought to be praying, fervently, that no one had noticed her absence. But the sun was too high in the sky for that.

She was out, at large, missing.

Her family would know.

What difference did one more hour make?

The more she remembered of the previous evening, the less she wanted to go home. The dreadful scene she had caused. The heartbreaking fight with her family.

The gossip columns would be endlessly discussing last night's scandal. She knew enough of London society and the London press to know what they would say. "One of those upstart Americans" had been discovered shoeless at a ball "in a positively heathenish manner" and clumsily faking a faint when any English rose would know how to do so with grace and elegance.

It would anger her family all over again.

No, Amelia was not in a hurry to go home.

And then, as she looked around the bustling streets on a rare blue-sky day, Amelia realized the following:

She had no idea where she was.

She had no idea *how* to return home.

This was a part of London that she was unfamiliar with—the houses weren't as grand, the people weren't dressed as fancily. They didn't stroll by idly on display; they rushed about with a purpose. This was the London she wasn't allowed to explore, and especially not on her own.

And this was everything she ever wanted.

This, she realized as she strolled down the streets, was a chance to explore. A chance to just *be* without the duchess reminding her to stand tall or wear a bonnet. Not that she had a bonnet. Or even a hairpin. Her hair was a vexing, tangled mess falling around her shoulders and falling into her eyes.

Perhaps she wouldn't go home just yet, she thought, weaving her way through the throngs of pedestrians. She'd take an hour, just one hour, to explore. After all, what difference could one hour make at this point? Perhaps she could find her way to the British Museum or the Tower of London. As long as there was no damask wallpaper or disapproving old dowagers, she would consider herself happy.

It was then that she spied a sign for a wigmaker. Amelia grabbed a fistful of her hair— thick curls that plagued her to no end and that foolish women with straight hair always claimed to envy—and didn't think twice about what to do next.

She slipped into the shop and spied a stout older woman at work. Her face was deeply lined. Her gray hair sprung from her head in a frizzy mess.

"Good morning," Amelia said. "Will you cut my hair?"

"Cut your hair?" she looked up, perplexed. Then she looked at Amelia's hair. The gleaming dark curls, cascading down to the middle of her back. "No."

It was a no that suggested Amelia was insane to consider such a thing, and this woman was doing her a favor by refusing the request.

"Yes," Amelia said firmly.

"No."

"Please."

"Perhaps the lady would like a wig instead," she said, gesturing to the ones available for purchase.

"Perhaps you can see that the lady has absolutely no need of a wig and would like you to cut her hair instead," Amelia said, as sweetly as she could manage.

"You are mad."

"Perhaps. Then you wouldn't wish to cross me, now would you?"

"Sit down," the old woman barked.

Amelia sat.

A fierce debate regarding how much hair to cut ensued. The wigmaker was aghast. Amelia was determined. She wanted it all gone—all of it!—and the old witch tried to persuade her to lop off just a few inches. Amelia insisted the scissors go higher and higher. The old woman muttered "madness" all the while.

To Amelia, it felt more like liberation. With each snip of the scissors, with each lock that fell, she felt as if she were letting go of her past— think of all the things she had seen and done with those curls falling in her eyes, or tumbling down her back. Now they were an ever-growing pile in some shop in London, and who knew where they would end up next?

"You must be an actress," the old woman said as she reluctantly chopped off most of Amelia's long curls.

"Perhaps."

"You are cutting all your hair off the better to wear wigs for your performances. That is the only logical conclusion as to why you would do such a hideous thing as cut off all this beautiful hair."

"It's possible," Amelia murmured.

"One of my wigs is used at Covent Garden for the production of *The Return of the Rogue.* You must go see it. Everyone is raving about the leading actress."

This was true; it had been mentioned in the gossip columns and in conversations at soirees. It wasn't clear which was more scandalous—the story or the lead actress. Amelia wished to see it but the duchess had forbidden it.

But the duchess wasn't here now, was she? Amelia bit her lip, smiling. What if this was her chance to see the play and this amazing actress?

Opportunities like these . . . Isn't that what she and her siblings said about the journey to England? It was. This seemed like yet one more opportunity she would be foolish to pass up.

When she reemerged from the shop a short

while later, she felt the sun on her neck and a weight lifted from her. Her head felt lighter. Her very being felt lighter. She felt renewed.

Her long hair would now be made into fashionable wigs, perhaps worn by actresses or even members of the haute ton who snubbed her, while she had a daring, scandalously short haircut that would give the ton something to talk about other than her shoes. Or lack thereof.

11:42 in the morning

Alistair followed a safe distance behind, newspaper in hand, as she wandered blithely through the busy street. He watched her peer in shop windows and examine the wares of street vendors. She moved at a slow pace at odds with everyone else's frantic bustling.

He saw her duck into the wigmaker's shop. What did she fancy, a disguise? It wasn't the worst idea.

He stood outside, pretending to read the newspaper, waiting for her. He learned that the ton had been beside themselves when it was discovered that Durham's heir was a horse breeder in the colonies. The haute ton's worst fears were realized when the family arrived and showed very little inclination to assimilate. According to this gossip rag, it sounded like they didn't even try.

As someone who spent a decent portion of his existence trying to make everyone in the haute ton forget (or at least overlook) his origins, let alone desperately hoping for their approval, this struck Alistair as foolish and arrogant. Or perhaps it was brave.

Either way, it was not something he was going to consider presently. He peered in the window of the wigmaker's shop and felt relieved when he saw that she was still there. He hadn't lost her, yet.

Now she was taking a seat.

What?

Now the proprietress was lifting a heavy pair of scissors. She couldn't possibly mean to—?

She did.

No.

Big chunks of dark brown curls were lopped off and fell to the floor.

What the *hell* was she doing?

Her hair, her glorious curly hair, had been chopped off haphazardly and she had just a little bob of curls around her head.

It was not fashionable. It was not *done*.

But there was no denying how fetching she looked.

He watched as the shopkeeper gave her a bonnet and helped secure the ribbons.

If he hadn't been staring intently at the doorway, if he hadn't watched the whole damn thing through the window, he would have missed her when she stepped out a short while later. She looked like a regular lady—except for that daring haircut and genuine smile.

The newspaper had deemed her wild, unpredictable, rebellious. And now he understood. Alistair continued to watch as she did at least six scandalous things at once—and spent his money, and *not* on a hired hack to take her back to respectability. There was only one thing to do: continue to follow her.

11:44 in the morning

So this was London. The streets were pulsing with the movements of people. So many people pulsing and pushing around her. The air was thick with the dull roar of people talking, of horses and carriages clattering through, of life just happening at a fast speed and a high volume. Then there were the cries of vendors, seeking buyers for their wares.

"Violets!"

"Oranges!"

"Fresh fish!"

Amelia had no need for fresh fish. She had no need for a posy of violets, either. But there was a girl selling them and she simply seemed far too young to be out alone on the streets, earning her keep by selling something as frivolous and delicate as violets.

Amelia hovered close to her, wondering. Where did she go at night? Did she have family, friends, or a suitor? For that matter, where did one find fresh flowers in London to sell? And what did she do when the violets were not in bloom?

"Violets would look so nice with your hair, miss."

Amelia smiled, because the girl knew to give her exactly the compliment she needed to hear at that moment. And she bought violets—possibly the last thing she *needed* at the moment, because she wanted to support this girl. And oh, she had a hundred questions to ask her, but as soon as she paid, the girl was on to the next customer, doling out compliments and extoling the virtues of violets.

Amelia moved on, knowing that the girl probably didn't have a place to return to, and certainly nothing so lavish or even comfortable as Durham House. She felt a little something—a pang, perhaps—at running away from such a comfortable residence and existence so she could muck about on the streets. But the thought, or pang, or whatever it was, retreated as quickly as it came, as Amelia's attentions were captured by the next new thing.

A similar scene was repeated with a woman

selling oranges. A similar scene was almost repeated with one of the mercury women selling gossip sheets—until Amelia saw a cartoon of herself on the cover.

Oh bloody hell.

She spun around, determined not to look, and she ended up bumping into a servant girl.

"I'm so sorry, ma'am," the girl said.

"Oh, it's all right. The fault is mine. I ought to watch where I'm going."

Amelia gave one last look over her shoulder at the wretched news rag. She would not spend her last coin—literally—on that rubbish. Thus, she lifted her nose high in the air and marched past. She was in the process of said marching past in a very dignified manner when a very rude person in a terrific hurry bumped into her.

She stumbled forward and caught herself, and turned to deliver a scathing setdown. Then her heart began to beat hard and fast.

11:50 in the morning

First, Alistair pretended to bump into her. Then he pretended not to recognize her.

"I beg your pardon," he said gruffly.

And then he slowed his pace and did a double take, allowing something like dawning recognition to assemble in his features.

She recognized him immediately.

"Fancy meeting you here, Mr. Finlay-Jones."

She smiled at him: such a sweet, artless smile. Already he felt terrible for deceiving her, even though he hadn't exactly misrepresented himself or behaved in an unbecoming way.

Yet. The day was young.

She was his ticket to everything he ever wanted—a way to repay his debts to the baron and maybe, even, a family. He would do well to remember that today.

"What a coincidence," he said, smiling, even though it was anything but. "I see you're enjoying the sights and offerings of London."

"Oh yes, I did mean to hire a hack and go home immediately. But there is so much to see. I suppose I got distracted." She smiled sheepishly.

"There is much to be distracted by in London."

"I'd love to see *all* of it," she said enthusiastically. The ton had not gotten to her yet. The aristocracy had not made her jaded, or taught her to sound fashionably bored.

No wonder they mocked her.

Even he felt taken aback in the face of such genuine enthusiasm. From a young age he'd been made aware that he was different and didn't quite fit in; from a young age he'd made every effort to act like the others in an attempt to belong.

Yet here was a girl who either didn't know or

didn't care that she was a misfit and she seemed *happy*.

Alistair wasn't sure what to make of that.

"Don't tell me you haven't seen the sights yet," he said, easily, spying an opportunity. "It's always the first thing most people do when they arrive here."

Her American-ness was unspoken between them.

His foreignness would have been as well, had it not been for his relatively pale skin and very English name.

"I have not seen the sights. I consider it a great tragedy," she said.

"I cannot imagine a greater one," he agreed. Then, "I don't know about you but I'm famished. Would you fancy joining me for a quiet breakfast while I persuade you to spend the day seeing all the sights of London?

He felt like a cad. Like the worst sort of scoundrel. It was an invitation no gentleman would ever issue and no lady would ever accept.

But he wanted so badly to fit in with high society, to have a sense of belonging and home and forgiveness.

And she, he could tell, very badly wanted a little adventure.

She hesitated. *Good girl.* She should say no. She should run away.

But he saw the wheels churning in her mind, probably calculating that she was probably already in trouble at home *and* she had already spent the night with him unscathed. It was just breakfast and she was most likely starving.

He could see each thought by the expression on her face.

Lady Amelia Cavendish would be terrible at cards.

Not that he knew her name.

"Yes, I'll join you," she said, giving him the kind of smile that made him feel utterly certain that fate and fortune changed their plans for him. He was back in their good graces.

"You know, I don't think I ever learned your name," he remarked, telling what would undoubtedly one of many lies today. He issued a silent prayer to the Lord for forgiveness.

"Oh! Right." She bit her lip, pausing thoughtfully. "It is Ame—Miss Amy . . . Dish. Miss Amy Dish."

He wanted to burst out laughing. But that would be rude to Miss Amy Dish and would interfere with his plans to woo her. So Alistair grinned and said, "It's a pleasure to make your acquaintance, Miss Dish."

And it was, truly.

Noon

Betsey had just returned from the shops to buy some supplies—cosmetics and such—before her mistress awoke after another long night of elegant soirees and such. But she was back now, still breathing hard from the rush, apron pinned on, cap in place, and ready to deliver breakfast to her Miss Randolph, who began each day abed, sipping chocolate and reading the gossip columns.

Betsey could only dream of lying abed past the first crack of dawn, or having a sip of chocolate or even being able to read well enough to enjoy reading the gossip columns, but there was no use grumbling about what one did or didn't have, her mum had always said. What mattered was a job well done.

So Betsey went down to the kitchens to get the silver tray with all the delicious things on it. The chocolate, the pastries. And the newspaper.

She paused over today's paper. On the cover was a cartoon that just happened to stop her in her tracks, because Betsey had seen that face just his morning on West Rose Street, after she was dashing out to buy more special ointment for Miss Randolph. But it was ridiculous that a lady of such social standing would be walking down the street alone, and at such an unfashionable hour, too.

She shook the crazy idea out of her head and thought nothing of it until Miss Randolph saw the front page and said something about it.

"Oh no she did *not*," Miss Randolph gasped.

"Beg your pardon, ma'am?"

"It says here that Lady Amelia Cavendish, of the American Cavendishes, fainted at Almack's and was discovered to be without shoes. How positively heathenish."

"I daresay I saw her this morning. Down on West Rose Street." She couldn't help it. The sighting of *her, there,* was just so strange.

"I'm certain you didn't. After this shenanigan, the duchess of Durham will lock her up. Or banish her to the country."

"No, I swear I did see her. I had gone down to West Rose Street to pick up that ointment you need for your—"

"We do not mention that."

"Anyway, I saw her come out of the wigmaker's shop and then a bit later I bumped into her and I said excuse me ma'am and she said that's quite all right and that she ought to watch where she's going. And I swear it. I saw her. And then I saw her with a man."

Miss Randolph's eyes were wide now.

"Betsey, tell me *everything*."

Chapter 7

In which the charade begins in earnest.

Noon-ish

Alistair led her past the Bull & Bear and the Queen's Head, where they might be recognized by debauched lords, refueling after a night of reverie. While it certainly wouldn't hurt his suit to be seen with her under such scandalously inappropriate circumstances, he had some notion of fair play. Until Death Do You Part was not something to take lightly; he had an idea that they might spend the day together, discreetly, and create some shared memories so that when they met again he wasn't just another fortune hunter, but one she had shared happy memories with.

He guided her toward the King's Arms, which

was just on the outskirts of Mayfair. He secured a private parlor for them, just in case.

He also dashed off a note to Jenkins and had a boy deliver it:

Come to the King's Arms urgently. Bring money. Agree with everything I say.

This morning he had watched as she easily took the last bit of cash he had on hand and spent it on frivolities like an orange and a posy of violets. He only hoped Jenkins arrived before the bill for the meal they were about to enjoy— preferably with money.

"This is very wrong," she said, taking a sip of the tea they had ordered that he could not pay for.

"The tea? Shall we send it back?"

"No. *This.*" She gestured to the room at large with a wave of her hand. "We should not be alone together."

This was undeniably, absolutely, one-thousand-percent correct.

But.

He had to marry. He had to marry *her*, in fact. And he did not see another way to make this possible without stealing these moments. He didn't stand a chance otherwise.

He dropped his voice and said, "I promise you, it will be our secret."

"Excellent. Because otherwise," she said drop-

ping her voice low and leaning in conspiratori-
ally, "we will have to marry. And I hardly even
know you."

"That is easily remedied. What would you like
to know?"

"Is Alistair Finlay-Jones truly your name?"

"Yes, it is. I was raised in Berkshire, attended
Eton, then Oxford." He neglected to mention that
he had been born in India, arriving in England
as a young orphan of eight. Thanks to his English name and lighter skin, the Baron had made
an effort to pass him off as purely English, with
mixed success. Alistair merely wished for a place
where he felt like he belonged, fully.

"Ah, yes, Berkshire. Not too far from London."
She sipped her tea. "You needn't look so surprised. Geography is one of the few subjects
taught to young girls. And I have a deep and
abiding interest in The Rest of The World."

"Are you well traveled?"

"Not nearly as much as I'd like to be. What
about yourself?"

*Yes. I have traveled all over Europe and other parts
of the world, looking for the feeling I felt when I opened
the door to my flat and saw you there.*

Gad, where had *that* thought come from?

"I only just returned from my Grand Tour of
Europe. Most gents take one year. I took six."

"I wish I could take a Grand Tour," she said
wistfully.

"It's a wonderful experience," Alistair said. And it was the truth, even though he often thought such freedom and travel would have been enhanced by knowing one had a home to return to. "But I've never been to America. What is it like?"

"Dangerous," she said gravely. "Between the wild bears that devour our horses and the constant attacks from native tribes or the dire paucity of luxuries and the deplorable lack of an aristocracy, we live a very mean, wretched existence."

"Is that so?"

"Not at all," she said with a laugh. "It's very civilized. Not that anyone here wishes to know that."

He was starting to see why the ton was not quite accepting of her. When she spoke there was always a hint of laughter, somehow, even when she was serious. Was she making fun? Or just amused? He didn't know, but her secret sense of delight made her beautiful.

"What brought you to England?"

"My brother—" she started, then stopped abruptly. She took a long sip of tea before replying. "My brother sent me to finishing school here.

"Why did you return to England after your travels?" she asked.

Alistair took a moment before replying. Not being a delusional fool, ignorant to the ways of the world and storybooks, he knew that she would eventually learn that his uncle had ordered him to marry one of the Americans. She would inevitably be livid. It was crucial, then, that he stick to the truth as much as possible.

Even though she had just blatantly lied to him, which, he had to admit, was smart of her. Going around declaring one's unchaperoned self as the sister to a wealthy duke was not wise.

He was glad, again, that he had been the one to find her. He had an agenda, yes, but it was a noble one. With him, her virtue and reputation would be safe.

"My uncle requested my assistance with his . . . business affairs."

"That is just a way of saying marriage, is it not?" He spit out his tea in shock and she laughed. "Ha! I'm right. I love it when I am right. And do allow me to guess: you are one of those unrepentant, avowed bachelors who must be dragged to the altar."

"Quite the contrary."

"How interesting," she murmured, merely lifting one eyebrow, he noted with a small amount of jealousy. He had *never* been able to master that.

It was then that Jenkins interrupted, thank God. He stepped into the room, newspaper in hand; to sip coffee while reading a newspaper was Jenkins's idea of heaven. And it just so happened that Alistair saw a familiar cartoon on the front page. Off all the news rags in London, Jenkins had brought *that* newspaper, with the damned cartoon of *her* on the front.

"Mr. Finlay-Jones," he intoned.

"Oh, hello there, Jenkins! What a surprise to see you here," Alistair said, for the benefit of the charade, even though it wasn't exactly a surprise. He rose to greet his valet. "I'd like you to meet Miss Dish. Won't you join us? We'll ring for more tea."

"I don't know what to say." Jenkins was clearly dreadfully confused. Alistair pursed his lips in annoyance and tried to give his man A Look.

"Didn't you read my note?"

"Obviously I have done so. Otherwise I wouldn't be here."

"Well then," Alistair said, clapping the man on the back. He may have gotten the note but he hadn't *gotten the note,* so to speak, so Alistair cut him off.

"You must be acting obtuse just to take the piss," Alistair said. What part of *agree with everything I say* was confusing? Jenkins was a smart man. He was also excessively morally upright at times.

Jenkins frowned. "Is 'take the piss' really a phrase you wish to say in front of a lady?"

He turned to Amelia. "I humbly beg your pardon for my unladylike language."

She laughed a lovely, genuine laugh and

Alistair looked over at his valet with a look that said *You see? She's lovely and we can't let her get away.*

"Oh please don't apologize on my account," Amelia said. "Like most ladies I secretly delight in very coarse and rude language."

"Like most ladies?"

"At least, I hope so. Otherwise I am dreadfully unfashionable."

The two gentlemen took seats at the table and Alistair poured a cup of tea for his valet, who was dreadfully confused at what was going on, but certainly disapproving of whatever it was.

"I doubt it. I wager that you're tremendously popular."

She shrugged and, "Not exactly, but I don't mind."

But he got the impression that perhaps she did mind. She certainly would once she saw what the newspapers were saying about her. And she would see *that* any second now, because Jenkins, obliviously, had set down the newspaper right next to his plate where anyone could see it.

"I thought ladies wanted to be popular."

"Oh many do. They fret over what is said in the gossip columns and simper with only the most eligible bachelors and make it a point to cut the ladies who are not popular. It is very dangerous being a lady in society." She caught herself. "So I am given to understand from my reading of the gossip rags, because I am in finishing school and would not know firsthand. Why, I'll bet we could prove my point by reading that gossip column in that very newspaper."

She started to reach for Jenkins's paper. Alistair couldn't let her see the horrid cartoon on the front page. So he accidentally tipped over his cup of coffee.

"Oh!" she cried out as coffee soaked the newspaper and spilled across the table.

"You mustn't be so clumsy Jenkins," Alistair admonished.

Jenkins looked as if he wished to swear vehemently. But there was a lady present so he bit his tongue and shot daggers with his eyes instead.

"Hell and damnation," Alistair swore. "Well, it seems I shall have to take your word for it. I don't have much experience with ladies myself."

Jenkins snorted.

"Somehow I don't believe that," Miss Amy Dish said. "And I share Mr. Jenkins's response. Even though ladies are not supposed to snort."

"You wound me. Both of you." Alistair pressed his hands against his heart for effect, drawing eye rolls from his companions.

"Well if you invited me out to flatter your delusions, you are sorely mistaken," Jenkins said flatly.

"Ah, Jenkins. Ever faithful friend."

"Friend." His voice verily dripped with sarcasm and irony and all that.

"Yes, my *dear old friend.*"

"Last I checked people didn't p—" whatever he was about to say—and Alistair was certain he was about to say something about friends aren't usually employed—it was lost. Alistair had hooked his boot under Jenkins's chair and easily flipped him over. The old man went sprawling on the floor and the chair followed.

"Oh!" Amelia shrieked. "Mr. Jenkins, are you all right?!"

She fled to his side and helped him up. Jenkins looked murderously at Alistair. Since he couldn't very well explain, Alistair grinned and shrugged while Amelia performed some bastardized version of a doctor checking for injury on a very unhappy Jenkins.

"I'll just go," Jenkins said, standing.

"No, do stay," Alistair said. "*Stay.*"

Glaring, Jenkins took his seat. Alistair turned to Amelia, back in her chair, sipping tea and that laughing sparkle in her eyes.

"So tell me, Miss Dish, what would you be doing right now if you weren't here?"

"Daydreaming about being here, probably."

"Is that so? *Here?* I find that hard to believe."

Here was a second-rate pub on the fringes of a fashionable neighborhood. It was not the stuff of daydreams.

"If not *here* per se, at least *out*. I spend far too much time . . ." she paused, searching for exactly the right words. "Indoors."

"I understand. Blink twice if you are being kept in a tower against your will, waiting for Prince Charming," he said, and she laughed. "But how are we supposed to climb up and rescue you, Rapunzel, if you chopped off your hair?"

"You noticed."

"Hard to miss. Rather fetching."

Jenkins snorted again, but everyone else ignored him.

"Thank you. The truth is, I've actually recently escaped from being held captive in the Tower of London."

"Miss Dish, are you saying that Jenkins and I are harboring a fugitive?"

"Do you have a problem with living dangerously, Mr. Finlay-Jones?"

"I have a problem with harboring a fugitive of the Lady variety," Jenkins said flatly.

"C'mon now Jenkins. Where is your sense of fun?"

"I haven't seen it in quite some time now."

"I haven't seen it either," Alistair said. Jenkins was not employed because he was amusing. But that mattered little when Alistair's future happiness sat to his left. "Miss Dish, now that you've escape from the Tower of London, how would you like to spend the day?"

* * *

How would she like to spend the day? Some girls would have said shopping on Bond Street or parading along Rotten Row (especially with such a handsome gentleman). A stupid, simpering miss would say, "Oh! I haven't thought about it!" mainly because such a stupid, simpering miss probably didn't think about much at all, ever.

Amelia sipped her tea, considering. She was not certain that she *would* spend the day with the handsome and charming Mr. Finlay-Jones—a sentence that sounded ridiculous as she thought it. Until this very moment, she had presumed that she would return to Durham House immediately upon the conclusion of this breakfast.

But now another possibility had presented itself. A very, very attractive possibility. Given the freedom to roam around London and explore, Amelia knew exactly what she wished to do.

Upon her arrival in London, she had purchased a guidebook and had spent hours reading all about the sights, treasures, and pleasures of the city. She had marked down the pages of things she wished to do. Alas, she hadn't brought the guidebook with her—suggesting she had departed in haste last night—but she remembered enough.

"I would like to see a show at Astley's Amphitheatre. I have heard it is marvelously entertaining."

In fact, she had suggested to the duchess that

they hire acrobatic performers from Astley's for the ball that they were planning to host and which was scheduled for . . . Amelia felt a flare of panic . . . a few days hence. (Phew, she need not rush home to decorate the ballroom. Yet.) But, it went without saying, that was not the sort of entertainment that the duchess considered proper.

"What else would you like to do?"

"I should like to stroll through the pleasure gardens of Vauxhall."

"A classic London adventure."

"Yes. And I would also like to see a play."

"You haven't yet been to the theater?"

"Allow me to clarify: I would like to go to the theater and stand in the pit."

"That is not an unreasonable list."

"Thank you. I didn't think it was either."

But the duchess, on the other hand, had been aghast at all the suggestions. She said that when Amelia was married, she could seek her husband's permission and escort to attend the theater in such a compromising manner. She had a feeling he, whoever he was, would have the same conventional opinion as the duchess.

"In fact, I think if one put their mind to it, one could easily do all of those activities. In just one day," he mused. Then he leaned in close to her and treated her to the kind of smile that made a girl throw caution to the wind and said, "The question is, shall we do it today?"

Of course they should not. Ladies and gentlemen did not do anything, not even breathe in the drawing room, without a chaperone or six. Jenkins hardly counted, though he was doing an excellent job of silently disapproving of the entire conversation.

The right thing to do was thank him for everything thus far—rescuing her from a dire fate, allowing her to sleep in his comfortable bed whilst he spent the night on that dreadful settee, and this lovely breakfast—and hire a hack and return to her family. Immediately.

She wasn't sure of the time but it was certainly late enough in the morning that everyone would have noticed that she wasn't home. She never missed a meal and breakfast at Durham house had surely come and gone. The sooner she returned, the better. Everyone would be livid, they would yell at her, and banish her to her room. Or force her to write thank-you notes, have her hair arranged, and change her dress at least three times.

But she had made it this far. She had managed to escape. Everyone was already mad at her. Amelia had this half-scrambled idea of graphing the intensity of her family's anger against the duration of her time out and gave up—Claire would know exactly how to plot the points and draw the line to show that one could only be *so* angry, so what then did it matter if she was gone twelve hours or twenty?

Or something like that.

There was also the matter of Mr. Alistair Finlay-Jones.

He has a handsome devil, there was no doubt about it. He wasn't like all the other poncey, stuffy lords she'd met so far. He was younger, and leaner. His gaze was sharper, his grin more charming, his humor like hers. His dark hair fell rakishly toward his eyes—those warm brown eyes with just a hint of sadness to make her wonder about what secret pain and tortured secrets he might possess.

Sometimes she got bored and read Bridget's novels about heroes with secret pains and heroines with the perfect, tender touch to heal all emotional wounds. They were vastly more entertaining than Claire's mathematical papers or James's agricultural treatises.

But never mind all that. There was a handsome man who made her laugh and was inviting her to spend the day exactly as *she* wished.

There would be hell to pay. And she would gladly pay it—later.

"Yes," she said. His eyes brightened. "Yes!" She laughed now. "Let's go have the perfect day."

"That is a terrible idea," Jenkins said flatly.

"I know!" she said excitedly. "But let's do it anyway!"

Chapter 8

In which a walk in the park is not merely a walk in the park.

Nearly one o'clock!

After leaving Jenkins to settle the bill, they stepped out of the Kings Arms and onto the street. Amelia—rather, Miss Amy Dish—craned her neck, looking here and there and taking in *everything*. If there was any doubt that she was new to the city and eager to see it, she dispelled it.

Alistair realized that the ton—a collection of people known to throw the most fabulous and expensive parties at which they stood around in satins and jewels and declared how *bored to death* they were—must be horrified by Amelia and her unbridled interest in the world around her. All that *enthusiasm* must confound them terribly.

She intertwined her arm with his and looked up at him.

"Shall we hire a hack to take us to Astley's?"

"We could. But it's a beautiful day—shall we walk?"

"That would be lovely." She smiled at him.

Arm in arm they strolled a few short blocks until they came to St. James's Park, in the southeast corner of Mayfair. It was smaller than Hyde Park and often less crowded. It had been remodeled since he'd last been; there were large swaths of grass interspersed with gravel paths and large oak trees providing patches of shade.

"I must admit I'm also keen to see the city. It's been so long," he said. Six long years without a stroll through the park, a ride along Rotten Row, a London ball, a drink at White's or an afternoon at Tattersall's.

"Why did you leave?"

It was an accident. I don't want to talk about it.

"Everyone goes on a Grand Tour," he explained. "It's the done thing amongst a certain set to take a year to see the sights of Europe and acquire a little continental polish."

"Why did you stay away? Six years is much longer than just one." She was quick, that one. He hadn't even realized what he'd said to give himself away and she'd pounced on it, asking the question no one dared ask because the answer was too complicated and awful and emotional.

Not that he would explain any of that to the lovely, intrepid, and curious woman on his arm. Alistair could see that she was one of those *determined* females who were like terriers when it came to men's secrets. If only he had noticed this earlier before initiating a line of conversation that would not end well for him. But what could he say? She distracted him.

"Nothing to come back to, really."

"What about your family? Or friends?"

"Truth be told, I don't really have much of a family."

"Much? So you must have some." Terrier indeed.

"Just an uncle," he said vaguely, trying to make it sound boring, so boring. He had no interest in discussing Baron Wrotham or even acknowledging him as family; in that they were in agreement. Alistair looked around the park, hoping for something interesting to point out—perhaps the horse guards were rehearsing or there was some other distraction to be found.

"Is he horrid?" Amelia asked very bluntly.

That was the thing about Wrotham. He was horrid but understandably so. He was a product of his time. And he was grieving. So if that made him brusque, distant, or cold, that was fine.

Perfectly acceptable.

Utterly understandable.

It just . . . well, Alistair wouldn't say it *hurt*.

But then again, here he was strolling arm in arm with the woman his uncle had commanded him to wed. So it certainly did something to him.

Not that it was a chore, being with Miss Amy Dish, with her charming smile and her sheer delight at something as simple as strolling in the park on a beautiful day.

Until this moment, that is, when she started asking questions.

"Mr. Finlay-Jones?"

"I'm sorry, I was distracted by that flock of pigeons. My uncle is not fond of me."

"Why not?"

Because I am a mixed-race burden upon his household and—well, Alistair swallowed—he still couldn't think about the other reason. He certainly wasn't going to explain the whole sordid affair to Miss Amy Dish. She would probably try to *soothe* him.

"It's a long story."

"I do have all day."

"Oh, look! The horse guards are rehearsing. Shall we go watch?"

1:07 in the afternoon

If Mr. Finlay-Jones thought he could distract her with the horse guards, he was only half right. She did marvel at all the men in uniform on horseback as they rehearsed their impressive routine.

But it did not escape her notice that there was some sort of drama between Mr. Finlay-Jones and his uncle. The more evasive he was—there was *no* flock of pigeons—the more curious she became. But as she said, she had all day.

So she turned and watched the horse guards for a while, though she found herself stealing glances at the man beside her. He was quite pleasing to look at—she had noticed that straightaway. But now she was becoming *aware* of him. It seemed she could feel the heat of him, which was absurd—it was probably the sun—but still . . . she glanced at his chest. It was broad, and flat, and she had the mad urge to rest her head there, listen to his heartbeat, feel the warmth of him.

When they continued on their walk through the park, arm in arm, she was *aware* of the muscles in his arm. Of all the asinine things. Of course he had muscles in his arms, everyone did. But she noticed them, felt them, and imagined them holding her.

Amelia knew she was not the first woman to have such feelings—Bridget detailed them extensively in her diary, which Amelia was fond of reading. But this was the first time she'd felt them.

The first time she noticed a man for something other than the terrible choice of waistcoat, or his weak chin, or nose red from drink, or overall sense of arrogance.

She had not met the best men in England.

Until Mr. Finlay-Jones. Who might have kidnapped her. Who clearly had a tortured relationship with his sole relative. Between his good looks and his dark secret and tortured past, he was, plainly, irresistible.

"And what will you tell your family of your whereabouts today?" he asked, interrupting her thoughts.

"I shall tell them that I was kidnapped and drugged and stumbled home as soon as I woke and could escape," she replied breezily. "And I will mention that on the way home, I fought off a band of ruffians thanks to the knife in my boot and that in order to avoid detection by the prying eyes of the ton, I traveled by rooftop."

"I imagine it would be difficult to jump across rooftops in a skirt."

"I love that that is the part you find outlandish."

"It is the part that I have the least experience with," Alistair said, "as I am not in the habit of wearing dresses or traveling by rooftop."

"Are you saying that you have a knife in your boot? That you have woken up after being drugged and kidnapped?"

Alistair sighed and smiled at a memory. "There was my eighteenth birthday, when I was brought against my will to the local brothel and plied with excessive quantities alcohol. I hardly knew my own name when I awoke the following afternoon."

"Against your will," she said flatly.

He grinned. Lud, but that grin made her giddy. Not that she'd let him know it. Instead she rolled her eyes and heaved a sigh. "Boys. Men."

"I find it hard to believe that as a young lady in finishing school, you have such experience with men that you can heave long-suffering sighs about their behavior," he said with a laugh.

"I have an older brother. He has friends. That is sufficient."

"I hope I might change your mind," he said softly. Seriously.

Suddenly they weren't joking anymore, which made her heart race.

She smiled up at him. "As I said, I have all day."

In which two gentlemen see something. Maybe.

Meanwhile, on a park bench nearby, there were two gentlemen—still dressed from the formal ball they'd attended the night before, and still drunk from the gaming hell they'd attended after that.

"I say, she's a fine bit of muslin," Fraser said, waving his hand in the general direction of a few women strolling in the park. Algernon took a look and didn't see anyone who fit that description.

"I say, you are most likely still deep in your cups," said someone who was probably still deep in his cups.

"Have a look. Have you ever seen short hair? *On a girl?*"

Algernon reluctantly had a look. Squinted.

Fraser watched her closely; she did seem familiar. Maybe. Perhaps. Where had he seen her? If he'd had more sleep or less to drink he might be able to place her. But it didn't matter.

Besides, who thought it was fun to watch the horse guards?

He watched her a little more—she did seem very familiar—and gasped like a shocked old matron as it dawned on him.

Horse breeders from the colonies—that's who cared to watch the horse guards!

Fraser looked again for the girl with short hair, out with a gentleman he didn't recognize. But she was gone and he couldn't confirm what he saw. It was probably nothing. And he had debts to worry about, not hicks from the colonies with unfashionable coiffures.

Beside him, Algernon started snoring.

Chapter 9

**In which our heroine runs off
to the circus. As one does.**

Just shy of two o'clock

It inevitably occurred to Alistair that if Amelia
was truly the sister to a duke—and niece to the
Duchess of Durham, a woman he remembered
as a terrifying dragon who regularly struck fear
in the hearts of grown men, and made babies cry,
probably—people would be looking for her.

Bow Street Runner kinds of people.

Perhaps even the king's own army.

Perhaps, even most terrifying of all, the duchess herself.

At the very least, there would be household
servants—whom he wouldn't have a prayer of

identifying and thus avoiding—roaming the streets searching for her.

It would not be a good thing to be caught together. Charges of kidnapping would swiftly follow, especially once other damning facts emerged: namely, that Amelia had no memory of how she came to wake up in his bedroom and that his uncle had essentially ordered him to marry her.

There was a chance that the duchess would insist on a wedding—which would certainly suit his purposes and there was no reason he should have qualms about it. *But . . .* it felt wrong to take advantage of a woman thusly, especially one as open, trusting, and kind as Lady Amelia.

Besides, entrapment was no way to begin a marriage.

His noble concerns could all be for naught; there was also a chance that Amelia's relations would refuse a match with him. He was hardly a catch—he was a mixed-race orphan who stood to inherit an impoverished minor title. Why would someone as lovely as Amelia wish to pledge her troth to the likes of him? What family would even allow it?

This was a quandary.

She was a quandary.

Alistair reminded himself that they only needed to spend enough time together so that when they inevitably met again, he would stand out amongst all the other desperate fortune hunters.

By that rationale, he could return her home now.

He glanced down at her. Even with her hair lopped off, she appeared feminine. With her short hair, petite frame, and delicate features, she reminded him of a fairy or a woodland sprite. Except he wasn't in the habit of lusting after fairies or woodland sprites.

Perhaps after Astley's, he would escort her directly back to "finishing school," otherwise known as her home.

He glanced at her again.

Focus. Focus not on her lips, or the dimple in her left cheek when she smiled. He ought to focus on avoiding anyone who looked like a Bow Street Runner or who eyed Amelia twice. She seemed oblivious to the fact that more than a few gentlemen took a long look or two at her—until they saw Alistair glaring murderously at them.

And above all, he had to continually focus her attention away from newsagents, people reading newspapers, people wrapping purchases in newspapers, newspapers that were trampled underfoot, and newspapers that were simply blowing in the wind begging for her to notice.

He didn't want her to see the scandalous and humiliating cartoon of herself on the front page of *The London Weekly.* It seemed like something that might be spirit crushing, and it just seemed wrong to crush the spirit of Miss Amy Dish, who was chattering away about something—he couldn't quite follow, but he did enjoy the sound of her voice.

Astley's loomed ahead—a tall domed structure surrounded by crowds of people milling about before the show—reminding Alistair to focus on his next problem.

Admission. Specifically, money for admission. He had none. Not even a pence.

According to his calculations, Amelia surely had some left in her possession.

There was obviously one course of action and it was *not* asking her to borrow a few quid. He would have to pick her pocket; fortunately he'd seen her slip a few remaining coins into her skirt.

The crowds were a help. It gave him a reason to draw her in close to him and wrap his arm around her, sliding lower, to her waist.

This was wrong. On so many levels, this was wrong.

But she fit against him so perfectly, her head nestled right below his shoulder. He could easily imagine them lying like that, lying other ways. Alistair made the mistake of breathing her in, and he was left with that heady, sated feeling of having just made love. So this was why ladies and gentlemen were kept at a distance.

This was no time to be distracted. Not by her

scent, or the feeling of her waist beneath his palm, or the desire to feel her all over.

The ticket takers were ahead, and—bloody hell—a pair of Bow Street Runners. Miss Amy Dish saw them at the same moment as he did. They were easily identifiable by their red waistcoats and blue greatcoats. Two of them sat on horseback, surveying the crowd in search of one lost heiress.

He felt her step falter. She lowered her head.

She was worried about being found.

And he was worried about losing her.

But her family knew where to look for her.

They knew her. Knew that she had likely run off to—if not join the circus—see it. For one hot second, he was jealous. He felt the burn of envy, the raw sense of heartache and longing.

When he ran off, no one had looked for him.

The baron was happy to see him go. And Elliot was dead and buried. He had friends, of course. But they had estates and families to manage, which left little time for chasing him across the continent. They had lives to live and Alistair? Well, he wandered and wondered about what his purpose might be.

And somehow all that running—all that searching and wanting for a feeling of home— had led to this moment, in which he was about to rob a runaway heiress under the watchful gaze of the magistrate's own representatives.

Alistair's heart pounded hard in his chest.

It was over in seconds.

He guided them into a thick crowd, pretended to stumble, falling against her. She grasped him to hold herself steady. His arms slipped around her waist . . . hand slid into the pocket . . . fingers closed around coins.

But he was more aware of her breasts against his chest, where his heart pounded. Those velvety brown eyes gazed up at his face. He was lying to her, stealing from her, and she looked up at him adoringly.

It slayed him, that.

Deception did not suit him.

After slipping the coins into his own pocket, they stepped apart, and laughed awkwardly. Alistair steered them toward the ticket taker on the far right, who wasn't in direct view of the Runners. He was a fat, jowly old fellow—he put Alistair in mind of a plump albino toad—and he had absolutely no interest in anyone or anything.

"Two tickets for my, uh, sister and I, please," said Alistair, handing over some of the money pilfered from Amelia.

A few steps later she laughed and asked, "Your sister?"

"You're right. I should have requested two tickets for myself and the unmarried young woman with whom I have absconded. And with whom I am traveling without a chaperone."

"This is such fun," Miss Amy Dish gushed.

Alistair wasn't sure if *fun* was the word he would use. Heart pounding and nerve-wracking? Yes.

Exhilarating and enchanting? Yes.

And terribly, terribly confusing.

Showtime

Astley's Amphitheatre was nothing short of spectacular. Three tiers of seats surrounded a circular arena and they were packed with all manner of people: from governesses with children of the rich and titled to families visiting London or those who had no other pressing engagements. High above them all hung a massive chandelier, lighting the merriment below.

The dull roar of the crowd hushed as the show began with a dramatic demonstration of equine feats. Fancily groomed and decorated horses wearing feathered headpieces pranced and galloped about.

The crowd gasped as the riders—*lady riders*—did the unthinkable: they stood on galloping horses' backs and performed acrobatic feats while the horses flew around the arena at a breakneck pace.

Alistair stole a glance away from the ring at the woman beside him. Amelia was leaning forward in rapt attention. Lips parted, eyes gleaming. He had the distinctly unsettling impression that she wasn't merely finding amusement in the performances.

No, he feared she was taking notes.

Of things to try.

Herself.

"I can do that," Miss Amy Dish said matter-of-factly as an equestrienne *stood* atop a horse as it cantered around the ring.

"Is that so?" He first felt a pang of horror as he imagined it and then a pang of empathy for her family.

"It is so. But I have been forbidden from displaying my prowess." Her dismay was evident. But he couldn't blame anyone for forbidding her to do it, if only for the stress to one's heart it would cause.

"Well, it is incredibly dangerous."

"Indeed, but I think my aunt's reasoning is that it necessitates the wearing of breeches," she explained. "In her book, scandal trumps mortal danger when it comes to things to fear."

"Is wearing breeches one of those wild American practices that have so horrified our refined English society?"

They both realized his mistake at the same time. He froze; she pursed her lips. God, he was an idiot. He might as well address her as Lady Amelia of America and inquire after her dowry and ask why she was parodied on the front page of the newspaper. He wracked his brain for something else to say and came up wanting.

She saved the day.

"I suppose it would be, if I were out," she said, choosing her words carefully. "But I am only at finishing school, you see."

"Right, of course. But can you do that?"

Someone dressed in an outlandishly exotic costume was juggling flaming swords.

"I would certainly *try*," she said with a wicked smile.

He absolutely believed her. It excited him, that. It shouldn't have. But there was no denying the frisson of something because she was a woman who did things. She acted. She took risks, courted danger, and flirted with scandal.

And he . . . didn't. Not anymore, anyway.

Once upon a time he'd been a hellion, like any young buck—there was no dare, wager, race, or expedition he would say no to. He lived for the thrill of danger, rejection, failure, and he lived for the thrill of triumphing over the fear.

And then Elliot was killed because of Alistair's need for excitement.

That put an end to that.

Ever since, he'd wandered, biding his time until he inherited. He tried to find peace with the tragic events that had made him Wrotham's heir. He was like so many other gentlemen, who simply passed the time until they inherited or married or something happened to them. It never bothered him until he sat beside a woman who was unlike other ladies.

But today, he had a purpose.

Her.

He liked having a purpose.

The dramatics of the flaming swords and juggling gave way to some lighthearted entertainment in the form of dancing dogs, who pranced and spun about upon command.

He was no better than one of those dogs. Alistair shifted uncomfortably in his seat. Aye, he had a purpose for the day, but it was not one of his choosing. Here he was, jumping on command and following the orders of someone who didn't even like him.

Amelia leaned in his direction, the better to see the performance below. He breathed her in. And he thought again about that moment when he arrived at his empty flat and it didn't seem so empty when she was there. And he thought perhaps there might be another purpose to this day . . . one that wasn't about what the baron wanted, but what Alistair needed.

The tightrope walkers were next. Everyone fell silent for this performance. A rope was stretched taut, high above the arena. And there was nothing to catch their fall. A violent spectacle of death seemed inevitable.

"I shall leave the tightrope walking to you," Amelia whispered, leaning in close. He felt the soft whisper of her breath.

"Afraid of heights, my dear roof jumper?"

"My skirts would get in the way. Besides, we need something for you to do in the circus while I'm juggling flaming swords and standing atop two galloping horses."

He felt, again, a flare of something—anger, jealously, rebellion? He did have a purpose—following Wrotham's orders and seeking his forgiveness. Wedding the woman beside him.

And maybe, just maybe, finding a person who felt like home.

Everything all came back to the woman beside him.

As long as he didn't screw up. He could perhaps make her fall in love with him . . . or hate him forever for this deception.

Like those tightrope walkers, one misstep could lead to certain disaster. But a dozen or two tiny, perfect steps could lead to triumph.

"Are you all right?" she asked him.

"Of course."

"For a moment I thought I might have hurt your feelings, but then I remembered that Englishmen don't seem to have any."

"Right." He cleared his throat. "That would be unseemly."

"Of course they do have *some* feelings," Amelia

continued, unaware of his turmoil. "Namely, hunger, thirst and horror at an excessive display of emotion."

"You seem very knowledgeable on the subject of Englishmen. For an American."

"I have made the acquaintance of many. They're a lot of pompous, intoxicated bores who don't seem to do very much except drink, wager, and pass judgment on young ladies."

He decided *not* to point out that a young lady in finishing school wouldn't have such knowledge.

But what could he claim to do beyond what she listed?

Woo innocent young ladies for selfish purposes.

Best not to say that aloud.

"I notice that you do not disagree with me," Amelia said. "I'm so often right. I just wish my family would recognize it more often."

Here she heaved one of those dramatic sighs that only young ladies can manage because only they can manage such depth of emotion.

Alistair was left with the impression that Amelia wasn't just running away from her home and family. She was seeking *something* in the guise of Miss Amy Dish. For all that she was enchanted by the display of Astley's Amphitheatre, he suspected dancing dogs and tightrope walkers weren't really what she was looking for.

Just like him.

He wanted to tell her to return home to her family, who undoubtedly loved her; he could just tell from the way she spoke of them in that teasing but loving way. And yet she was his ticket to finding that feeling of home and belonging for himself. If he could just marry her he could both atone for the mistakes of his past and secure the future he longed for.

The show at Astley's had been everything her dog-eared guidebook said and more. Amelia had witnessed gravity-defying feats, charming little dancing dogs (oh, how she wanted one!), and the juggling of flaming swords. To say nothing of the dramatic feats performed atop horseback and all the other activities in which the performer risked his or her neck for everyone's entertainment.

But it was the tightrope walker who had Amelia holding her breath. Because even with her feet firmly on the ground, she felt as if she were performing high in the air, with an audience watching, and everyone waiting for her to fall.

Just one misstep could ruin her.

The only thing to do was keep moving forward, to take one step and then another.

If she paused, she would fall.

If she hesitated, she would fall.

Today, she vowed not to hesitate.

With an extra spring in her step and sparkle in

her eye, she linked her arm with Mr. Finlay-Jones as they strolled along the Thames.

"I feel my life would be complete if I only had one of those dancing dogs." Amelia sighed. She felt Alistair stiffen beside her. Had she said something wrong?

"I'll see what I can do," he murmured.

She noticed that he spoke, if however vaguely, of a future encounter. He couldn't be so terrible if he planned for them to meet again, right? Thus far, he had been a perfect gentleman—as far as she knew. It mattered; Amelia wanted him to be good, a gentleman, because she liked him. His company was enjoyable and he seemed more than happy to indulge her whims to see the city. He wasn't like any of the other stuffy, boorish gents the duchess had introduced her to with the absurd hope that Amelia would want to marry one of them.

That reminded of her of what awaited her at home—the duchess, the pressure to marry, the horrible suggestions of future husbands.

"Where shall we go next?" Amelia asked. "Vauxhall?"

"Wherever the lady wishes," he said, which were words any lady loved to hear. "Or you might wish to return home." Which were words she was less thrilled to hear.

Of course she would go home. Eventually. Naturally she should go home immediately. But the sky was blue, the air was warm, the man with her was quite handsome and said they could do whatever she wished. He was not giving her grief for, say, being discovered at a ball free of her footwear.

"Not quite yet . . ."

She thought of the tightrope walkers, halfway between one ledge and another. Turning around and going back was an impossibility. One had to simply keep moving forward. Somehow, it seemed the same for her.

"Your family must be worried."

Oh, Lud. Amelia glanced up at Mr. Finlay-Jones. He seemed genuinely concerned. She found herself imagining a dramatic scene involving her worried family in the drawing room:

"I should have never insisted she wear shoes," the duchess wailed, clutching a perfectly starched linen-and-lace handkerchief to her dry eyes, because duchesses do not do anything so human as cry.

"And I should have taken her to the British Museum instead of my horridly dull lecture at the Mathematical Society," Claire lamented. "I almost bored my sister to death and now she might be actually dead."

"Don't say such a thing," Bridget cried. "Although then I would have something else to write about in my diary besides Darcy and Rupert."

"When she returns," her dear brother James said in her imagination, "I vow to buy her another horse and allow her to ride astride whenever she wishes."

"What is a little scandal compared to Lady Amelia's happiness?" the duchess asked. *Indeed.*

"Yes, they are probably worried. I ought to send word that I'm alive. But I am not yet ready to return."

"You do know how lucky you are to have a family that cares about you?"

Gah. He had turned serious. And sentimental. And it made her nervous.

"Of course," she replied flippantly. "Doesn't everyone?"

"No." He said this so darkly. She paused.

"Your uncle doesn't care for you?"

"No." Darker still.

"Why is that?"

She saw him shrug as if there was really nothing to say, and certainly nothing deeply emotional. It was an evasive maneuver, one she'd seen James employ a time or two or ten. Amelia found it at once amusing and exasperating that these men thought a casual shrug signified, oh, nothing to see here. When in fact the opposite was true. It signified to her, a person who wanted to know everything, that she ought to dig deeper.

So she said, "Ah, I see."

"What do you see?"

Mr. Finlay-Jones sounded nervous, which meant she was right. And she would have to explain.

"Some Tragedy Hath Befallen, leaving you

both estranged. You are both broken-hearted but too proud and angry to admit to grief."

Mr. Finlay-Jones stared at her in mute horror. It wasn't the best look for him; she far preferred when he gave her that charming smile. And then she thought it was very troubling that it was only early afternoon and she had already catalogued his expressions and developed preferences. And that they involved charming smiles that, if she were a lesser woman, would make her weak in the knees.

"I see that I am right," she said. "You needn't tell me about it now. I have all day."

And then she shut up. It pained her to remain silent, but she persevered. She had learned, as the youngest sibling, how to manage others and cajole them into providing information they rather wouldn't.

A moment later, when she had been admiring the blue of the sky and marveling at the grossness of Thames water, and wondering if *grossness* was a word, Mr. Finlay-Jones finally got his tongue back from the cat.

"There's nothing to tell," he insisted.

"Right."

"My uncle and I simply don't get along."

"Of course."

"It doesn't really signify."

"I would never presume that it would."

"We haven't even spoken for years, except for this morning."

"I missed that."

"You were asleep."

"So while I was sleeping, you were meeting with your estranged uncle for the first time in years about nothing in particular."

He didn't answer, except to say, "Why do I feel the need to prove myself to you?"

It wasn't entirely clear if the question was addressed to her, to himself, or to the universe at large. Amelia, being Amelia, answered without thinking.

"Because you might be falling for me."

He laughed. Oh God, he *laughed*. Was that friendly laughter? Awkward laughter? Was he laughing at her? Since when did she care if anyone laughed at her? She hadn't cared when she was twelve and fell out of a tree and exposed her unmentionables to her entire class at school, and she hadn't cared last night when she'd been caught shoeless and dignity-less in front of the entire haute ton.

"Is that so?" he asked, laughing. Still.

She glanced over at the Thames and considered launching herself into its gross waters. But no, that is something Bridget would do.

Amelia was fearless and didn't care one whit what anyone thought or felt about her.

Except . . .

Oh dear Lord, she seemed to care what Mr. Finlay-Jones thought. No, felt. *What did that mean?* Best not to think about it now.

She would not be one of those girls who mooned over what a boy thought and she would not believe herself unlikeable. But now she desperately wished to know if he was falling for her. Or not.

"Well, what other reason do you have for eschewing all your work and responsibilities to spend the day with me?" she pointed out. "You either must like me. Or," here she paused dramatically and dropped her voice as low as it would go, "you have an ulterior motive."

"An ulterior motive?" He quirked his brow, teasing her. "That sounds dastardly."

"Doesn't it?" Then she stopped and turned to face him. Mr. Finlay-Jones's face was becoming familiar to her now. But that didn't mean that she knew him. It was entirely possible that he had ulterior motives. According to the duchess, most men did. Her heart started to thud a little harder at the thought. How did she come to be in his company, anyway? "But the question is, Mr. Finlay-Jones: Do you have an ulterior motive?"

Their eyes locked. His were a warm shade of brown and fringed in black lashes. And she thought about all those silly stories where the characters could read The Truth and Deep Emotion simply by gazing into someone's eyes. For the first time she thought perhaps it wasn't completely ridiculous.

They stood like this, gazing like idiots at each other, for a long moment. One in which she became aware of her heartbeat and that she was holding her breath. The truth was, she didn't *want* Mr. Finlay-Jones to have an ulterior motive regarding her. He was the first man in England she had *liked* and it would be such a pity to lose him to an ulterior motive.

"And what if I do have an ulterior motive?" he asked.

"I shall be devastated and will hold a grudge. You might wish to know that I am a champion grudge holder."

"I believe you," he murmured.

There was another long moment. It felt like an eternity.

Finally he broke into a grin—that grin—that she couldn't resist mimicking

"Why wouldn't a man want to spend the day with a pretty, charming girl?"

Really, why wouldn't he? It was only logical.

"And what of your responsibilities?"

"Honestly, I haven't any."

"You said you returned to England to help your uncle who hates you with his business affairs."

"It's complicated. Which is why I'm eager to avoid it."

He was more complicated than she had originally thought. Earlier this morning, Amelia had taken one look at his him and thought him handsome. In conversation, she found him charming. Quick witted. In possession of a sense of humor. But not complicated.

She had him pegged as the sort of man who spent time wagering on horse races and games of chance, the sort of man whose main activities were lounging about, being roguish, and flirting with women of questionable morals.

Which wasn't to say he wasn't that. Just that he might be more. He had a Secret Pain and a Tortured Past. He could have an ulterior motive. It was entirely possible—nay, even likely—that he had an ulterior motive.

She started to fret.

Would he blackmail her into marriage? Kidnap her and hold her ransom—dear God, what if he'd already sent a ransom request to the duchess?

But then again, how would he even know who she truly was? She'd given him a fake name and a fake story and he seemed to believe it. But then again, how did she come to be in his flat?

But for all he presented himself as a carefree rogue enjoying a beautiful day with a pretty girl, Amelia detected that there was something *more*. She was desperate to know what it was. There was no way she could discover it whilst locked in her bedroom at Durham house.

"Let us go to Vauxhall. I have been in London

for weeks now and have yet to go. This might be my only chance."

"That can't be true."

"After I return home, I doubt I shall be ever allowed out ever again. If I am destined to be a spinster, held captive against my will until my dying day, it's imperative that I see Vauxhall today. With you."

Chapter 10

**In which our hero and heroine
explore the pleasure gardens.**

3:36 in the afternoon

Vauxhall was best seen at night, when thousands of lanterns hanging from the trees illuminated such attractions as the famous rotunda, concerts, hot-air balloon rides, and the infamous dark walks where young ladies, chaperones, and their virtue were often lost. It was best to approach Vauxhall by the boat that ferried people across the Thames; the other entrance for those walking was far less magnificent.

But the lady had insisted on Vauxhall today, this very afternoon, and they were already on the south side of the river, having walked through St. James's Park and over a bridge to Astley's.

Alistair purchased two tickets for their admission, which left him with very little. Which made him nervous. It was one thing to steal his own money out of the pocket of his own companion; he didn't have it in him to steal from a stranger.

"We ought to have come tonight," Alistair said as they strolled through the gates. They were not the only ones who had decided to come out and enjoy the lovely afternoon at the gardens. "There are concerts and fireworks."

"And those dark walkways where romance happens. Or so I've heard."

"That is one way of putting it. I thought young ladies aren't supposed to know about such things. What are they teaching you at school?"

"Oh, nothing interesting. Nothing that compares to this!"

They set off down a well-worn garden path, one he trod many times before—usually at night, usually whilst in his cups, probably with female company on his arm. It was just something one did while in London and he never thought of it while abroad.

But this time was different. Amelia delighted in seeing Vauxhall for the first time—every statue, water fountain, flower garden, or what have you. He viewed those things through her eyes now. Her delight was contagious, even to a seen-it-all, done-it-all, wrecked-it-all scoundrel like himself.

Alistair was also seeing *her*. Her expressions were so animated that her features were never quite still. She was constantly looking around and thinking and feeling, and not trying to hide any of it.

He caught her delicately biting her lip while in thought.

Or she pursed her lips in annoyance when someone walked slowly in front of her.

She kept reaching up to feel her hair, running her fingers through the cropped mop of curls, as if she couldn't believe what she'd done, that it was all gone. He wanted to run his fingers through her hair . . . and pull her close and lower his mouth to hers and . . .

No. Not today.

Yes, he intended to marry her. And yes, today he had to make her fall at least at little bit in love with him. That was the whole point of this day—if he were to have a fighting chance for her hand in marriage, he'd need to stand out from all the other fortune hunters vying for her attentions.

But he was not supposed to fall in love with her. He could not let love and lust addle his brain when he was so close to achieving his life's purpose of making amends with the baron and atoning for Elliot's death.

Besides, she was a *lady*. And he was not a completely unscrupulous scoundrel. Alistair was determined not to ruin her any more than he—or she—already had, simply by being together.

There would be no kissing, no claiming of mouths, or any of that. Not today.

3:47 in the afternoon

They wandered through the garden paths. Overhead, the sky was blue, though gray clouds in the distance were ominously—and quickly—moving in. Alistair did not believe in signs, but damn if those clouds didn't make him think he shouldn't be outside, brazenly strolling through a park with a proper young lady.

They paused before a statue of a Greek or Roman god who had declined to fully clothe himself, revealing a body that would make a mere mortal keenly aware of his lesser status.

"In Rome and Athens, statues such as these are everywhere. The place is riddled with ancient ruins. And in India they are even more . . . indecent."

He thought of the statues he'd seen of gods with dozens of arms and goddesses with breasts bared, and other gods and goddesses engaged in romantic, copulatory acts. He imagined legions of English ladies swooning at the sight.

"How romantic and exotic," she said, though he thought of them as just hunks of rock someone had hacked away at. "I so wish I could see them."

"Perhaps when you marry, your husband will bring you to Rome on your honeymoon."

"I will never marry," she said darkly. Flatly. With a note of finality.

That gave him pause. Her determination not to wed certainly conflicted with his plans to atone for his sins and secure his future happiness.

He stood there, still, not quite hearing her as she chattered away. He wouldn't just have to convince her to marry him, but to marry *at all*. Bloody hell.

He forced himself to focus on what she was saying.

"I know, I'm supposed to want nothing more than to be chosen by a man and to have a passel of brats. But that doesn't excite me."

As if that was all that marriage was. That was the thing with sheltered women and virgins. They just didn't know about . . . the rest of it. The lust, the longing, the pounding heart, the taste of a kiss, the luxury of early-morning lovemaking. But then again, no one ever told them.

He wasn't about to start.

"And a pile of old rocks and stone does make your heart beat faster?" Alistair asked skeptically, with a dismissive wave at the statue before them.

"Well . . ."

"Do you really long to see what this man looks like without his fig leaf?" He asked. She blushed.

For all her bravado, she blushed. Then she recovered.

"The thought does keep me up at night," she said, looking him in the eye.

"I can just imagine you lying in bed, swathed in moonlight, thinking wicked thoughts about a statue's . . . secrets," he murmured, wanting to see her blush again.

But she didn't blush. She gave him a teasing smile and said, "Wide awake and wondering if perhaps a real man wouldn't be more revealing."

Alistair coughed.

"I wonder . . . Would his skin be as cool to the touch?" She reached out and rested her palm on the statue's chest, right above the heart. "And would a real man be as hard?"

He stifled a groan. This was wrong. It made him want to do wicked things that he swore he wouldn't do, less than an hour ago.

"We should go see the rotunda," he said. "It is famous."

"Well if it's famous . . ."

And off they went, away from the secluded paths where anything might happen and into the dark, cool, and most important, *populated* interior of the rotunda.

Everything echoed. Their steps, their voices, the voices of people a few feet away. It was a terrible time and place to have a conversation, especially one of a personal nature. But he couldn't imagine a woman not wanting to marry. And he feared what it meant for his future plans, which involved wedding her. She did mention sisters . . . but now that he thought about it, he wanted *her*.

Her plump little mouth, her mop of curls, her enthusiasm for everything and the way she didn't seem to care at all about the things he obsessed over, like fitting in. He. Liked. Her.

His heart started to beat a little harder at the thought—damn, what a warning that he was getting in over his head now. It was just marriage, just to a girl. He had to do it for Elliot's death and the Baron's need for funds and the aching loneliness he'd always lived with.

But Amy . . . or Amelia . . . or whoever this girl was had started to work her way under his skin and was heading swiftly in the direction of his heart.

"You really don't wish to marry?" Alistair asked.

"Not particularly, no," she replied with a shrug. "I would miss my family."

"The family who you are running away from?"

She pursed her lips. So he had hit a nerve. Alistair watched her closely.

"I'm running away from finishing school," she said finally.

"Right, sorry," he said.

"Marriage is a terrible bargain for a woman. We give up what little rights and freedom we have. I shouldn't want to be owned by anyone or beholden to anyone."

She had a point. But it wasn't like that if there was love, right?

He thought it too early in the day to begin speaking of love to her.

"I'm curious, Mr. Finlay-Jones, why it matters to you whether I wish to marry or not?" There was nothing coy about the way she asked or her manner of asking. Such a forthright question asked for a forthright answer.

I owe a debt to someone I can probably never repay but your hand in marriage would be a start.

Also, he had started to fancy her. It was hard not to.

Of course he didn't breathe a word about any of that.

"It doesn't matter to me," he said with a shrug. "It's just . . . curious. I seem to have misunderstood women."

"Or a woman," Amelia corrected. "We are not all the same. Like snowflakes, each one is different if you care to look. And you should know by now that I'm not just any other stupid, simpering English girl."

"I knew that from the moment I met you," he said softly.

"Pity I can't remember it."

4:03 in the afternoon

Having observed the rotunda—it was round—
they exited and recommenced their strolls
through the gardens. In this moment, everything
was perfect. She was out-of-doors instead of in
some stuffy drawing room. She had the company of a man with whom she could be herself,
and who had a strange effect on the direction of
her thoughts.

She had just become so aware of his mouth.
The full lips so often stretching into a charming smile. She had never before given so much
thought to a man's mouth, wondering what it
would feel like, or taste like, to press her lips to
his.

His dark hair had the stubborn habit of falling
forward into his eyes and she constantly wished
to push it aside, run her fingers through his hair,
perhaps caress his cheek. Perhaps pull him close
to her for a kiss.

She'd never entertained such thoughts
before—certainly not home, in America, when
the boys she knew were . . . just boys. In London,
most of the men the duchess had introduced her
to inspired revulsion or, at best, boredom. Never
this tingly curiosity to touch, to taste, to feel, to
know.

She'd never experienced such awareness of a
man—the heat of him when she got close, the

muscles of his arm when they were linked, the sound of his laughter and the constant wondering of what it would be like to kiss him.

Amelia wasn't sure what to do with these thoughts and feelings.

Did he feel the same? She wasn't sure. Once again, her gaze darted at him, quickly. She leaned slightly against him, savoring the feel of him. But he didn't seem to notice or respond, and she was at a loss.

So she tried to focus on the moment. This glorious, wonderful, liberating moment.

But her thoughts did stray to her family at Durham House. She was sorry her siblings were probably worried—though they knew her habit of running away and returning—and she wouldn't have entirely minded their company. They were a fun bunch when they didn't have the duchess trying to make them diamonds of the first water or whatever nonsense.

Well, no, actually. She *would* mind having company. She tightened her grip on the arm of Mr. Finlay-Jones. She did not wish to share him.

"I was walking through Mayfair," he said, apropos of nothing and distracting her from her thoughts. "It was late, and I was, I confess, a bit drunk."

"What are you talking about?"

"The moment we met." *Silly.* He shook his head and half smiled. "You really don't remember, do you?"

"Not one bit. You'll have to remind me."

"I was singing."

"Oh, let me hear you sing!"

She watched with glee as Alistair seemed to consider it. *That* was why she was falling for him. Anyone else would say it wasn't seemly and give her a dismissive look for even making the request. *Amelia, gentlemen are not in the habit of singing aloud when the mood strikes them.* But no, Mr. Finlay-Jones looked around to ascertain that there were not many people about who would mind terribly if a gentleman broke into song.

And then he sang. His voice was a lovely, rich baritone. She smiled dreamily and closed her eyes as snatches of memories came back to her: leaning out the window, the cool night air on her face, hearing a man's voice in song, faintly. She remembered the longing to feel as free as she did in this moment.

And then she paid attention to the words. They were tremendously impolite.

A country John in a village of late,
Courted young Dorothy, Bridget, and Kate,
He went up to London to pick up a lass,
To show what a wriggle he had in his a . . .

Amelia laughed and shushed him when people started looking their way and frowning in disapproval. Lord, perhaps the duchess was rubbing off on her after all.

"What?" he asked, feigning innocence. "That was the song I was singing the night I met you."

"I am horrified."

"No you're not. It is exactly the sort of song you would expect a drunken young wastrel to sing whilst walking down the street at a late hour. You wished you knew the words so you could join in. Now repeat after me:

*"O when he got there it was late in the night
Two pretty young damsels appeared in his sight."*

She laughed again, nervously now, and sang along with him. They gazed into each other's eyes. It would have been a romantic, swoon-worthy moment if the lyrics weren't so absolutely filthy and if he hadn't stopped to ask, "Has anyone ever told you what a terrible singing voice you have?"

She swatted his arm playfully, then grudgingly admitted yes.

So much for the romantic moment. But then again, whoever said love and romance were proper and polite all the time?

"I think I remember your voice," Amelia said. "I think I remember leaning out my bedroom window and listening to you sing."

"My wonderful voice must have lured you out. You did say something about the sirens."

"I'm ever so glad to know that my knowledge

of Greek literature remains when I am out of my wits. I shall have to write to my tutor and let her know."

"And then suddenly you were there on the street," he said. She could see how this all happened. She'd been captivated by his voice and snuck out of the house. It wasn't entirely out of character for her. But why could she not remember it? "You were stumbling about like a drunkard."

"Like this?" Amelia feigned stumbling around drunk, swaying to and fro and taking one step forward followed by three steps to the left and one step back. Then she sort of accidentally on purpose bumped into him and then reeled back, spinning around.

He laughed at her impression. "Are you sure you don't remember?"

"Barely."

Truly, she barely did. She remembered the horrible fight with the duchess and her siblings. A vision of hairpins skidding across a marble floor. The sensation of a cool glass of water. And then, vaguely, the feeling of night air on her skin and his voice.

A girl didn't forget a voice like that.

But then . . . nothing.

"Then you collapsed into my arms," he said softly.

"Like this?" she asked. Then she collapsed into

his arms. He caught her. Of course he caught her. He caught her with his strong arms, and made her feel weightless.

"Like this?" She gazed up at him; he wasn't smiling. His eyes were dark, lowered, focused on her lips. She wasn't smiling either. Because this was the moment that it—whatever it was between them—was no longer just a lark.

This was the moment it became real.

"Yes." His voice was rough.

"How forward of me." She meant to tease, out of habit, but the words only came out as a whisper.

"I didn't mind," he said. And then, "I don't mind."

"Good," she whispered. But she really meant *yes* to the question in his eyes.

And he understood.

And lowered his mouth to hers.

Amelia felt a spark the instant his lips touched hers. This! This was what she had been missing, this was what she had been craving, what she had been seeking. He tasted like excitement, adventure, like mystery. He made her feel alive, tingling skin, pounding heart and all.

His lips were firm and she yielded to the gentle pressure, opening to him, willing, so willing to explore this. Every tangle and thrust and gasp. Every beat of her heart. As he pulled her close, the sparks turned to a slow burn of pleasure.

She never wanted to let him go.

The time?

This was not supposed to happen. This was not part of the plan. This was a pounding heart, soft lips, a sweet taste, a kiss. And yet this kiss felt inevitable. Like he was powerless to stop it and could only surrender to it.

Not that Alistair minded.

Noble intentions beat a quick retreat, because a man didn't have a kiss like this every day.

When it was just a kiss, this one, for a moment, right now *and no more*, a man slowed down to savor every second of it. The taste of her. The feel of her, warm and luscious and pressed against him. The way he could plainly tell that she wanted him. It made him a bit dizzy, so he held on to her tightly, pulled her close, completely forgot about plans and intentions. Instead, he kissed her deeply as if nothing else mattered.

A moment too soon?

First it was the thunder that interrupted. Low and rumbling and not so subtly hinting that it was time to wrap this up. But oh, Amelia wanted this kiss to go on forever and ever. Apparently so did he. Because thunder, and now lightning, be damned. He kissed her—tangled tongues, soft laughter, bodies pressed together—and didn't stop.

It was only when voices—human voices, of adults and children—interfered that they hastily broke the kiss. Alistair—she would call him by his given name now, after that intimacy—helped her to stand on her own two feet. She swayed slightly and this time, she wasn't pretending to be drunk. His kiss had actually made her knees weak and disrupted her center of gravity. She reached out and placed her hand on his chest to steady herself and beneath her palm she felt his heart pounding.

This wasn't nothing to him.

He might have ulterior motives but the kiss well and truly affected him. That kiss made her want to believe that he did not simply wish to spend the day with a pretty girl, that this was the day that she finally fell in love.

That kiss almost made her desperately want to ignore that all this—the man, the day, the grand adventure—was too good to be true.

"We should go," he said finally.

"Yes, we really should."

Neither of them made any move to leave, even though the thunder issued another warning. The intruding people rushed past, in a hurry to find shelter.

"This is improper."

"An egregious violation of propriety," she agreed.

"You are trouble."

"And you like it," she blurted out. But she meant, *And you like me.*

He was serious for a moment—agonies—and then his lips drew up into a seductive smile.

"Yes, yes I do," he said. She knew he really meant that he liked her. *He liked her!* The truth of it made her warm up from the inside out. Not many gentlemen liked her—she was too imprudent, impudent, improper, just too much.

But this man liked her.

Gad, she was surely starting to fall for him now.

Time to go, surely

Alistair was vaguely aware of the thunder and more aware of *her.* He couldn't tear his gaze away from her dark eyes and her impish smile with lips reddened from his kiss. They might have stood there all day, gazing like love-struck morons into each other's eyes, were it not for the arrival of the Bow Street Runners.

A flash of red that caught and commanded his attention. He turned to look, and confirmed his worst suspicions.

He held his breath and watched as one, two, three, a dozen appeared. They marched in uniform down the garden path, sweeping their gazes down each little walkway.

Without thinking it through, Alistair swept Amelia into another kiss so their faces wouldn't be visible. He turned their bodies so they might appear as just another couple . . . *Nothing to see here, do carry on* . . .

Thunder rumbled again, loud, insistent, and ominous.

Is this when and where and how it ended?

His heart pounded hard in his chest.

Alistair's goal for the day had been met: he would no longer be just another gentleman in the ballroom to her. If they were to part now, and meet again at a soiree, she'd certainly give him a special smile and favor him with a waltz or two. He'd continue his courtship *properly* and they might, just might, get married and live happily ever after.

Everything he wanted was just within reach.

And other flash of red intruded upon his vision. Another Runner. There must be dozens of them, fanning out all over Vauxhall and all over the city. Odds of escaping undetected were low.

But Alistair wasn't ready for this day to be over. He wasn't ready to part with her just yet, not when he could still taste her on his lips and his heartbeat hadn't returned to its normal pace.

"A rainstorm seems imminent," he said. "And we are out-of-doors."

"Exposed to the elements."

"At nature's mercy."

Neither of them moved. They stood there, gazing stupidly into each other's eyes, and the thunder grew louder, more instant, and lightning cracked in the distance. The Bow Street Runners picked up their pace.

"Shall we stroll toward shelter?" he suggested. Perhaps they'd find some out-of-the-way building; they couldn't stay in the open and risk discovery.

"Yes, it wouldn't do to be caught in the rain," she replied.

"Let's find a place to wait out the storm," he suggested, forcing his voice to stay neutral. Wouldn't do to sound the alarm about the Runners and let the runaway heiress know that he knew that she was a runaway heiress.

4:29 in the afternoon

Amelia saw the Runners but quickly decided not to say anything. Dozens of men in uniform did not search the city for one wayward girl running away from finishing school. But dozens of men in uniform, under the command of the government, did, apparently, search for dukes' sisters who were missing.

She didn't want Alistair to know the truth about her. Not yet. He would insist on taking her back to Durham House, where her brother would kill him. In the meantime, Alistair would become formal and proper and stop kissing her. Their wonderful rapport and perfect day would be over. She wasn't ready for that just yet.

Best to continue to allow him to believe she was just Miss Amy Dish.

Arm in arm, they strolled quickly along the paths, taking turns to avoid Runners. Amelia took care to keep her head down to help escape detection. The thunder had become louder, more insistent, and she was glad of it because it covered up the pounding of her heart. The sky had darkened considerably too.

The lightning came next—a terrifically loud and bright crack. It was instinct to look up and turn toward the noise and the light. And it was instinct that doomed her. Her face was turned up and exposed at just the moment a Runner turned and saw her.

He murmured something to his companion, and both men started stomping toward her.

"I wonder what is down here," she murmured, turning and pulling Alistair down a different pathway. He did not resist turning left with her. Nor did he protest that right turn, another left, a turn around and a quick kiss in the bushes before another dash down a pathway to the right. As soon as they'd lose one Runner, another would appear. She was haunted by those red coats trailing her, and afraid of being caught.

It did not escape her notice that Alistair seemed just as keen as she was to avoid the Runners. She wondered if perhaps they weren't after her, but him.

Or was he just trying to avoid being caught in the imminent rainstorm? They were walking at such a brisk pace that they were nearly running and she was too breathless to ask.

There was more thunder, more lightning. And then, with one terrific burst, the heavens opened up and unleashed a deluge upon them. They were both soaked in an instant. Amelia shrieked, Alistair did not.

Suddenly, finding shelter was the most important thing and the Runners were the least of her concern.

4:41 in the afternoon

Alistair dared to breathe a sigh of relief when he and Amelia had not only managed to evade the Runners, but also to find shelter from the storm in a pavilion. A crowd of people had gathered, all seeking protection.

When it seemed they were safe, they turned to each other and burst out laughing. She shook out her wet curls and he laughed harder. A rivulet of water trickled down her cheek and he wanted, badly, to lick it. Then kiss her.

But there were people present.

Just average, everyday people. Women in dresses, men in hats, children with governesses, begging for sweets. And—here he gulped—a few men in those telltale red coats.

One of whom was threading his way through the crowd, his black beady eyes fixed on Amelia. He came and stood close, far too close for comfort. Though he didn't look at her, the Runner leaned in and murmured into her ear.

"Lady Amelia?"

She stiffened. A flush of pink suffused her cheeks.

"I don't know what you mean."

"Come with me."

"I beg your pardon?"

The Runner placed his thick, gloved hand on her arm.

That is when Alistair stepped in.

"Sir, unhand me!" Her voice was a strangled whisper, as she did not wish to draw attention to herself.

"You heard the lady," Alistair said in a voice so low and fierce he almost didn't recognize it as his own. There was no denying the surge of possessiveness he felt upon witnessing that man's hand on his woman.

"Who are you?" the Runner asked gruffly.

"This young woman's protector." Truer words were never spoken.

But the Runner wasn't buying it. He started to pull Amelia away, despite her protestations. The crowd had swarmed around—there was no other entertainment—watching this agent of the crown attempt to take and subdue a spitfire of a woman.

Alistair threw a punch.

It connected solidly with the man's jaw.

And with that, all hell broke loose. More Runners arrived, streaming in with the rain. The crowd became swept up in the melee, pushing, jostling, and swatting at one another. Out of the corner of his eye, Alistair saw Amelia grabbing a parasol from a young woman and using it to thwack one of the Bow Street Runners.

In the midst of the drama and confusion, with everyone's attentions occupied, Alistair and Amelia took the opportunity to flee.

Hand in hand, they dashed along the garden paths, seemingly taking one wrong turn after another, skidding into each other as they tried to stop, getting tangled up as they tried to turn around.

"How do we get out of here?" Amelia cried out over the rain and thunder.

"I have no idea. Did you not take a map?"

"When would I have taken a map? I thought you knew the way since you've been here before."

"Six years ago, at least. While drunk. In the dark."

"We will have to talk about your habit of wandering around drunk in the dark," she said in a nagging, wifely way. "But another time."

Eventually they managed to find a way out of Vauxhall, but not after what felt like an extended scenic tour of every last walkway. He'd never been so reckless as to start a fight or run like a madman through a public space; it was not the done thing by someone who was eager to fit in and aware that the ton needed only the slightest reason to exclude him.

Yet even though he wore rain-soaked clothes and his lungs burned from the exertion of running through the entire damned park, he felt exhilarated. For a moment there, it had been him and Amelia against the world and they had won.

The rain had tapered off to a slight drizzle, but Amelia was still vibrating with excitement and glee. Her heart was pounding hard and she was gasping for breath but . . . That. Had. Been. Fun.

She giggled, recalling the shocked expression of the Runner when she smacked him on the head with a parasol. Oh, the duchess would have been *aghast* had she seen it! Just imagining the duchess's reaction made her giggle more. It felt so splendid to laugh and run and feel the raindrops on her skin. It felt almost as good as kissing Alistair.

And then she noticed that Alistair was no longer running alongside her. She paused, noticing that he had slowed to a walk.

"What are you doing?"

"Walking," he said, stating the obvious. "We are already wet straight through. Why rush?"

"That is an excellent point," she said, falling into step beside him. She slowed and turned her face up to the raindrops. They were warm and plump and felt wonderful on her skin. "I need to catch my breath anyway."

And so they walked through the rain, hand in hand, aware of the curious and flabbergasted stares of people huddling under makeshift shelters.

"Doesn't it feel so *defiant* to be walking slowly in the rain?" Amelia asked.

They walked like that for a while, as if a little water never hurt anybody. Every step of the way, their hands remained clasped together until it just felt right. She used to hold James's hand. Or one of her older sisters. But it never felt like this. Like her fingers belonged intertwined with another's. With his.

"You know, this is the second time I have found myself soaking wet in public this season," she remarked.

"The second? And here I thought I was your first."

She laughed a little. "The first occasion was at a garden party. We were rowing. I might have rocked the boat."

He paused. "Might have?"

She grinned. "Definitely."

"Scandalous."

"But also refreshing."

"Like this?"

"This is better. So much better." And she looked down at their hands and back up at him. He smiled at her with such sweetness and longing and, she suspected, *feelings*.

In which Lady Boswell never.

"Well I never," Lady Boswell huffed.

"That was very exciting, Grandmother."

"No, it was not, Matilda," she admonished vehemently. One had to swiftly disabuse a child of such ideas as soon as they took hold. Otherwise, her granddaughter would end up like . . . that girl and her companion who caused the melee. Given the presence of all those Bow Street Runners, she assumed they were probably criminals. "It was a stunning lapse of elegant behavior and I'm certain terrible things are in store for that girl. That's what happens when you cause scenes. So you mustn't get any ideas, my dear."

But Matilda was already dashing out into the rain, spinning around and knocking into people who dared to venture out from the gazebo, the recent site of a shocking brawl. In broad daylight! At Vauxhall!

"Stop running!"

"But she is running," Matilda said, pointing to the girl dashing through the rain, making her escape. A Bow Street Runner dashed after her, but then tripped on a parasol lying on the pathway and sprawled face-first on the ground.

Lady Boswell could not be certain, but that girl looked familiar. She'd caught a glimpse of her during the brawl, and again as she dashed past during her escape. The girl looked back at them, and the scene she was leaving behind.

"I daresay she looks like one of those Cavendish girls," Lady Boswell murmured to herself. "But that cannot be; the duchess would never allow it."

Lady Boswell strained to get a glimpse of the gentleman. She noted only dark hair and a figure a bit taller than average.

First, she wrangled her granddaughter. Then she approached one of the Runners in the red coats.

"Sir, what was the meaning of all this?"

"We're looking for a runaway lady," he said.

Lady Boswell gasped. Her brain, frantically churning to put all the pieces together.

"Dammit, Watson, don't you know what *discretion* means?"

Watson cleared his throat and apologized. His superior stepped in to add, "There is nothing to see here any longer, ma'am. Our apologies for the disturbance."

Nothing to see here indeed. Hmmph.

Chapter 11

**In which our hero and heroine embark
on an awkward ferry ride.**

4:52 in the afternoon

*A*listair stood at the front of the ferry they
had boarded to take them across the Thames
and back to the north side of the river. She stood
beside him, finding amusement by listing to
herself all the rules she was breaking: she was
out without a chaperone, she was soaking wet,
she was alone with a gentleman, she had been
kissing said gentleman, which perhaps meant he
wasn't a gentleman. Thus she was out, unchaperoned, with a scoundrel. And kissing him. And
liking it.

Not to mention publicly brawling. Best not to
mention that.

Beside her Alistair was silent and she wondered if perhaps she shouldn't have mentioned that she made a habit of causing scenes and scandals. According to everyone, men didn't want to marry women prone to trouble or embarrassing episodes. She didn't think he was the sort to care—they got along splendidly and he had even encouraged her participation in that brawl—but now he was silent. Pensive.

And in that silence she realized that she wanted him to think of her as marriageable. At least, not dispensable. Not the sort of woman one frolicked with and then forgot. She wanted him to remember her and this day.

Actually, she didn't want it to end.

She glanced over and found him gazing at her. He drank her in with those dark eyes of his. The way he was looking at her . . . well . . . it felt a little bit wicked and still quite wonderful.

"You are looking at me," she said.

"Yes."

"You are looking at me like you are having thoughts about me," she said, a roundabout way of asking.

"Mmm." He just smiled. His eyes sparkled. Her heart did a flip-flop followed by a cartwheel.

"But I cannot tell what you're thinking," she continued. "And you are obviously thinking something by the way your eyes are sparkling, and by that dreamy half smile."

"My eyes are sparkling? I'm not sure what that says about my masculinity."

She scoffed. "We're not talking about your masculinity, which is not in question, but what you're thinking. About me."

It had suddenly become imperative that she know what he thought of her. Did he consider her a terrible hoyden with whom he'd have a spot of fun and then forget? Or was she more?

"I am thinking that you remind me of me," he said. "Or rather, the way I used to be."

"Used to be? Do tell."

"Before I had to grow up."

"Oh."

Her voice was flat. If there was one thing she hated, it was being called *childish*, which was what he just said, in so many words. She'd heard it all her life, especially when her siblings didn't want to explain something to her or wanted to leave her out of an activity.

When they arrived in London, it seemed all the duchess ever said to her was, *You must grow up, Amelia. You must act like a proper young lady. You must put away your childish notions and start to think about marriage.*

She had to dress like a woman, stuffed into corsets that molded her into the prefect feminine shape—but still remain completely innocent. She was supposed to be witty and provocative but also ladylike. She had to ride sidesaddle at a walk when she really wanted to wear breeches and stand atop a galloping horse.

She was caught between these states of childhood and womanhood, neither one quite satisfying her. And now Alistair saw her as childish, and it gave her the mad urge to put on lip paint and sway her hips and say seductive, womanly things. She wanted him to see her as a woman, not a wild and silly girl.

Lud, she must like him. She must *like* him. She must *like* him in a way that wasn't childish at all.

As if sensing her distress, he tried to verbally dig himself out of the hole.

"Which is not to say that you are childish. Quite the contrary in fact." Here, she noted, that his cheeks reddened. So proper, so English of him to blush at such an indirect way of saying that he noticed her person. "I wouldn't have . . . we wouldn't have if . . ."

She knew what he meant to say: he wouldn't have kissed her like a woman, as he'd done, if he'd found her at all childish.

This whole conversation had suddenly become unbearably awkward. Her emotions had flared; that made him uncomfortable. As they were on a boat, she could not walk away. She loosened her grip on the railing and considered launching herself overboard, escaping into the murky depths of the Thames. And why not? She was already soaking wet.

Finally, after a long moment of excruciating silence, Alistair spoke.

"I lost someone."

"How very careless of you to lose a whole person," she quipped, because if they could just stick to lighthearted, easy banter it would be so much easier.

"You know what I mean," Alistair said seriously. "He was my best friend. Like a brother. My only family. Before that moment I didn't know loss, or that sense of responsibility that dulls everything. When I thought everything was a possibility. So you remind me of me, before I knew those things and when I lived like nothing could ever go wrong."

Like she was an innocent. Who hadn't lived. But whose fault was that?

"It's a wonderful quality," he said. "I miss it."

"I'm sorry about your loss," she said.

"It's not your fault. It was my fault."

"I'm sure it wasn't anyone's fault. And you're not the only one to have lost people."

"But . . ." He changed his mind about whatever he was going to say. "Never mind."

Alistair's hand found hers and their fingers intertwined in a now familiar way and they stood there in silence for a while. She wanted to say that it was companionable and wonderful—*look at us, we can be so comfortable in silence together*! But she could not. The silence felt awkward and uncomfortable, like they were both teetering on the edge of a cliff debating whether to dive into the waters below.

Like they were tightrope walkers, pausing before taking that next step.

She burned with curiosity to know who he had lost, and why it was his fault. But it seemed like asking him wouldn't end well. He would either brush her off, and she would feel pushed aside when she wanted to be closer to him, or perhaps he would tell her a heartbreaking tale, tugging on every last one of her heartstrings and leading to an emotional entanglement.

She might be falling for this man, but there was still a certain *something* warning her to keep her distance.

Besides, if she were to ask him, he might ask the same of her. To speak of loss and locked-away secrets was to open up in a way she might not be ready for. He could ask her why she was in England. Why she was running away from school. Wouldn't her parents be worried about her? Oh, they were dead? How long, and how, and what few memories did she have of them . . . ?

She sighed. Perhaps it was immature of her, but she didn't want to talk about any of it. She didn't want to cry like a child, on a ferry, into the starched cravat of a man she barely knew.

Too many questions. One would lead to another and her carefully constructed story might unravel. Perhaps it was the same with him.

Besides, who wanted to speak of such serious things on a carefree day?

But, Amelia thought as the ferry approached the shore, perhaps it was time for her to grow up, just a little. Especially if—here she stole another glance at Alistair, all dark-eyed and dreamy—if it involved kissing.

Alistair was kicking himself, figuratively speaking, as they disembarked and walked back toward Mayfair, back to their regular lives, back to rules and responsibility and away from this horrid charade that had somehow gone much farther than he had intended—too far, even. He had said the wrong thing earlier and it was plain to see how just a few words could plunge her into despair. Her gaze dulled, and drifted away from him.

At least he could see what she was feeling and could try to make everything better, instead of ignorantly carrying on and inadvertently making everything worse. But in his efforts to explain himself and console her, he started talking about Elliot. Sort of. And thinking about Elliot had him in a state of despair.

He wanted to know who she had lost, but he didn't want to ask, because he didn't want to explain about his stupid, idiotic, *childish* behavior leading to Elliot's death.

Feelings. They were messy, complicated things that were best ignored.

"I suppose we ought to do something about these wet clothes," he said. And then he mentally kicked himself *again* because God, if that didn't make him sound like some sort of lecher. "And perhaps we should return home. You have been gone quite a long time now."

"And you have business matters to attend to," she added.

Right. He was attending to those business matters right now. Not that he could say that. He wasn't a complete idiot.

After disembarking from the ferry, they found themselves on a fairly desolate stretch of road on the north side of the river. The rain had sent people seeking shelter indoors and many had yet to venture back out.

"Do you think we'll be able to find a hack?" Amelia asked anxiously, peering to the left and then to the right and then back again. There were almost none to be seen, at the moment.

He did not. The streets were empty. The few hacks passing by were already carrying passengers.

"We might have to walk," he suggested after a few moments in which they had no luck in securing transportation.

"It seems far though, doesn't it?" she said, quite reasonably. "I have never felt so far away from home."

This, from a woman who had lived, until recently, on another continent.

"We managed the walk this morning," he pointed out. "In fact, I daresay we had a pleasant time of it."

She looked at him curiously, as if wondering *why* on earth he would argue with her about something as mundane as taking a hack back home when they were both uncomfortable in wet clothes and tired from a long day of walking halfway across the city. But he wasn't arguing so much as providing an alternative mode of transportation when their first choice seemed impossible.

"Yes, but this morning we were in dry clothes," Amelia pointed out, now sounding quite peevish.

Oh God, she wanted a carriage. Ladies always wanted a carriage. They never wanted to walk and they especially weren't keen to walk when the conditions were not optimal: a cloud in the sky, too much sunshine, rain the day before or the threat of rain tomorrow, imperfect footwear, an inconvenient hour, a distance just a bit too far, the temperature a degree too high or low . . .

"I doubt we'll find one, especially with the rain," he said. "Perhaps we could procure horses." He was not hopeful of this, even as he suggested it.

"But what if it starts to rain again?"

"We are already wet. Besides, there are no hacks to be had."

"I'm sure we can find something. And I have money to pay for it."

But she didn't have money. He knew this because just hours earlier he had robbed her of it and spent it on admission to the amphitheater and Vauxhall Gardens.

He watched as she reached into her pocket, three, two, one second away from discovering it empty.

"My money!" Frantically she dug around in her pockets, turning them inside out. "I have been robbed!"

He said the first thing that came to mind.

"Calm down. It will be all right."

"Calm down?" she echoed in the sort of calm fury that was more terrifying that the shrieks of a hysterical woman. Very well that was the *wrong* thing to say. It was so wrong, if he had three wishes, he would use one to take the words back. "How can you tell me to calm down in a moment like this?"

"Because I am just a man who doesn't know what to say in a moment like this. I only said the first thing that came to mind. I don't mean it at all. Do not calm down."

That gave her pause. In that pause, she took a breath. And that calmed her down marginally.

"Let us walk back to my lodgings and try to secure a hack along the way," he said gently. "We can have a meal by the fire as our clothes dry. And then I'll see that you get back to school safely."

"That is a terribly scandalous idea." She sniffed. "But one I find very enticing at the moment."

Returning to Alistair's flat was a terribly scandalous idea. It was beyond scandalous. But she had to admit it was also enticing. The prospect of removing this sodden dress was all she could think about. That rainstorm—and their insistence in reveling in it—meant that each layer was soaked, right down to her skin. The wet fabric was heavy, and cold. She wanted to remove it all and sink into a hot bath.

She suddenly had a new respect and even longing for the comforts of Durham House.

She and Alistair walked along in silence and she considered somehow finding her way home directly. This was more complicated that it seemed: she still did not know the way and now she had the lie about finishing school to maintain.

Lud, this was quite a situation.

She needed a good pot of hot tea before she could sort it all out. Never mind to have the strength required to contend with the inevitable brouhaha when she returned home.

Yes, she simply needed to let her dress dry, warm up before a fire and sip a fortifying cup of tea. Then she would concoct a story to get herself home.

One thing at a time. One small step in front of the other, just like the tightrope walker. One step closer to removing this wet and wretched dress.

It dawned on her just then that she would require Alistair's assistance with the dress. Alistair, who had been walking beside her quietly—and with whom she'd been exchanging those sly, darting glances. Was he looking? Oh goodness, he was looking! Quick look away! But . . . her gaze was drawn back to his eyes, his mouth.

She remembered the feeling of his fingertips upon her back as he did up the buttons this morning and shivered at the anticipation of that feeling once more.

He would see her bare skin, inch after inch of her back, exposed. He would probably get Ideas of the sort that ladies took great care to ensure a man did not get. Lusty thoughts. Wicked thoughts.

And then what?

Her lusty thoughts and wicked thoughts dared to consider what then. Amelia wasn't certain of much, other than that her skin suddenly felt hot, which was remarkable considering this cold, wet dress. She became aware of the beats of her heart. Did it always beat so quickly?

What would he do when confronted with her, in a state of undress? Would he take advantage—or would nothing happen? After all, had he not had every opportunity to ravish her already?

There was another question demanding attention with every shiver, heart pound, and blush: What would *she* do when alone with him whilst in a state of undress?

She ought to get into a hack right this minute. But she had come this far. In for a penny, in for a pound—was that how the saying went? Perhaps she might as well go all the way . . .

Chapter 12

In which they are alone now and there doesn't seem to be anyone around.

Sometime after five o'clock

The flat was empty when they returned. God only knew where Jenkins had gone off to, which was probably for the best. He'd been introduced as a friend, and friends didn't help friends deal with their attire. Valets did. Only gentlemen had valets. He had not presented himself as the sort of gentleman who had a servant; to reveal one might raise questions. Alistair did not wish to be caught in a lie, at least not now. This day had gone much farther than he had ever dreamt and much farther than necessary.

He wanted to quit whilst he was ahead, but wasn't sure how to end their day together. How was he to escort her back to Durham House in broad daylight, whilst maintaining the charade that she would be returning to finishing school?

Alistair would sit and think about this whilst Amelia changed.

And she had to remove her dress, just as he had to change his attire as well. Their clothes were wet. They would have to be removed, lest they might contract a fever and die.

Thus it was not a stretch to say that the removal of their attire was a life-or-death matter.

Alistair's mind went places, like, oh, say, places under Amelia's dress. Because he was not a gentleman. He was a man, tortured with emotions, caught in a ridiculous lie and entangled—possibly entranced—with a pretty woman who was presently in his flat. Alone.

He thought of her lips and he thought of her skin.

Skin he would *not* see and would *not* caress and would *not* taste.

He had done enough damage to her reputation and marital prospects today. He would not take her innocence.

Besides, if they were to marry—and the idea was becoming less and less about the baron and more and more about his desire—he wanted their wedding night to be special. Meaningful.

He went into the bedroom to see what Jenkins had left about that she could wear.

"I apologize that I do not have extra dresses lying around the flat. But you can wear this while yours dries." He handed her one of his shirts and a pair of his breeches. They were not even remotely going to fit her.

"You don't seem to have much lying around at all." She glanced around and he did too. There was a bare minimum of furniture that came with a furnished flat: the delicate, rickety settee and a mismatched chair or two; the large bed and wardrobe; a small table and chairs in the kitchen. There were no paintings or knickknacks or any such item that would indicate this was someone's home.

"I only just arrived in town."

"But you have hardly any luggage."

She was right. He traveled light, given that he didn't stay in any one place for very long.

"The bedroom is through there. You can change. I'll see about making some tea."

He turned to go.

"I need help with my dress."

He paused. Stupid ladies' dresses, always demanding someone's attentions. Stupid dress of hers, demanding that he undo button after button, exposing her soft, pale skin.

Resolve. He needed resolve.

"Turn around."

His voice sounded brusque and bothered by the task. But the truth was that this *day* had already gone farther than he had intended it to. He'd meant to simply share a meal or enjoy an innocent walk in the park. His only goal had been to have one little excursion, one harmless secret that they could smile about when they met again.

He wanted to stand out from all her other suitors, that was all.

And yet now they were here, alone, and he was undressing her, all whilst engaged in an epic battle between his honor and his baser self.

He would marry her, now for reasons beyond Wrotham, beyond even matters of her reputation and his honor.

It was because of that moment when he'd opened the door to his flat and found her there waiting. It was because of the way his heart beat faster with the appearance of her dimple when she smiled, because of the sparks of delight when she laughed, and the feeling of connection when her fingers were intertwined with his.

It might be something like love.

There was also the matter of the deep-seated feeling of righteousness he felt at this exact moment, when his fingers fumbled with the buttons on her dress. There was something so elementally simple and right about this: a woman in his home, the intimate act of undressing.

And then, of course, the lust.

It had been smoldering all day and was now sparking with each button.

Alistair flicked open the top button. Then the next, then the next.

Inches of milky white skin were exposed.

She was holding her breath.

So was he.

He undid one button after another. With the last one, he forced himself to turn away. If he looked, he would want. And if he wanted, he would have to resist.

Alistair had this notion of a proper wedding night.

The proximity of her bare skin, her lips, *her* was making him forget.

"Tea," he said, voice rough, apropos of nothing. "I'll just go see about tea."

He somehow managed to do so without setting the kitchen afire. She appeared just as he was pouring a second cup. It was only then that he noticed Jenkins had procured another issue of that blasted newspaper with that damned cartoon of her on the front page.

He didn't have a chance to get rid of it.

And then he promptly forgot all about it when he glanced up and saw her standing in the doorway, wearing his clothes. The shirt was open at the neck and she had rolled the sleeves up to her elbows. His breeches were far too large for her, but she had found an old cravat and used it as a makeshift belt. Her feet were bare.

The whole moment felt so domestic.

He had just one thought: *this is what it feels like to be home.* Even in this empty flat. This was the feeling he had sought from England to India and a dozen places in between. This is the feeling he ached for, this is was the reason why he wanted—no, needed—to marry her.

That, and those lips he wanted to kiss. And those clothes he wanted to strip away from her body.

"What are you reading?" she asked.

"Just some rubbish," he said. "Tea?"

"Please." She smiled, and pulled out a chair and sat down at the small table. He joined her and started to move the newspaper.

"No—I want to see it."

Alistair watched her nervously as she took in every last detail of the cartoon: the stocking feet and little shoes cast aside, the fake faint, the chieftain's headdress and stars-and-stripes dress, the riding crop. It was over the top, ridiculous—and it declared, with each detail, that she Did Not Belong.

He knew the feeling.

Alistair waited for her to say something, probably to the effect of "that poor girl" or "what a horrid newspaper." But no.

"That is not the right size and style riding crop."

"Is that something you learned in finishing school? I thought they only taught young women how to arrange flowers and paint watercolors of kittens."

"Kittens are remarkably difficult subjects to portray. They never stay still, especially if you give them a ball of yarn. But no, that is not something I learned in finishing school."

"They must have noticed you missing by now."

He had to say it. If only to ease his own conscience, he had to give her every opportunity to leave.

"Indeed. Hours ago, probably."

She gazed pensively down at the newspaper, not quite meeting his gaze.

"They must be worried."

"Yes." She fingered the newspaper, looking once more at the cartoon. It was her. It was so undeniably her.

"We both know I can't stay much longer," she said softly. When really, she should never have been here at all. She ought to be tucked into her room in a Mayfair mansion with an army of maids and lady relatives standing guard around her.

"You have already stayed longer than you should have," he said softly.

Every second that she stayed, dressed in his clothes, sipping tea in his kitchen, was another second that he wanted to remove said clothes and carry her off to the bedroom. It was another second his better judgment had to fight his desire.

He glanced at the open vee at the neck of the shirt. And then glanced down. He was only a man.

Alistair forced his gaze back to her face.

"Should, should, should. That's all a lady ever hears. Though sometimes it's should not, should not, should not."

He leaned forward, half smiling. "And what would you do if there were no rules?"

She looked down at the newspaper and smiled ruefully.

"I wouldn't wear any shoes, like this girl. At the very least, I wouldn't wear stupid pointy-toe shoes that were a few sizes too small and made not by a cobbler but by someone with a fetish for torturing young ladies," she said. "And I would wear clothes like yours," she added.

"They suit you."

"I feel like I can move in them. Breathe in them. Just be in them." To prove her point, she stood up and started dancing and spinning around the kitchen, like a manic pixie or—a society miss on the run who had finally escaped stupid pointy-toe shoes and everything else that confined her.

She was laughing and smiling and he couldn't help but respond in kind.

"And I would travel all over the world," she said, pausing to catch her breath. "I would see everything. And I would probably kiss you."

5:27 in the evening

There. She had said it. While she was spinning around like a madwoman and rambling on about all the things she shouldn't or couldn't do but wanted to, she went and gave voice to the desire. It'd been simmering all day. And their kiss in the gardens had done little to nothing to satisfy her.

What she didn't say was that she would do more than kiss him. Much more. All of the more. She couldn't help but admit it, now that they were warm and alone. He made her feel things—a spark, a tingle, a new dawning awareness of all the sensations her body was capable of—and she ached to feel them all, intensely and completely.

Amelia wasn't worried about how Alistair would react. He was a man, she was a young, not-hideous woman, and those two things usually added up to one thing that even sheltered, innocent society ladies had a clue about.

So of course she had to say it. At this point, when she was wearing his clothes, standing barefoot in his kitchen after a long day together, there was really no reason not to.

So she said it.

And I would kiss you.

And then she carefully watched his expression. The changes were nearly imperceptible. His eyes darkened, and his gaze dropped to her lips. His grip on a chair back tightened.

There was a long moment of silence. Doubts did not creep in . . . but anticipation blossomed slowly, intensely, surely. Now she was thinking about it, imagining how his lips were firm but yielding against hers. How she felt the slight scratch of his stubble against her cheek and the manliness of it thrilled her. She imagined how his mouth, and that stubble, and his hands, would feel elsewhere.

Of course, this was another thing she should not think about.

But Amelia knew she wanted this. No matter what anyone said. Just imagining it had made her skin tingle in anticipation, heat pool in her belly, and something tighten within.

Now he was just leaning against the wall, gazing at her with an expression she couldn't interpret.

She felt herself pout.

Wasn't he supposed to stride across the room in two long masculine strides and sweep her into his muscled arms and crash his mouth down to hers? Wasn't he supposed to be dying to ravish her? Wasn't his jaw supposed to be clenched and his knuckles white, all due to his tremendous self-control, battling with his raging desire for her?

It seemed that Bridget's books were *wrong*. It seemed all the warnings were wrong. It seemed that her reputation would be ruined and she wouldn't have any romance to show for it. And she wanted to know all that, to feel all that.

Finally, after it felt like eternities had passed, when it had probably been only half a minute, he said something.

"You're a bit too far away for kissing."

"Yes, I know. You're supposed to stride across the room and sweep me into your arms and have your mouth crash down on mine."

He smiled slightly. Oh God, he was laughing at her. Laughing! She had made herself vulnerable and he had laughed. Her options were to throw herself out the window, or scowl at him. So she scowled.

"Am I now?"

"So I've been told." She punctuated this with a shrug designed to convey that she honestly could not even care less.

"By whom?"

"You are ruining the moment. If you don't wish to kiss me, just say so. I'll think that you're odd, and I'm sure some other gentleman will want to."

5:29 in the evening

Of course, just when a man decides to be honorable and restrained is when a beautiful woman demands a kiss. Just a kiss. Just his mouth claiming hers in a sweet declaration of desire. As if that was all it ever was. When done right, it was only the beginning. And Alistair did not want to begin what he could not and would not finish today.

He had an old-fashioned notion about a wedding night. About asking her properly to be his wife. About not irrevocably compromising her—at least not more than he had already done. After a scandalous meeting and even more scandalous courtship, he craved the stamp of respectability on their relationship.

A kiss would complicate that. Because when he kissed her again, he wasn't sure that he would be able to stop there.

But desire for him was plain on her face. He could see in the flush of her cheeks and the darkening of her eyes, and the way she slowly slid her tongue over her lips.

And then she introduced the idea of another gentleman kissing those lips, threading his fingers through her curls, knowing the curve of her breast, or hearing her soft sigh of pleasure.

And that was just not to be born.

The hot streak of jealousy surprised him. When had he begun to feel possessive of her?

If he was going to lose her, it would not be because he had some noble idea of refusing to do what he desperately wanted to do.

He stood.

Gazes, locked.

Breath, stopped.

Then he strolled across the room in just two long, powerful strides. He pulled her against his hard chest and his mouth crashed down on hers.

"Oh!" It was a sharp gasp, a quick sigh and then only the sound of his pounding heart.

Oh, he was attuned to her wishes. He was so attuned to her everything—the quickness of her breath, the soft little sounds she made when he kissed the gentle slope of her neck, the way her little fists grabbed a handful of his shirt and pulled him closer—that he knew he wasn't pushing her beyond her limits. Society's limits, yes. But those had ceased to matter hours ago.

He slid his fingers through her hair, cradling her head as he kissed her deeply. It was a kiss meant to erase the notion of another gentleman from her mind. Yet Alistair found this kiss might be ruining all other women for him. Her taste, her scent, the way she fit in his arms and the way she kissed him back with such unconcealed pleasure . . . well, a man didn't find such perfection every day and he didn't let it go when he did.

The kiss went on longer than he meant to.

Probably. Who had any notion of time when kissing a pretty girl? For that matter, who had any notion of propriety or decency or rules at a moment like this? He was aware only of his heart pounding, blood pumping, desire raging.

And then he paused for a moment.

"How was that?" God, he was breathless.

"Perfect." Her voice was but a whisper and her lips were so plump and red. He wanted to claim them again.

"Good. Because it is just the beginning."

"You know, I've been on my feet all day."

Words. She said words. It took him a moment to process.

"You poor thing," he murmured.

She gave a coy smile, a very pointed glance and said, "I might like to lie down."

His brain was hardly working but he still understood an invitation to bed—to making love—when it smiled, murmured and batted its eyelashes at him.

And even with his reduced mental capacity, his better judgment was still functioning and communicating with the rest of his brain. He should send her home immediately and untouched.

Right now.

This very minute.

But apparently she wasn't the only one desperate to just be and feel and love without rules or limits. She pressed her palm against his chest, sliding it down his abdomen. She bit her lower lip. And then her fingers hooked on the waistband of his breeches.

Alistair was going to marry her—if he didn't die first. It was entirely possible that he was already halfway in love with her. If not, it was only a matter of time.

Therefore . . .

He groaned. There was no therefore. There was no rationalizing his way into lovemaking or anything like it. This was all wrong and improper and he should have put a stop to it hours ago and . . .

But they had made it so far, therefore . . .

He was falling in love with her and had every intention of marrying her, therefore . . .

Then she stood on her tiptoes and pressed a gentle kiss on his lips. He felt the length of her pressed against him.

He was hard, so hard, therefore . . .

It was the sweetest, gentlest kiss that undid the last shred of his resolve. With some vague notion that they would continue kissing—JUST KISSING—lying down on his bed, he scooped her up in his arms.

"Where to, my lady?"

"What are my options?"

"That horribly uncomfortable settee." They both looked at the tiny, horribly uncomfortable settee. "Or my bed." Then, realizing how that sounded, Alistair added, "which is also horribly uncomfortable."

They both looked over at it—and the feather mattress, soft pillows, and blankets. They both knew that it was not horribly uncomfortable at all.

"At the risk of sounding horribly forward, let us to the bed," she said.

It was just a few steps to the bed.

He lowered her onto it, half wishing it were their wedding night. She'd be in white, perhaps with flowers in her hair and his ring on her finger. But he was getting ahead of himself, ahead of them.

He took a step back and exhaled.

She peered up at him from the bed. She reclined, leaning on her elbow.

"Aren't you going to join me?"

Yes. No. He shouldn't. But oh God, he wanted to. In order to make himself feel right about it, Alistair made some promises in his heart. He was going to marry this woman. Protect her. Love her. Do all the right things.

But first, he shut the bedroom door.

Then he joined her on the bed.

"Amy . . ."

"No. Don't say any more." She pressed a finger to his lips, stopping him from speaking. Well, he tried to delay the inevitable.

But this little minx and her boundless enthusiasm, curiosity, and need to explore was going to be his undoing.

She pressed a kiss to the soft skin just below his jawbone. He was aware of her breathing him in. So it was going to be like this, a slow, sensuous exploration. Next, her lips found the base of his neck, the hollow of his throat, the bare vee of his chest exposed by his open shirt. Her hands fumbled with his shirt.

What the hell. He sat up enough and pulled it off, letting it fall carelessly to the floor. The way she gazed down at him was almost as erotic as her touch. Her brown eyes widened, darkened. And her lips curved into a sensuous half smile. She liked what she saw.

She ran her palms along his chest. He hissed when her thumbs caressed his nipples.

She smiled. *Oh you like that do you?*

Then she teased his nipples with her mouth, her tongue, and he groaned. Her hands went lower, brushing along his breeches, and caressing his rock hard arousal.

He had never been this hard.

Especially once he felt her touch.

Thoughts of sending her home had long since given way to thoughts of feeling her hand around the hot, hard length of him. Or feeling her around him.

She teased him with her soft touch, here and there and all over his body as if she were memorizing it or claiming it. When he could tolerate it no longer, he flipped her onto her back and rolled on top of her.

"You are trouble," he whispered.

"But you like trouble," she whispered back.

And there was no denying that.

* * *

Amelia had but one thought in her head: *Yes, this.* She loved the feeling of his hot, bare skin under her palms or, better yet, her mouth. And there was something about his scent that went straight to her head and chased away all and any thoughts. Except for *yes, this.*

She couldn't quite explain this desire to explore him and to know him, intimately. It wasn't merely curiosity about a naked man, though there was certainly some of that. It wasn't merely a desire to be wicked, and break the rules and do just one more Thing That Proper Young Ladies Would Never Do.

She just wanted to know him, all of him. From the thoughts in his head and his earliest memories to the feel of his skin and the way he tasted when she kissed him.

And now she knew the way he felt on top of her. His body was strong, heavy with muscle. Alistair propped himself up on his arms, caging her in. He gazed down at her with those dark eyes, fringed with ridiculous lashes. *Two could play at this game,* his eyes seemed to say.

She smiled back. *I won't stop you.*

He pressed a kiss at the hollow of her throat and start moving lower. *Yes, this.*

And this. His palm pushed the shirt up, sliding the fabric along her skin, followed by his hand. Skin to skin. It felt intimate. It felt right.

And this. He lowered his mouth to her décolletage. And then lower. And then the blasted shirt was in the way. In but a moment it was gone.

And oh God *this*. He took the dusky centers of her breasts in his mouth. She arched up into him. He laughed softly. *You like that don't you?*

She gasped. *Do not stop.*

And then she writhed a little bit beneath him because he was heavy and *hard* and she felt him pressing against her intimate place. Even with the layers of fabric between them, just the *feel* of him there did something to her. She felt something tighten in her core. She felt a warmth blossoming and taking over. *Yes, this* became *Yes, more.*

Or not.

"We shouldn't," Alistair gasped. "I have . . . honorable . . . intentions."

Oh yes, those. She had forgotten.

"However . . ." There was a wicked gleam in his eye, one that made her heart beat faster.

"What do you have in mind?"

He didn't answer her, just slowly worked his way down her body, pressing kisses along her belly. Oh . . . he paused, glancing up at her, seeking permission. She didn't know what he wanted or what she would be agreeing to, because if she was imagining things correctly . . .

Alistair lightly pressed his lips to the soft skin below her belly button, then gently flicked the skin with his tongue, teasing her with a hint of what was to come. Oh. Yes. This.

At some point, her breeches came off. Gone. Good riddance.

Then he moved lower, and pressed his mouth there, gently teasing at the soft folds.

She gripped the sheets, twisting them in her fists.

Her breath was short, shallow. Feeling. There was so much feeling. So much *good* feeling but . . .

A release. She needed a release. There was too much heat and tension and feeling all building inside of her.

"I think . . ." Her voice was a hoarse gasp she hardly recognized.

He lifted his head just enough to say. "Don't think."

"But I need . . ."

She needed more of him. She needed to feel him.

"Tell me what you need," he murmured. At least that's what she thought he said. She was having trouble concentrating. So much wanting. She wanted him to continue, but also pause. She wanted to hold him, but she didn't want him to move.

"I feel like I'm going to explode."

And then he stopped. He stopped! She was left throbbing, wanting, *needing*, and he stopped.

"Why did you—"

He silenced her with a kiss. Oh, *this*.

But still, she felt incomplete. Unfinished. She wanted *more*.

Alistair had long ago learned that every woman was different. And that was the fun of it, if you asked him. When it came to lovemaking, half the fun of it was that slow, teasing, exciting process of discovering what would make a woman go wild.

And Amelia was discovering what gave her pleasure now, with him, for the first time. He was the lucky bastard who would get to show her and hold her as she learned for the first time all the pleasure her body was made to feel.

It's supposed to stop here. Ah, yes, another intrusion from his better judgment. *Stop now before you ruin her irrevocably.*

But he couldn't stop now, not before she had her release. He was starting to know her. She'd be irate for days otherwise.

So he kissed her, bringing her back to that wonderful mindless place—he knew because she softened against him, and gave those little mewls of contentment.

Then he slid his hand down, finding the bud of her sex and with the lightest, slowest touch began to stroke. He felt her writhe, pressing into his hand. He grinned into the kiss. *This,* she liked this.

"I love this," she whispered. "But I want more of something . . ."

He pressed a little harder.

"I feel . . ." She gasped as he slid his finger inside. She was wet. And warm. And God he wanted his cock inside her.

Think of your wedding night.

He got even harder, if such a thing was possible.

Okay, do not think of your wedding night.

Focus on her.

He focused on her. Kissing and teasing her neck as his fingers kept up a steady rhythm, in and out, and stroking the bud of her sex. He listened to her breaths, each one coming faster, shorter, shallower, harder.

"I want . . ." she panted. "I need . . ."

He knew the feeling.

She was close and she didn't know it yet.

I want. I need.

Wait. Stop now.

Shut up.

She was close, so close. It was time to send her over the edge. He shifted so he could take one of her nipples into his mouth. He sucked and teased with his tongue while never once wavering from that steady rhythm. In and out and in and out and . . . her sighs of pleasure were like a caress; they only aroused him more. The way she writhed against his hand made him ache to be inside her, to give her *more*. He wanted to bring her to the brink and then beyond.

So he didn't stop.

He kept going, stroking her with his fingers, teasing her with his mouth. He didn't stop until she was bucking a little underneath him, crying out in pleasure. He vaguely heard words like *yes* or *God* or *this yes*. He felt her clench around him as she came.

She wasn't the only one out of her lust-addled mind. Alistair didn't know how it had happened, but between all the sighs and moans and touches and groans they had tangled themselves up. He was on top. His cock was poised at her entrance, he was dying to be inside her, and his resolve was . . . gone.

Yes this. Yes this. Yes this. Yes this. Yes this. Yes this.

Thoughts. She had them. *Yes this.* Or just the one.

Something marvelous had just happened to her. She couldn't catch her breath and any second now, surely, her heart was going to burst right out of her chest. So she had to tell him now.

"I want . . . this," she gasped. "I want . . . you."

It was as if those were the magic words he needed to hear. She felt him hard, there. Then harder and deeper still. And then she felt him fully inside her. Hot. Throbbing. Aching.

Wanted. She wanted.

Then he began to move, each slow thrust stoking the fire that had been building and simmering inside her. Any little lingering thoughts of should or shouldn't or what time is it . . . all were burned up, reduced to nothing. Only one thought, again and again, with each thrust: *Yes, this.*

And then she couldn't even put those two words together.

He moved inside her, thrusting deep and slow. There was nothing but the soft clink of tooth against tooth as they fumbled for a kiss. She felt the slick sheen of sweat on his back; she licked it off his neck. His fingers threaded through her hair, grasping tight, holding her close. There were grunts (his) and gasps (hers). Limbs were tangled. He was on top, and then she was on top and then somehow they ended up on the far end of the bed. And still, he moved inside of her, moving faster now, harder now.

She sensed that he might be close to that marvelous earth-shattering I-had-no-idea moment she'd experienced. Amelia wrapped her legs around him, arched up. He groaned in pleasure. She felt a spike of triumph.

They kissed. They moved together, mostly. She held on for dear life as he thrust hard and fast and shouted out. Then he collapsed on top of her. A few quiet, possessive grunts. A few last shallow thrusts. One last deep kiss.

For now.

Who cares about the time at a time like this?

It was raining again, a soft drumming of raindrops on the windowpanes. They were warm and dry inside, tangled up in arms, legs, and sheets. Clothes were strewn about the room. The air was thick with the scent of rain, the scent of sex. The city outside seemed so distant. There was only the two of them, in the room, in this bed.

"This has been the perfect day," Amelia said softly, tracing a line up and down his arm with her fingertip.

"Even though you were robbed, caught in a rainstorm, and ravished?" Alistair teased. There was *nothing* like being able to lie contentedly, naked, with a woman and tease her, knowing she would smile just like that, sweetly, giving him a peek of that dimple in her left cheek.

"Because of those things. And this moment." She rolled closer and buried her face in his neck, breathing him in. He heard—and felt—her whisper, "I don't want it to end."

He held her close and in a soft voice said, "Maybe it doesn't have to."

Chapter 13

**In which our heroine returns
~~home~~ to finishing school.**

Or does she?

Six o'clock? Or seven?

Evening was settling over the city when they set out once more. This time, they went together. The destination was Durham House—not that Alistair knew that. Amelia made sure he thought that he was doing the gentlemanly thing by escorting her back to finishing school. How she was going to manage the deception was something she ought to figure out immediately, but no ideas came to mind.

That lovemaking had slowed her wits. She felt

like a ninny with the way she was already longing for him, and his touch. She had become the
thing she had always mocked in love stories and
poetry.

Amelia walked slowly, like one of those
pokey pedestrians in Vauxhall who had vexed
her earlier. Then, she had been in a rush to see
everything. Now, she wished to prolong her
time with Alistair. In the course of the afternoon something had changed; it was no longer
about running away, but wanting to stay with
him.

She knew their moments together were dwin-
dling.

The idea of elopement was preposterously
premature. Staying another night was too much
and besides, she was beginning to feel the tug
of home. The clock was ticking on her time with
Mr. Alistair Finlay-Jones and their one perfect
day.

There had been no discussion or mention of if
they would meet again, as if it were understood
that this was the only time they would ever
spend together.

After all, what could possibly happen?

He knew her as Miss Amy Dish, finishing-
school student. A gentleman could not call on a
young lady there—even if said school actually
existed and even if she was actually enrolled in
said school.

To see him again was to reveal her true identity.

She was not ready to risk that.

The clock was ticking on their time together. Alistair knew this. So he walked slowly and dragged his feet as he escorted "Miss Amy Dish" back to "finishing school." He was curious to see how she would maintain the charade, though he wasn't exactly eager for the moment they would part.

Alistair hadn't said anything about seeing her again.

The words were on the tip of his tongue, wanting to be spoken. It seemed impossible that he would never see her again. But a gentleman couldn't call on a young lady who didn't exactly exist at a school that was certainly fictional.

To see her again was to reveal the deception: that she was truly Lady Amelia Cavendish, sister to the Duke of Durham. And that he'd known all along.

He would be revealed as the worst sort of scoundrel. How on earth could he justify that he had lied to her all day, all over London, and then made love to her?

It was unforgiveable.

He realized that now that it was too late to do anything about it. Damn.

He would have to take the secret to his grave.

They *would* meet again—even if she didn't know it and even if he didn't speak of it—and he would have to act surprised to see her and hurt that she had lied to him all day, all over London, and then made love to him.

But could he maintain such a lie for a lifetime? It hurt his head to consider it.

A few hours ago—it felt like a lifetime—the plan had been so simple—forge a connection, stand out from all the other fortune hunters. He had by all accounts been successful, yet he had the sneaking suspicion it would lead to his downfall.

They walked along in silence, lost in their own thoughts. Amelia really wished he would say something, because all this thinking was ruining her mood. They would have to say goodbye soon, any minute now really, and it would be the end.

Forever.

Probably.

Not only had Alistair not said anything about calling upon her, he hadn't said anything about marriage. She had meant it when she said she had no intention of marrying. But she knew that Real Gentlemen issued proposals after making love to a gently bred woman.

Perhaps he didn't think she was a gently bred woman. And why would he, when she'd practically ravished him?

Perhaps he wasn't a Real Gentleman, which mean that she had ruined herself on some scoundrel. How tragic. How melodramatic. God, she could at least be more inventive than that.

But then she thought about his bare chest—the ridges of muscles, the soft skin darker than her own, the smattering of hair. And then she thought about the rest of him, naked, without even a fig leaf, and she decided she couldn't regret a thing.

This man was her downfall.

She was ruined, gloriously so.

She was without virginity and without proposal.

Which was beside the point because she suspected that she would not be allowed to marry him anyway.

There was plenty of evidence to suggest that Mr. Alistair Finlay-Jones could be classified as a fortune hunter. She was clued in by the nearly empty flat, devoid of things and servants. There was also his willingness to squire around an heiress all day, humoring her by calling her Miss Amy Dish when he certainly had to know, thanks to that stupid cartoon in the newspaper, that she was Lady Amelia Cavendish.

She stopped short and groaned as it all dawned on her. Dear God, he must know.

"What is it?" he asked.

"Nothing," she replied. Because she couldn't

even introduce that line of conversation; if there was the slightest chance that he was clueless, she wouldn't dare risk giving up her disguise.

In the end, it wouldn't matter either way.

The duchess would not consider him a suitable match. There was the fortune hunting. And lack of title. She didn't care one whit. But she had learned that her wishes weren't all that counted. If he wasn't suitable, the duchess would think that Amelia could at least do better: a higher-ranking title, plumper pockets.

But it was all beside the point because he hadn't said anything about meeting again.

So this was it, then. They were a few city blocks away from the end of the most wonderful day of her two and twenty years.

It was the day she met the man with whom she could be herself.

She slowed to a stop—it wouldn't do to get closer to Durham House and risk him seeing.

He pushed one wayward curl away from her face and tucked it behind her ear. She felt a pang in the region of her heart—how could they share such an intimate gesture and yet never see each other again? What a cruel fate that would be.

That stubborn curl, cut short, fell right back into her eyes.

It seemed like ages ago that she'd gone into the wigmaker's shop and chopped all her hair off. That reminded Amelia about the play the wigmaker had mentioned—*The Return of the Rogue*, the one the duchess said wasn't proper for them to see.

And then Amelia had an idea. Lust, love, and kisses must have addled her brain—the part where logic and reason resided, not the part where adventure and pleasure lived. She fancied more moments with him—especially since this was likely her only chance—and the sun hadn't quite set yet, there were still things she wished to do and see, and they were already out . . . she had made it this far.

Why not *more*?

It was the line of thinking that so often got her in trouble.

It was also the line of thinking that had led to the very best day in her entire life. It had led her to Alistair, a man who didn't seem interested in trying to constrain her. Unlike everyone else she met, he held her hand and asked what was next and then said, "Let's go."

For that alone, she loved him. Never mind the lovemaking . . .

"I have an idea," she said, grinning at him.

"Why do those words strike fear in my heart?"

"Oh, don't become a stick-in-the-mud now, Alistair," she teased.

"Me? A stick-in-the-mud? Might I remind you how I spent the day?"

"Every moment is burned in my memory," she

said earnestly. And then, smiling at her idea, she asked, "But what if we continue the day?"

He paused. A long pause. *Don't become sensible and proper now!*

"All right, tell me this idea of yours," he said reluctantly. But she saw the fire in his eyes.

"The theater."

"I'm certain even in your finishing school, you are allowed to attend the theater," he said, in a surely-you-can-do-better kind of way.

"Yes," she said impatiently. "But not in the pit. And not a performance by Eliza Barnett."

Everyone in London was raving about her. Correction: many people were raving about her, but others had deemed her performance unsuitable for a variety of reasons, classifying it as "inappropriate for ladies." Amelia wanted to see a play in the pit, down with the people, and not in a box all high and mighty above everyone. And she wanted to see the performance that had scandalized and polarized the haute ton.

Tonight was her only opportunity.

"No," Alistair said flatly.

"Oh, please." Oh, God, she was begging. But the words were out of her mouth before she could catch herself.

"You have been gone far too long. Your fam— schoolmates and teachers are likely worried."

Yes, but . . . of course they were worried. They had been worried all day. It would be a worry mixed with fury, a noxious combination of emotion that she was in no rush to encounter. Not when she was, perhaps, falling in love and had just hours left in this one perfect day.

And there was another unsettling truth.

"What if we never see each other again? What if these are the last few precious hours we could spend together? Would you really have them be mere minutes?"

"We will see each other again," he said firmly as they stood on a street corner and London rushed around them. But how? And when? And how would they explain it?

"How can you be so certain?"

"London is a small town. In spite of its vast size and thousands upon thousands of inhabitants."

"I see."

He must have grown weary of her. More than once James or Claire had remarked how *tiring* she could be. Somehow, within a second, this fear that he'd grown weary of her spiraled into a panic that she was unlovable.

Or worse: he had gotten what he wanted from her—her virtue—and was now no longer interested in her.

How crushing, because she was starting to wonder if she might be able to love him—that is, if she wasn't halfway in love with him already.

How mortifying, because that meant the warnings were right.

How devastating, because that meant she had been a silly fool.

"I promise," he said, which somehow only made things worse. Again, she wondered if he knew the truth about her.

He was content to part ways now because he had enough information to ruin her or ensure a wedding or a nice settlement to keep quiet.

Silly. Fool. Miss Amy Dish was a silly, cork-brained ninny.

Amelia ought to be rid of her immediately.

"Then let us say goodbye here," she said, horrified by the tremble in her voice and a wobble in her chin. She would not be a silly girl who cried on a street corner over a boy who she'd known but one day.

"I want to see you home safely," he said softly, but she no longer believed that. Did he wish to confirm that she would enter Durham House? Did he have notions of escorting her right up to the front door and popping in for tea with the duke and duchess?

She imagined the worst: *By the way, I ruined Lady Amelia . . . how does Tuesday work for the wedding? It doesn't? Wouldn't the ton like to know that . . . ?*

Amelia allowed that, in her haste, she might have gravely miscalculated him. Them. Everything. She didn't know, and she hated that. The seeds of doubt had been planted and she couldn't quite bring herself to completely disregard them.

"My school is nearby," she said firmly. In fact, Durham House loomed in the corner of her vision. "We are in Mayfair. I'm certain no danger shall befall me between here and there. If it does, I shall scream and someone will come to my rescue."

"I want to see you again." He reached out for her hand. She glanced up at him. His gaze was dark, serious. Her heart thudded. She believed him, but she had doubts about his reasons.

"Someone once said that London is a small town," she replied. His eyes flashed. She had cut him with the flippant retort, throwing his words back at him.

"Amy . . ."

And she had lied to him. He would discover it. It was best to end things now.

However . . .

There was something like love starting to bloom in her heart and she couldn't bring herself to bring this day to a close now, and forever.

"Let's leave it up to fate," she suggested. "If we happen upon each other, then we'll know it's meant to be. But if not . . ."

If not, then this was goodbye. Forever. This would be a perfect, sweet memory uncomplicated by whatever might happen—or not happen—after.

"Thank you, Alistair, for a perfect day." Amelia stood on her tiptoes and pressed a kiss to his lips. To hell with whomever might see. When a girl was as spectacularly ruined as she was, why not indulge in a bittersweet goodbye kiss? Why not, indeed. Amelia turned, and walked away.

It could not end like this. In all of this madness and deception they had found something beautiful and true, the first tender steps toward something like the love of a lifetime. And she just thanked him with a polite kiss on the lips and walked away, off into the night.

Just like she had arrived.

It hadn't even been four and twenty hours and yet it felt an eternity. He could scarcely remember life as it was yesterday, or even this morning. He'd been a nobody with nothing to do.

Then, he'd been a man on a mission and then, sometime in the late afternoon, tangled in her arms, he felt like someone in love.

Not even four and twenty hours later. Madness, that.

But now her steps were straight and assured—she was not intoxicated—and he was transfixed by the sway of her hips. The desire to have her again surged through him.

But that wasn't the reason Alistair followed her. It could not end on a sudden note of bitterness. They had shared something real and lovely and he wanted it to stay that way until the end. It could not end yet. He would not leave their future happiness up to fate.

It could not end that like this. He'd sensed her retreating; he should have asked what she was thinking and then tried to assuage her worries.

But that would be more lies, would it not?

No, I'm not a fortune hunter.

What? You aren't Miss Amy Dish!? I had no idea.

That was why he followed her, stepping swiftly off the pavement to cross the street and nearly being run over by a charging horse because he was paying attention only to her delectable bottom and not the rest of his surroundings. Clearly, he could not live without her.

He had to make things right, now, so that they could be right when he saw her again.

He would see her again.

Alistair threaded his way through pedestrians, always keeping his gaze fixed on Amelia. Finally, he caught up with her.

"Let us go to the theater."

She eyed him for a long moment in which his heart thudded in his chest. What had he done? What had he said? How had it suddenly gone from right to wrong to over?

"We'll go see the play and stand in the pit with the unwashed population of London. It'll be terrible but we'll be together."

Alistair's heart surged when he saw the smile tugging at her lips and the reluctant grin.

"Well if you insist, Mr. Finlay-Jones."

"I do, Miss Dish." He took her arm and escorted her in the direction opposite Durham House. "I also insist on supper first. Thanks to you I have worked up quite an appetite today."

For supper, they ate steaming hot meat pies and drank mugs of ale in a private parlor at a pub. They dined on credit; he may have had to drop Wrotham's name to ensure they would be taken care of and as a way to ensure the barmaid that money would be forthcoming. He had an IOU from cards the other night; he'd return and pay on the morrow.

Amelia noticed none of it. She had that wide-eyed delight again, the way only an heiress on the run could be delighted by the prospect of a meal in a dingy London pub. It was a novelty to her, a part of the daily drudgery for everyone else, or even a special treat for those in especially hard circumstance.

"I should be wining and dining you," he said, immediately regretting the suggestion that she was wealthy, a Lady, and not Miss Amy Dish, finishing school runaway.

"I have plenty of that at . . . at my school."

"When I was at school, we were served gruel that would have made this seem like the finest food in the world. I shan't tell you more or it'll put you off your supper."

She implored him for details. He obliged. She
made faces of grotesque horror and he laughed.

"It's much more refined at a ladies' finishing
school," she said. "As you may be able to imagine. I doubt you know better than I, although,
I wouldn't be surprised if you regaled me with
stories of sneaking into a girls' school to take lib-
erties with the French teacher."

"You know me so well," he murmured. Even
though she didn't know him at all. For instance,
she didn't yet know him to be the terrible liar that
he was turning out to be. "And you are going to
be in tremendous amounts of trouble when you
return," he said, gazing at her with those eyes of
his.

"Oh, I am aware. Which is why I am still here."

"Delaying the inevitable, are you?"

"Well, who says I will return?" She coyly lifted
one brow.

"You cannot simply vanish. You must wish to
return for a new dress."

"I'll just purchase a new one," she said with a
shrug. As if it were that simple. And for a duke's
sister, it was.

This little throwaway comment got him thinking the sort of depressing thoughts that made a
man question everything.

He had lived off the small inheritance from
his father, as any gentleman would do. Before
he'd reached his majority and control over the

funds, much of it been absorbed into Wrotham's pockets, presumably for Alistair's education and other expenses.

He suspected "other expenses" were gifts to Wrotham.

For the past six years, Alistair had supplemented his annuity by playing cards and winning wagers with other idle aristocrats abroad; his winnings were invested and produced a modest return, enabling him to live and travel in a certain style.

But he didn't have nearly enough—or the prospect of earning enough—to support her in the style to which she had recently become accustomed. And while some men might have no compunction about spending their wife's dowry, Alistair found it all a bit unsettling. He wanted *her*, not the money she came with. But he wanted her to be happy, and he wanted to be the one to provide such happiness.

What if he could not provide for her?

Perhaps marrying her wasn't such a good idea after all.

What if he came to dread coming home because he couldn't bear the fact that he sponged off his wife for their very existence? Or what if all of his time and energy became devoted to digging the Wrotham barony out of the financial hole it was currently in—so much so that he forgot about his wife?

He would be one of those husbands who spent an inordinate amount of time at the club and someone would inevitably stroll in and tell him, "I say, Jones, did I just see your wife standing atop a galloping horse as it leapt over the serpentine?"

He would mumble something about how that sounded like her and how, once upon a time, he would have been there, encouraging her antics.

But that was *later*. This was *now*.

And he really should have thought of this *before* he made love to her.

Alistair managed to push such troubling thoughts aside and chatter amiably with her for the rest of the meal. All of his attentions were then focused upon getting her to the theater without being seen, causing a scandal, or getting in trouble. It occurred to him that they'd gotten away with so much today; some sort of scandal was certainly inevitable, the consequences of which would certainly be enormous. And hopefully enjoyable.

Amelia had been to Covent Garden once or twice before. The duchess had them all dress in some of their fine gowns made of silks and satins, all embroidered with jewels and glass beads that shimmered in the light. Then the lights in the theater went dark and no one saw what they were wearing. Amelia lived for the performance onstage and endured the tedious socializing during the intermission.

She remembered looking down at the pit, where one could converse loudly and freely and didn't need to quit fidgeting and sit still, for Lord's sake. They were closer to the stage, to the action. The group had seemed to pulse with excitement.

Meanwhile, Amelia was trussed up and sitting still high above them all, like a princess locked in a tower.

Was.

Tonight she followed Alistair into the pit, taking care to keep her head ducked lest anyone recognize her. But she still managed to take it all in: the hot crush of bodies, the energy in the thick air, looking up to the stage rather down upon it.

"Let's go in and find a place to stand where you can see," Alistair said, pulling her close to him in the crush. He clasped her hand so they wouldn't become separated, a distinct possibility given the way the crowd surged and jostled around them.

"I am so excited for this."

"I don't see why. Everyone smells like they haven't had a bath in weeks."

"Or ever," Amelia said, but cheerfully. Yes, everyone around them smelled and was shabbily dressed. But the crowd was chattering and boisterous, happy to have an evening's entertainment. They bought oranges and drank ale. When the lights dimmed and the curtains parted, they finally hushed, attentions fixed upon the stage.

Eliza Barnett was a revelation. Her voice was sweet and her movements elegant; she embodied the character, breathed life into the role she portrayed. There were no cracks in her performance, something Amelia, who could never quite play a role consistently, admired.

In the role of Aristocratic Young Lady she broke character all the time.

In the role of Runaway Schoolgirl, she was certain she'd slipped up here and there with her story. Alistair must know.

Alistair. He stood behind her so close that she could feel his warmth. If she were to rock back on her heels, she would brush against his chest. She knew that his chest was broad, muscled but not overly so, a light smattering of hair across his smooth skin. She knew it—could envision it, had touched and tasted it. What an intimacy she had never imagined, and what an intimacy she would certainly imagine again and again once . . .

. . . once this ended. She supposed it had to end at some point. But Amelia didn't want to think of that now, so she turned attentions toward the actress onstage, achingly aware of Alistair behind her and unsure of just how little time they had left.

In which they are discovered.

The hour is late

There was a commotion during intermission. At first Amelia thought it was the natural movements and shuffling of people taking advantage of the break to step outside or procure a beverage. But she heard a certain hum of people murmuring. There was even a stir in the aristocratic occupants of the boxes high above it all.

Curious as anyone else, Amelia turned. She saw a familiar figure cutting through the crowd. One who was beyond out of place here. One she could not fathom had any business in this place. Yet there he was—impeccably tailored, expression inscrutable—heading directly her way.

Lord Darcy.

He was otherwise known as Dreadful Darcy, according to her sister Bridget's diary, which Amelia read faithfully each day. Bridget was in love with Darcy's brother, Rupert, who hadn't kissed her yet, and she had an ongoing list of Things She Disliked About Lord Darcy.

There was much to dislike about him; he was the perfectly turned out, exceedingly proper, high and mighty aristocrat who embodied the haute ton's opinion of the American Cavendishes. Which is to say, he didn't think very highly of their family at all.

All of which begged the question of what he was doing here and why he seemed to making a beeline for her.

Amelia turned away, ducked her head.

"We have to leave. Immediately."

"Why? Are you not enjoying the performance?"

"We're about to be discovered."

"Bloody hell."

"My unladylike thoughts exactly."

Alistair protectively wrapped his arm around her as they threaded their way through the crowd toward the nearest exit. But the force of all the people moving and churning through the space was too much and in a split second, they were separated.

She looked around frantically, not seeing him anywhere. Amelia wanted to call out for him, but thought better of drawing attention to herself as a lone female, lost in a crowd. She moved toward the exit, hoping they might connect there.

But then she encountered an obstacle: one in a silk waistcoat and starched cravat with a perfectly tailored jacket.

Reluctantly she lifted her eyes and confirmed her worst suspicion. Darcy. Here. Staring down at her. One look at his expression and she didn't even consider pretending not to recognize him.

"Lord Darcy! What brings you here?"

"Would you believe me if I said the theater?"

he asked dryly. Of course she would not believe him. Her heart started pounding. But he couldn't be here for her, could he? That was absurd. It would suggest an intimacy between their families that she hadn't been aware of. It would mean that she was in unfathomable amounts of trouble. Oh, God, and who else knew?

"You are not known for enjoying amusements," she replied, trying to be lighthearted, as if this really wasn't such a big deal at all.

"You agree, then, that I have another reason to be here," Darcy said. He had this way of speaking that just dared her to challenge him and yet she found herself tongue-tied and unable to defy him. "Specifically here, in the pit, and not up in the box I usually reserve."

Neither one of them dared to lift their faces in the direction of the private boxes above.

"It is quite altogether a different theatrical experience when one . . ." Her voice trailed off when she saw that he wasn't paying attention. In fact, he was looking at something, someone, just over her shoulder. He was looking with something like surprise, and perhaps anger.

"Finlay-Jones," he said flatly.

"I'll be damned. Darcy."

Alistair came to stand beside her.

It wasn't awkward *at all*.

Very well, it was tremendously awkward.

Amelia watched as the two men had some sort

of *moment* in which some information was surely communicated via inscrutable male faces, but was absolutely not articulated. She did not understand. Did they even know each other?

"Are you two acquainted?"

"Yes."

Both men spoke at the same time.

"So Alistair Finlay-Jones is your real name," she said with no small measure of relief.

"It is," both men said at the same time. There had been a nagging suspicion that something was not quite right. But if she knew his name, his real name, then maybe everything was fine. She would have a chance of finding him again.

"Who would lie about their name?" Darcy asked, confused.

"Certainly not *I*, Miss Amy Dish."

She gave Darcy a pointed look. He gave no indication that he caught her meaning. No wonder Bridget found him exasperating.

"How are you acquainted?" she asked, changing the subject.

"School friends," Alistair explained.

"What a small world," she remarked. She should have figured that all the English lords went to the same school. After all, they belonged to the same club, attended the same parties, etc., etc. . . .

Gah. They knew each other. Her mind reeled with the implications of this—what it meant with regards to Alistair's status and what it meant for her.

For them.

The likelihood of meeting again.

It was hard not to think of the words *marriage* or *special license* or *outrageous scandal*.

But it was hard to get a thought to stick when Darcy was looking at them, radiating disapproval.

"I am shocked to find you both here," he said, glancing from one to the other. "Together."

There was nothing to say to that.

"I suppose you have come to take Miss Dish back to school," Alistair said smoothly. Had Darcy been less Darcy his lips would have twitched at the ridiculousness of her fake name, her fake life. But he gave no indication of being even the slightest bit amused by the situation.

"Right." Of course, Darcy wouldn't correct Alistair's assumptions, so as to protect her reputation.

"What if Miss Dish is not yet ready to return?" Amelia asked. "We are only at intermission and I wish to see how the play ends."

"I think we can all agree that you have seen enough," Darcy said flatly.

Amelia turned to Alistair. Surely he wanted just a few more precious moments together. He held her gaze for a moment. A long moment of gazing into his dark brown eyes. She didn't like

what she saw. He was letting her go. He was setting her free.

Whatever this was, it was over.

She liked what he had to say even less.

"He is right. You should go with him."

Just like that . . . *you should go. I'll just pass you off
to another man as if I didn't claim you for myself just
this afternoon. As if we didn't fall half in love. As if it
were just one and only one perfect day, and that's all.*

She waited a moment—a long, endlessly excruciating moment—for him to say something about
seeing her again or simply, *Fear not, this day meant
something to me, too.* But no, he said nothing.

Amelia felt something rising up in her throat;
she swallowed and fought to keep control of her
voice. After all they had experienced together
today, all he had to say was *You should go with him?*

"So this is how it ends."

"No," he said softly, daring to lightly caress her
cheek under the pretense of pushing one wayward curl aside. "This is just the intermission."

**In which our heroine has a heart-to-heart
with the most unlikely gentleman.**

The hour is even later

Amelia had to admit it was a relief to sink into the
plush upholstery of Darcy's carriage after a long

day on her feet. Why, she and Alistair must have walked from one end of London and back again. Darcy sat beside her in the curricle and picked up the reigns. Then they were off, through the city streets, on her way home.

She found her guidebook on the seat. She recognized the dog-eared pages and leather cover and the gold engraving of the title: *Burton's Guide to London*.

"What is this doing here?"

"Lady Bridget left it behind," he replied, much to her surprise.

"Bridget was here?"

"Yes."

"With *you*?" Amelia fully turned in her seat to face him. Darcy sat still, facing straight ahead.

"Yes."

"Just the two of you?" She did not attempt to hide her intrigue. Bridget hated Darcy. She wrote extensively about it in her diary.

"Yes. Lady Amelia—"

"Just the two of you? *Alone?* Without a chaperone?"

Amelia gaped at him. Darcy. And Bridget. Who would have thought? Amelia was about to question him further, but figured she would get much more information from reading Bridget's diary in the morning.

"I daresay you are not in a position to judge others about the presence of a chaperone, or lack thereof," he replied in that haughty way of his before changing the subject. "Everyone has been searching for you all day. Discreetly, of course."

Amelia flipped through the guidebook, noting all the pages she'd folded down and the sights she'd circled with ambitions to see them. It was clever of them to use this to track her down. Or perhaps it wasn't clever; perhaps her family just *knew* her so well.

That brought a lump to her throat.

Now that she was away from Alistair, away from that spell he cast over her—to be fair, one she most certainly welcomed and encouraged—she remembered her family. It felt like years—decades, even—since she had seen them. And in all of her two and twenty years, she had never spent this much time apart from them.

"Your family is very worried about you," Darcy said, which she knew to be true, but it made her feel guilty to hear him say it. "Gravely worried."

"I know," she muttered. Then she braced herself for a lecture, because Darcy seemed like the lecturing sort, and he delivered.

"Yet you stayed away for the better part of a day, without sending word. You have taken incredible risks with your own safety, your reputation, and the reputation of your family. That is remarkably careless, foolish, and inconsiderate behavior on your part. I would expect better of you, Lady Amelia."

Well, Darcy did not disappoint on the lecturing front.

And she *knew* all those things. She wasn't an idiot. But she had for one day managed to push it all aside because . . .

"I wanted to do something for myself," she said softly. "Just once I wanted to do what I wished and not give a care for what anyone thought. Just once I wanted to have a day of fun and adventure instead of stupid morning calls in the afternoon and changing my dress three times and attending the same old parties with the same old people. I wanted a day for myself. I don't expect *you* to understand."

Darcy wasn't an idiot and thus didn't ask what she meant by that. He was Noble Duty To Others personified.

"I do understand," he said, in a voice full of *feeling*, which surprised her. "In fact, I understand completely. Perhaps more than you will ever know."

This shocked her and she turned once again to look at the man beside her, trying to reconcile this calm and understanding man with the heartless snob she read about in Bridget's diary.

"But aren't you going to tell me that I am horribly selfish? That I should sacrifice my happiness for others? Aren't I going to receive a longer lecture?"

"For all that you have made foolish decisions, I

do think you are aware of the fact," he said. "Besides, I suspect the duchess will do a far better job of it than I."

"I suspect I shall confirm that shortly," she muttered. When no other lecture seemed to be forthcoming from Darcy, Amelia turned her thoughts to Alistair. His eyes. His lips. The way he touched her. Their perfect day.

And the uncertainty of what would happen next.

"About Mr. Finlay-Jones," she said. Beside her, Darcy nodded. "You know him."

"I do." When Darcy was not forthcoming with any other information, Amelia prompted him. "Well? Is he a terrible scoundrel? A villain with nefarious intentions?"

"Do villains ever have intentions that aren't nefarious?"

"That is an excellent point. But do answer the question. Have I . . ." She paused, struggling to find precisely the right words . . . have I . . . *fallen in love with* . . . *given myself to* . . . She gulped. "Have I spent the day with a villain?"

"No."

"So Alistair Finlay-Jones is his real name, he has spent six years on the Continent, and he is not a villain?"

"True, true, and true."

"Well that is something at least."

But she was not consoled. Now that she thought about it, she knew so little of him: he had business with his uncle, but who was his uncle and what had transpired between them? What did one do on the Continent for six years and why would one stay away for so long?

She knew how he tasted, what his fingers felt like entwined with hers, and that she could be herself with him. It had seemed so important hours ago, but now she wondered if she had risked her reputation and future on a man based on something as little as how he kissed.

There was so much more to know about him. And yet, he had said nothing of another opportunity with which she might discover it.

"I have known him to be a gentleman," Darcy added. She noted the *past* tense. Then Darcy coughed awkwardly and asked, "Do I need to revise my opinion?"

Then she blushed furiously. Never in a million years did Amelia ever imagine that she would be having this conversation with this man.

"Lord Darcy, are you very politely inquiring if you need to duel on behalf of my honor?"

In the dim light of a passing gas lamp, she saw him redden slightly.

"Either way, you will have to marry him," Darcy pointed out. "The duchess was surely hoping for a more prestigious match, but if today's events are discovered, you will be ruined. Your whole family's reputation will be tarnished. That is, unless you marry."

But Alistair thought her Miss Amy Dish, student at a finishing school that didn't exist. He wouldn't be able to find her.

Or would he? She glanced at Darcy—her one connection to Alistair. Darcy could certainly find him and ensure that they were wed, whether they wanted to or not, just so they could avoid a scandal.

Whether she was *ready* for that monumental step or not. Yes, she ought to have considered this earlier, etc., etc. . . . but it was only now that she dared to really consider it.

What a terrifying prospect. Marriage. Forever. She wasn't sure she wished to marry, ever.

"Those aren't good enough reasons to promise a lifetime to someone," she said stubbornly. It was certainly more complicated than that, but she didn't want to think about it now. She didn't want to be pushed into the Right Thing or the Done Thing. She had meant it when she said she had no intention of marrying. But if she did . . .

"Oh? Than what is?"

"Love, Lord Darcy."

"Do you not love him?"

"We have known each other but one day," she pointed out, not ready to declare her new, half-blossomed love to *Darcy*, of all people.

"Much can happen in one day," he said thoughtfully, and upon that they could agree.

Chapter 14

**In which our heroine returns to
the bosom of her family.**

Nearly midnight

Finally, Durham House came into view. The stately mansion rose up against the night sky, nearly every window lit from within. Amelia recalled her impression upon first seeing the house: nothing so grand and palatial could ever be a home. And yet, the people she loved most in the world where behind those walls, sitting vigil by the candlelight, waiting for her.

At Amelia's request, Darcy waited in the carriage while she alighted.

She paused, there, taking a deep breath and squaring her shoulders, facing that house, and everything it represented. Shoes that pinched, tightly laced corset, riding sidesaddle at a walk instead of riding astride and galloping on horseback. Reputations and polite conversation about the weather. Footmen in matching livery and multiple forks at every meal. Mean-spirited cartoons about her when she got it all wrong. Marriages for the sake of reputation, not love.

She vowed that she would not return for *that*.

Amelia was returning for her family. Because she loved them and because she had put them through enough worry. Because she had spent the day with someone who didn't seem to have much family of his own, for better or for worse.

And because, though she belonged with them, she might belong with Alistair too, and how to reconcile all this belonging was something to sort out in the morning.

With love for her family firmly in her heart, Amelia knocked on the door.

Pendleton opened it, and gave no indication that her homecoming nearly four and twenty hours after her disappearance was anything remarkable. But that was an English butler for you.

Once he saw that she had returned home safely, Darcy nodded in the darkness and drove off. And within seconds of stepping into the foyer, her siblings were rushing toward her.

"Where the hell have you been?" James demanded. But his voice was muffled by her hair, as he pulled her into a fierce embrace.

"What did you do to your hair?" That was Bridget.

"Do you have any idea how worried we were?" That was Claire.

Before Amelia could reply she was engulfed in the fierce and loving embrace from all of them, all at once.

They finally stepped back and parted, revealing the duchess standing in the doorway between the drawing room and the foyer. Her spine was erect, and her eyes were bright. She smiled, revealing relief.

"Really, where have you been?" James demanded, slightly shaking her. "We've been looking *everywhere* for you."

For once in her life, Amelia found herself at a loss for words. Her brother looked so worried, and dare she say it, older than he did yesterday, undoubtedly because of her.

She did feel guilty. Now, especially.

And yet her day with Alistair was *hers*. She had no wish to share it and have her memories picked over by others or to be chastised for all the perfect little moments of the day. She wanted to preserve the memory of the happy day.

"I've been out. Exploring."

"Were you alone?" Bridget asked, pointedly.

"Do you have any idea how bloody worried we were?" Claire demanded, ever the older sister.

"I'm sorry to have worried you all. Truly."

Amelia spoke earnestly. "I didn't mean to run away. I honestly don't even remember how I did it. But then I was out and . . . and then I was waking up . . . I was safe, I promise."

But still, her siblings and the duchess exchanged loaded glances.

"It must have been the laudanum," Claire murmured.

"What laudanum?" Amelia asked. She looked from face to face at all the sheepish expressions.

"We might have slipped some laudanum into your water," Bridget explained in a small voice.

"We?"

"We simply wished to calm you down after your . . . excitement last night," the duchess said in the no-nonsense way of hers.

But it all started to make sense now. Her own family had drugged her! Any untoward emotion, any expression of feeling, any display of behavior that went beyond simpering was something to be drugged away. No wonder she had run away.

That ameliorated some of her guilt at running away since she was clearly out of her mind—involuntarily—when she'd done it.

"I told him I wasn't drunk," Amelia muttered.

"Told who?" James demanded.

But Amelia wouldn't answer. She slowly climbed the stairs and plodded down the hall to her bedroom. Once inside with the door shut behind her, she opened the window and leaned out, looking at the night sky.

The city was quiet; there was no one singing tonight. There was no romantic baritone singing bawdy ballads to lure her out. Amelia gazed out over the dark outline of the city, dimly lit from starlight. She thought of all the people and places she had seen today, from the lowly girl selling violets to the triumphant actress upon the stage. There was a whole world out there, pulsing with activity, and today, at least, Amelia had been a part of it.

And somewhere, out there, was Alistair.

**In which our hero broods and sips
brandy, as heroes are wont to do.**

Was it midnight yet?

There was a pounding on the door of Alistair's flat. It couldn't be Jenkins, who had retired for the evening. It could not be Amelia; even she wouldn't dare to run away, alone, at this late hour, again. Besides, those were a man's heavy fists pounding at the door, demanding entry.

Alistair opened the door to find Darcy glowering on the other side.

Of course it was Darcy, Lord Protector of Propriety, the Right Honorable Gentleman, the defender of virtue, etc., etc., etc.

"Do come in," he said as his friend pushed past him into the flat. "Make yourself at home. Brandy?"

"No thank you."

"What brings you here?"

He was answered with a sharp look. *Don't be an idiot.*

"Tell me everything that happened," Darcy said, "beginning with how you came to be in the possession of Lady Amelia Cavendish."

"I think I will have a brandy," Alistair remarked. He poured himself a drink and sat down on the uncomfortable little settee. Darcy paced. Alistair wondered why he cared so much about the fate of one wayward American girl.

"Do you believe in fate, Darcy?"

"No."

"I don't either. Or rather, I didn't." He paused thoughtfully. Was it fate that had brought him and Amelia together? Or was it merely luck? "As I was walking home from the club last night, she literally stumbled into my arms. I thought she was drunk. You know I couldn't very well leave her on the street. So I brought her home."

"She spent the night here." Darcy's horror was evident.

"Do consider the alternatives. Leaving her on the street, depositing her on the doorstep of some unsuspecting family and fleeing the scene . . ."

But Darcy had no time for that.

"You will have to marry her."

"And this is where fate enters the picture," Alistair said with a laugh. "Marrying her was the plan from the beginning. No, the middle. At any rate, I found her last night and Wrotham ordered me to marry her this morning."

"Which is interesting, truly, but does not explain why I found you both at the theater this evening."

"She wished to spend the day doing all the things she hasn't been permitted to do."

"I do not want to know," Darcy said flatly. Alistair decided not to confirm Darcy's worst suspicions. "You must marry her *soon*. If word of this gets out, she will be ruined and the entire family will be shunned. In fact, not even the duchess could smooth their entry into society. A scandal like this would ruin them all."

"I have not been out of society so long that I have forgotten how it works. If a man so much as sneezes in the vicinity of a gently bred female of virtue, he will find himself at the altar. As it happens, I have every intention of wedding her."

There was just the tricky bit of revealing that he knew she had deceived him from the beginning. And God Forbid that she ever discover he'd been *ordered* to secure her hand in marriage.

But he'd gone over all that in his mind all day long. Darcy paced before him, evidently incredibly vexed by the whole situation when Alistair couldn't fathom that he had reason to be. Or did he?

"The question is why the family's reputation matters to *you*."

Darcy gave him a dark look, but Alistair had known him too long to fall for his Lord High And Mighty routine, which terrified everyone else. Instead, he sipped his drink and wracked his brain for what Darcy gave a damn about.

Then the answer was suddenly, blindingly clear.

"You're in love with her."

His quick no wasn't quick enough. Alistair's stomach dropped. He wouldn't have a prayer of marrying Amelia if someone as esteemed and *rich* as Darcy was interested in her. God, and he would be considered Amelia's rescuer while Alistair was just the scoundrel who had ruined her.

"That is why you were searching for her."

"Lady Amelia?" Darcy burst out laughing. "No, I have no feelings for her, other than polite concern for her welfare."

"I don't suppose the family includes sisters?"

"Two, in fact. But this is not about me." But it was; Alistair saw that now. The potential scandal would ruin *all* the sisters' prospects. This was starting to make sense to him now. "This is about you," Darcy continued. "And the fact that you absconded with a young lady of virtue and squired her all over town. Anyone could have seen you."

"No one saw us."

"How do you know?"

Alistair shut up and sipped his drink. The truth was that he didn't know. He'd been so long out of town, he wouldn't recognize most people—or be recognized by them. And frankly, he wasn't paying attention to anyone or anything other than the captivating Miss Amy Dish.

"Someone will have seen you. They always do. Word will get out. It always does. If you have any sense, you will wed her properly and publicly before anyone learns the truth about you and Lady Amelia."

Chapter 15

In which our hero has a choice to make.

The following morning, Alistair awoke to a missive from the baron.

Come at once.
—WROTHAM

He dressed and departed quickly, allowing time to walk there, which also provided the opportunity to gather his thoughts. He knew Wrotham would want to speak of his quest to marry his heir into the Cavendish family, but how much was Alistair prepared to say?

In a very limited period of time he had, perhaps, exceeded the baron's expectations. Any word about Amelia would certainly help to ensure a wedding. She *had* to marry him now.

He had, essentially, completed his task. All that was missing was the ring on her finger and the announcement in the newspaper. It would take nothing more than a quiet conversation with her brother, the duke. Or just a well placed "rumor."

But Alistair *liked* her. She was amusing and challenging, pretty and charming. He could even love her. He might already be halfway there. Above all, he didn't want her as his wife by trickery or scandal. He wanted a union of two hearts in love. Gad, that was a treacly, overly romantic thought unbefitting an Englishman.

But there it was.

Rutherford once again asked for his card and asked him to state the nature and purpose of his visit. Alistair sighed, procured a card, and said the baron was expecting him.

"I did not see you at the Carsingtons' ball last night," the baron began by way of greeting when Alistair stepped into the library.

Oh bloody hell. It was only then that he remembered he had promised to attend so that he might make the acquaintance of Lady Amelia. Instead he had squired her to the theater . . . after bedding her. This would please the baron to no end, if he were to ever learn of it. But Alistair would die a thousand painful deaths before providing such information. She was *his*.

"Something came up."

"I can't imagine what is more important than

doing your duty to the Wrotham estate." Then, with a withering glare, he added, "It's the least you can do, given what I have done for you."

This he wanted to protest, but this he could not protest.

The man had given him a home, an education, and something like a family. The man had raised him alongside his own son.

Alistair had visited his mother's family in India; he had seen how radically different his life might have been. He would not have had his gentleman's education, enjoyed the friendships that he did, or traveled so extensively. He would not have met Amelia and he never would have found himself in this position . . .

. . . standing on a well-worn carpet, receiving a setdown he didn't even deserve from his uncle even though he was a grown man of thirty.

Something hot, like anger, flared up and he had the urge to defend himself to his uncle. Alistair wanted to see a spark of approval in the old man's eyes for once.

Just once.

Anything but that perpetual frown of disappointment.

"I went through all the bother of securing an invitation for you and you don't even have the decency to attend. I will not be embarrassed by you."

Unspoken words hung in the air, understood:

I will not be embarrassed by you *any more than I already am*.

And there it was again: the angry urge to tell the Baron everything. *Everything*. That he had not only made the acquaintance of the American girl but had made her *his*.

The baron thought he had failed; well, Alistair had exceeded expectations. He could be at Durham House issuing a proposal now, were it not for this interview in which he had to bite his tongue and allow this man to think him nothing, useless, a bother.

Because he cared for Amelia. What had occurred between him and Amelia yesterday had been true and genuine; it was not to be callously used as fodder to seek Wrotham's approval *for once*.

And yet the urge remained.

Alistair did not wish to consider what that meant, or what it said about his character, because he suspected it wouldn't be flattering.

But then maybe this internal struggle was entirely beside the point, given what Wrotham said next.

"At any rate, I suppose you heard the gossip," Wrotham said cryptically. "Everyone is talking about it."

Well if that wasn't the sort of thing to make one start to panic and deeply regret not taking a moment to peruse the gossip columns this morning.

Heard *what*?

Talking about *what*?

Talking about *whom*?

He had his suspicions of course: rumors of a young heiress spotted strolling through St. James's Park in the company of a gentleman, young scandalous lady seen kissing a gentleman in Vauxhall Gardens, a young lady causing a melee between Bow Street Runners and a crowd of bystanders.

Rocking back on his heels and biting his tongue, he waited for the baron to confirm or deny if those were the rumors being discussed. Alistair didn't dare volunteer the information.

But if he did . . . if he'd started a rumor . . .

Wedding bells.

It would be so *easy* to have everything he ever wanted. A wife and family. The baron's approval. *With just one word, one well-placed rumor . . .*

"I daresay the ton has never seen a more scandal-plagued family," the baron said and Alistair froze, waiting. The baron interrupted his needlessly long, dramatic pause to issue a sigh. Alistair balled his hand into a fist, so anxious was he, waiting to hear *what*, now that he knew *whom*. "But then again," the baron said, *finally*, "we can hardly expect a pack of American horse breeders to behave as befits the most civilized people in the world."

Such kind words for his (hopefully) future in-laws.

Visions of their day flashed through his brain, each one more scandalous than the last, and each one giving way to imagining the worst of what the ton would be saying.

Did you see her dining alone with TWO gentlemen?

Did you see her dashing through the rain?

Did you see her smashing a Bow Street Runner on the head with a parasol, taken from an innocent old lady bystander? Well. I. Never.

Gad, he could practically hear the old matrons of the ton huffing.

"But I suppose this bodes well for you and your suit," the baron said, giving voice to the words Alistair hated himself for thinking. "Though how you are to meet them if they all cancel their appearances due to sudden illness which leaves one of them bedridden I know not."

Alistair dared to breathe a sigh of relief. They had not been seen.

"What, exactly, happened?"

"They did not attend Carsingtons' ball last evening. They were expected," the baron said, and Alistair wanted to laugh that such an inconsequential thing could be deemed such a horrendous offense. It was as if the ton was, collectively, determined to resist the Americans no matter what they did or did not do.

It was a feeling he was not a stranger to; the difference between him and Amelia was that he hadn't given up on trying to assure his place.

Which was why he was here. And not with her.

"At the very last minute, the duchess sent word. The hostess was furious. All anyone could talk about is how they were expected to be there and had reneged on their word."

"What a horrible tragedy," Alistair mumbled.

"It is said one of the sisters had taken ill," the Baron added, and that finally caught Alistair's attention and made his pulse quicken as he considered the implications. "Bloody females always being indisposed," Wrotham muttered. "Silly female complaints."

Alistair elected to disregard that.

If it had been put about that Lady Amelia had been ill . . . his mind churned at a furious pace considering every implication and evaluating how he ought to proceed . . .

If he were to propose this morning and announce a betrothal shortly thereafter, someone was sure to notice that neither he nor Lady Amelia were known to have met. He had not officially returned to society. They had not attended the same ball, nor had he been sighted at calling hours. That someone who would inevitably notice would also inevitably comment upon it.

There would be questions about whether she had been ill. Or was the entire family lying in an attempt to defray a scandal? What were they trying to hide? And Alistair knew there was still a chance that they had been sighted. It may not have been in the papers this morning, but what would tomorrow bring?

One little remark, combined with one possible sighting of Lady Amelia on her day out, plus a splash of speculation, a dash of insinuation, and suddenly there was a massive scandal.

That would bring him everything he ever wanted.

That was not how he wished to begin his married life.

Or was it? Time soothed all wounds, did it not?

"At any rate, I have secured another chance for you," the baron said smugly. "They are hosting a ball in a few days' time. I pulled a few strings to obtain an extra invitation. You will go, you will make her acquaintance and you will wed her. Do not ruin this, too."

It was the *too* that slayed him.

Such a little throwaway word. Too. Also. One more thing.

But it referred to one big thing, one tremendous loss, and one reason for what he was about to do next.

In which our heroine languishes in the drawing room, as lovesick heroines are wont to do.

The next day dawned as if nothing had changed, as if nothing remarkable had happened the previous day. As if Amelia hadn't tasted freedom. She woke in her bed, alone. She dressed with the assistance of a proper lady's maid and daydreamed of Alistair buttoning—no, unbuttoning—her gown.

She went downstairs for breakfast with the family and discovered that she simply didn't have much of an appetite.

Afterward, she joined her sisters, the duchess, and Miss Green in the drawing room. Her thoughts strayed to yesterday . . .

The girl with the violets, the woman with the oranges, the people on the streets. The circus performers and the Bow Street Runners in Vauxhall Gardens. The sun on her face and the feeling of endless possibilities.

And Alistair.

And all those strange, tingly, wonderful things he made her feel and that put a blush on her cheeks. Lud, she couldn't think of *that* while in the company of the duchess in the drawing room.

Fortunately, she was distracted by conversation demanding her attention.

Unfortunately, it was about her scandalous day. The duchess was obsessed with the potential consequences—disastrous ones, of course. She'd been reading the newspapers all morning, line by line, in search of any speculation or gossip that would need to be quashed immediately.

"And *The London Weekly* is hinting at an exposé tomorrow," Josephine said. "I shudder to think what their gossip columnist has dug up. She is ruthless."

"No one saw me," Amelia said. She was languishing on the settee. Love. She was almost certainly in love.

"That you know of," Josephine said, leveling a stare over the pages of *The London Weekly*.

"And I didn't do anything scandalous," Amelia added, which was possibly the farthest thing from the truth and the biggest lie she'd ever uttered.

"Were you out-of-doors without a chaperone?" Josephine asked, blinking frequently, and they all knew where this was leading.

A staring contest and battle of wills ensued between the duchess and Amelia. Of course she was out-of-doors without a chaperone. But she couldn't admit it. She couldn't say one single thing; any detail revealed would be like a string they could pull that would unravel the whole ball of yarn.

For a second, Amelia imagined telling the duchess that she had been *inside* without a chaperone. Inside, behind closed doors, with a man, and a complete lack of attire.

Good Lord, she should *not* be thinking such thoughts with so many people around!

As she stared into the cool, unblinking blue eyes of the duchess, she heard her sisters whispering about who would blink first.

In the end, it was Amelia who blinked first as

she tried to dismiss the intimate memories; those were to be saved and savored in private. She wanted to keep everything about the previous day to herself, her own special memories of the day she fell in love. They were not to be fodder for speculation or conversation.

Also, one didn't just *say* aloud in the drawing room the things they had done. Her heartbeat quickened at the memory. Her cheeks were suffused with a telltale blush. Lud, but love and lust had wrecked her.

Love?

Aye, she might love him. Because he was wonderful and troubled and she wanted to make him happy. Because he seemed to like her just as she was. Because her heart beat faster at the thought of seeing him again And . . . just because.

Did love really need a reason?

Someone pointed out that her cheeks were pink.

"*Her* cheeks are also pink," Amelia noted immediately, hoping to deflect attention from herself. Which is why she turned the tables on Bridget, who had spent the day with Lord Darcy. Now *that* was something to discuss. "What did you get up to yesterday, Bridget?"

"I spent the whole afternoon traipsing around London searching for *you*."

"In the company of Lord Darcy," Claire added, with a smug smile.

"Dreadful Loooord Darcy," Amelia teased.

Dreadful Lord Darcy, who'd tracked her down and returned her to her family. Who had actually understood her after all. And who said she would have to marry Alistair. Who was not here to issue a proposal.

"You know his reputation," Bridget said, speaking of Darcy. "You can imagine how tedious the day was. We went to Hyde Park before being caught in a thunderstorm. Then we returned. Nothing remotely interesting occurred."

Amelia glanced over at Bridget and saw that her cheeks were still quite pink. And she had been writing in her diary and dreamily staring off into space. Surely that meant *something* had happened.

Pendleton, the butler, opened the door.

Was it Alistair? Her heart lurched.

Had he found her? How—through Darcy? What would it mean if he had? How would she explain it?

It was remarkable how many thoughts and feelings one could have in the space of a heartbeat, in the passage of a just a few seconds.

"Lord Darcy is here," Pendleton said. "Are you at home?"

The five ladies glanced around the drawing room—which was strewn with Miss Greene's embroidery things, a stack of newssheets, and some pillows on the floor. Claire was slouching in the chair. Bridget nearly spilled ink on her open diary. Amelia was lounging—languishing—on the settee with her ankles exposed. Bridget's hair was a mess, having hastily been pinned up. A tea tray was on the table, but one that had been devastated by five parched and famished ladies.

They all glanced at each other, panic wild in their eyes.

"We shall need a moment, Pendleton," the duchess said, utterly poised in spite of the mess. "Send a maid for this tray and please bring round a fresh one."

The embroidery was shoved in a basket, which was shoved behind a turquoise upholstered chair. Amelia sat up like a lady with a stack of books on her head, Claire put her things away, and Bridget shoved her diary under a seat cushion and pinched her cheeks.

"They're already pink, Bridget," Claire said with a smirk.

"Is it because of Loooord Darcy?" Amelia asked, drawing out the ooooo's just to vex her.

"Do shut up, Amelia."

"Language, Lady Bridget," the duchess admonished.

Then all the ladies stood and turned their attentions to the door.

"Good day, Lord Darcy," Claire asked. "To what do we owe the pleasure?"

"I have come to see how Lady Amelia is faring," he replied. "I am glad to see that you have returned safely."

Ah. She understood: they were not to speak of the previous evening. She was not to let it be known that he had discovered her or escorted her back. Otherwise, he would have mentioned it. But why keep it a secret?

"I am quite well, thank you," Amelia answered. Even though she wasn't quite well; she might be in love with a man whom she might never see again. Perhaps she might get word to Alistair, through Darcy, if she could snare a moment alone with him.

"I am glad to hear it."

"We are so grateful that you accompanied Bridget on the search yesterday," Claire said.

"It was my pleasure," he murmured. His eyes locked with Bridget's for an intense gaze that Amelia noticed. Something had definitely happened yesterday.

"I do hope we can be assured of your discretion," Josephine drawled.

Darcy glanced at her, then to Bridget.

"Of course. It would be a pity for a lady's prospects to be tarnished because of unfounded rumors."

Were there rumors about her already? No one had seen her, right?

"You're a good man, Darcy. Now how is that scoundrel of a brother of yours?"

"As much as a scoundrel as ever, in spite of my efforts to keep him from the falling over the brink into disaster and ruin."

"He is fortunate to have your support," Josephine said. "But what he really needs is a wife."

"He is thinking of taking a wife, finally," Darcy said.

"Bridget has taken a liking to him," Claire said, smirking.

There wasn't even the slightest shift in tone when he said, "Indeed. I have noticed."

"What of *your* prospects, Darcy? Have you proposed to Lady Francesca yet?"

"Pardon me if I will refrain from gossiping about my personal affairs," he said diplomatically. Amelia wasn't the slightest bit interested in his personal affairs; she wanted to know why he was really here. Did he have news from Alistair? What if there wasn't any news from him?

What if she had fallen in love with a man she would never see again? It was a distinct possibility. Probably. It certainly *felt* like it.

"I ask only because I have three girls to get married off."

"I will never marry," Amelia stated. Translation: she probably couldn't marry now. The only man she could wed had probably disappeared. He certainly wasn't *here*, proposing.

"What happened yesterday?" Claire asked.

"Nothing," Amelia declared. But that wasn't quite right. So she added, "Everything."

And something between nothing and everything was the truth.

Chapter 16

In which our hero and heroine meet (again).

In Amelia's humble opinion, this party would have benefitted tremendously from tightrope walkers. Amelia stared up at the massive chandeliers in the ballroom, imagining a rope strung up between them and performers from Astley's putting on a show for the hundreds of guests that had been invited to the ball at Durham House.

The duchess said planning a ball was one of those essential tasks for ladies of their station. Amelia had been delighted with the prospect of planning an event unlike all the other tedious ton affairs, hence her suggestion for tightrope walkers, fortune-tellers, and fireworks. But all her suggestions had been deemed absurd and ridiculous.

As a result she and her sisters (and the duchess, really) had thrown a party just like all the others: a crush of all the same people, an orchestra stashed away behind screens and potted palms, champagne, and lemonade. And always, always the same conversation repeated endlessly.

Tonight, however, no one was speaking about the weather. All the conversations were about her sudden, dire, deathbed illness and her sudden miraculous return to those amongst the living. The duchess's lips were pinched furiously in a straight line.

Amelia thought of engineering a relapse just to be excused. Perhaps she might faint again—because that had worked out so well before. She stifled a snort of laughter.

Last week she had been informed in no uncertain terms that ladies did not snort with laughter.

Instead, she endured.

And just when she thought she would truly perish of boredom, Amelia spied a reason for her heart to keep beating.

Mr. Alistair Finlay-Jones.

Her heart lurched when she saw him. Here. In the flesh. Or rather, in a set of evening clothes that made him look so devastatingly handsome and dashing.

He was *here*!

This was a wonderful thing and terrible thing, all at once.

Any moment now, she would reveal herself to be a liar to the man she loved. Miss Amy Dish indeed. He would know for certain that she was a lady, a duke's sister, who was clearly not in finishing school.

And he would know that he had only to say the word and they would be wed—or her family would be ruined, forever. She was torn between wanting to launch herself into his arms and wanting to avoid him all evening.

There was only one thing to do: sip champagne and pretend he wasn't there.

An hour later

Amelia had never thought of herself as the nervous sort; she tended to brazen out all and any situation in which she found herself. But Lud if she wasn't on tenterhooks all night as she waited for the inevitable moment in which she and Alistair came face to face once again, brought together by Fate after all. Or perhaps it was Darcy. She couldn't think of any other reason for him to be here, or connection that would have secured his invitation.

She was aware of him through endless conversations about the state of her health.

She was aware of him as she waltzed and danced with a half a dozen unremarkable gentlemen.

She was aware of him as the duchess dragged

her all over the ballroom, ensuring that she spoke with all their guests, particularly the male ones with titles, fortunes, and spotless reputations.

Amelia noted that Alistair was not in that group.

But then there he was, in attendance with a couple whom she didn't recognize. Her heart pounded so hard in her chest, she was certain that everyone could hear it, even over the orchestra.

The duchess performed introductions. Amelia hardly heard a word she said.

"May I present Baron Wrotham and Baroness Wrotham," the duchess said in reference to some squat, pale old man and his lovely young wife. "And his nephew Mr. Finlay-Jones."

He hadn't lied.

And his eyes glimmered with recognition.

Just one word from those sensuous lips of his and she would be ruined forever. She might have fallen in love with him, but she wasn't at all keen to find herself an object of scandal and wed, within the week.

"My niece, Lady Amelia Cavendish."

She caught the spark in his eyes. Just a quick flash of . . . something.

"It is a pleasure to make your acquaintance," she said, holding her hand out for Alistair. And then adding, under her breath so only he could hear, "For the very first time."

"I assure you the pleasure is all mine," Alistair murmured as he kissed her hand.

"We are so glad you have recovered from your recent illness," the baroness said kindly. She wasn't much older than Amelia.

"Of course we understand about females and their delicate constitutions," the baron said in a patronizing way that rankled Amelia. "Though you seem to have made a remarkable recovery from whatever ailed you. We are so glad of it; I'm keen for you to make the acquaintance of my nephew. He came all the way back from the Continent to meet you."

Amelia froze.

Her heartbeat slowed.

Her brain resisted the implications of that statement, but there was no denying it.

He had known who she was before they ever met.

And that meant . . . oh Dear Lord, what did that mean? She didn't want to think about it, she didn't want to know, but there was no denying that it wasn't good. It meant that their day hadn't been special or even a delightful twist of fate. It had been a nefarious scheme all along. She thought she'd been taking control of her life but she'd just been a puppet all along.

Her gaze flew to Alistair.

Alistair winced. Confirmation.

By some miracle—or perhaps a lifetime of brazening things out—Amelia turned to the baron, and managing to keep her voice light, she said, "Oh? Is that so?"

"Indeed," the baron boasted. "Why, just the other day, I encouraged him to make your acquaintance. I do believe that was the day you had fallen ill, but better late than never!"

Ah, so their time together might not have been a lovely twist of fate but the scheme of a fortune hunter.

Her heart beat hard.

She balled her hands into fists. As if *that* could stop her heart from breaking. Lots of little cracks as she thought of all the little moments they shared. Lots of little breaks as she realized her trust had been misplaced and her perfect day had merely been his perfect opportunity.

Amelia carried on in a voice that was honey-laced with venom.

"I wonder how he knew about me. Certainly nothing written about me in the gossip columns would impel a man to travel such a great distance merely to make my acquaintance."

Alistair opened his mouth to speak—she imagined he would know just what to say to assuage her suspicions—but she had no interest in whatever excuses he would offer. So she turned to the baron and gave him her full attention. Even a smile to encourage him to reveal more. And she watched Alistair out of the corner of her eye.

"I wrote to him saying how splendid a match between our families would be," the baron said proudly.

Beside Amelia, the duchess harrumphed. Amelia did too. For once, she and her aunt were in agreement.

But her heart was pounding, pounding, pounding in her chest.

She had fancied herself in love with him and . . .

She had given herself to him and . . .

She had risked scandal and the reputation of herself and her family and . . .

Alistair was just another fortune hunter, deceiving her all damned day and night at the behest of his toady old uncle. She thought she could be herself with him, but he was probably just encouraging her so that he could wed her for her dowry or some other awful reason.

He might not even *like* her at all, and she had given herself to him.

She felt sick—like she might actually and truly faint for once.

She had fallen for him and—Amelia lifted her gaze to his and what she saw broke her heart—he did have an ulterior motive all along. And he had lied when she asked him about it.

He wasn't trying to hide the truth now: He had known her real identity from the beginning and he had an incentive—*orders*—to make a match with her. And what better way to do that than compromise her.

She felt betrayed. She felt humiliated. She felt sad for what she had just lost.

Not only had he just broken her heart, but he now also possessed information that would destroy her and her family.

"And now here he is, so pleased to become acquainted with you," the baron said, blindingly oblivious to the hole he was digging and her ever-increasing distress.

As panicked as she was, Amelia still took a moment to marvel at how the man had been so close to what he obviously desired—a match between her and his nephew—and how he destroyed any chance of it with every word he spoke.

Or perhaps not.

Just one word from Alistair . . .

She would find herself married to a liar. A deceiver. A blackmailer.

"How are you finding London, Lady Amelia?" Lady Wrotham said, mercifully changing the subject and reminding everyone else of her presence.

"To be honest, Lady Wrotham, the city has held few attractions for me."

"You must not have had the opportunity to explore then," Alistair said. And she did not care for the wicked gleam in his eye. "There are many wonderful sights in London. Vauxhall Gardens, Astley's Amphitheatre . . ."

How dare he allude to that! She wanted to murder him.

"Perhaps if I had suitable company," she replied. "It wouldn't do to see such wonderful sights with any old scoundrel."

"What about a particular scoundrel?"

He quirked his brow and gave her a hint of that charming, wicked smile. She wondered about the etiquette for throttling a gentleman—did a lady take her gloves off for such an endeavor or leave them on?

"Obviously Lady Amelia will not be consorting with any scoundrels at all, whatsoever," the duchess said in her this-topic-of-conversation-is-closed voice.

"Have you not met any appealing prospects?" Lady Wrotham asked kindly, utterly oblivious to the frisson of tension between Amelia and Alistair. "I imagine a girl as lovely as you must have many."

"I haven't met anyone whom I would consider pledging my troth to," Amelia said. She glanced at Alistair and saw him clench his jaw. "All the gentlemen I've met in England thus far are so . . ."

"Dashing?" Alistair supplied.

"I was going to say disappointing."

"Well, the night is young," the baron said jovially. "And you have only just met my nephew.

I daresay he would love to become more intimately acquainted with you."

Amelia started coughing. She braced herself to hear a response like, *Actually, Lady Amelia and I are already acquainted. Intimately.*

"It seems fate has brought us together," he said softly, having the nerve to gaze into her eyes. The. Nerve.

"Fate?" the duchess echoed with a decidedly unromantic tone.

"Fate is tremendously overrated," Amelia said.

"It wasn't fate," the baron said. "It was my idea."

Everyone ignored him.

Alistair fixed his gaze on her and said, "Lady Amy, may I have the honor of a dance?"

"It's *Lady Amelia*," the duchess corrected.

"I beg your pardon," he said to the duchess, but not to Amelia.

She did not answer immediately and his invitation hung in the air, awkwardly, overheard by those nearby.

A long pause was the least he deserved.

A long pause in which she considered what would be more satisfying—giving him the cut direct, or giving him a piece of her mind when he would have to listen to every last word of her outrage.

She smiled at the prospect.

But it seemed Alistair knew better than to see

just the upturn of her lips; aye, she knew he detected the furious sparks in her eyes.

She knew, because he gave her an *apologetic*
smile. Which only made her more furious because it indicated that he knew all along and that
he knew it had been wrong. And he had taken
advantage of her anyway.

"Amelia . . ." He murmured her name in the
sort of lovesick, longing, I'll-die-a-thousand-
deaths-to-have-you-forgive-me sort of way.

He swept her into his arms and it took a her-
culean effort on her part to ignore his scent, the
way his arms felt around her, and to banish anything remotely like a romantic feeling.

She succeeded. Barely.

Alistair didn't even know where to begin. She
was obviously—rightfully—angry. With him.
With Wrotham. With the lot of them. Her impul-
sive day of joy was revealed to be an opportunity
seized by a fortune hunter.

Of course she was angry. He had half expected
this to happen, but he wasn't fully prepared for it,
perhaps with the vain hope that she might never
discover Wrotham's orders. Within the span of a
waltz, he needed to win her back. After he had
broken her trust, possibly irrevocably.

Bloody hell.

Let the scrambling and groveling begin.

"Amelia." He murmured her name again,

marveling that now he could say it. The truth was out. He felt some relief, in spite of her anger, which he hoped would blow over.

"Don't do that," she snapped. "Don't pretend to be tortured with longing and heartsick when everything we shared is obviously one big lie."

"So says Miss Amy Dish," he dared to murmur, to tease. Her anger flared.

"I might have lied about my name—a trifling thing—but you knew who I was all along. When did you discover it, anyway?"

"That morning. I had known when I returned to the flat and you were leaving."

He remembered opening the door to find her there, awake and smiling and his salvation. If he didn't screw this up ... he could still wake up to her smiling, find salvation, happiness, everything ...

"And the night before?"

"Truly a coincidence. Dare I say it was fate?"

"It was laudanum," Amelia replied. Laudanum? That made more sense than brandy. "And fate can go hang itself."

"I only took you to my lodgings because you would not tell me where you lived. As a gentleman, I couldn't leave you on the street alone at night."

"As a gentleman." She sniffed. "That's a bit rich, coming from you." He gave her a sharp look; Englishmen did *not* take kindly to having their word as a gentleman questioned. No man did.

"I carried you home," he said. "Nothing untoward happened. Though in the interest of full disclosure, I did leave you to sleep on the settee."

"And you call yourself a gentleman," she retorted. "To leave a lady to sleep on that rickety scrap of furniture and allow her to think you'd sacrificed your comfort for hers. Mine. A gentleman. Ha!"

"I'm sorry."

"We didn't accidentally encounter each other on the street the next morning now, did we?"

"No."

"And the perfect day of all the things that I wished to do?"

He heard the catch in her voice; was he going to take that happy memory from her?

"It was real," he said honestly and fiercely, eyes flashing with passion. "It was all real."

She blinked quickly and turned away for a second. Tears?

"And when you lied about having an ulterior motive? I *asked* you."

"I panicked. I had already started to fall for you and didn't want to lose you so soon." It was the truth.

"Hmmph. Was it all your uncle's idea or did you come up with that plan on your own?"

"He wishes us to marry; there is no denying that," he said. "I knew that I, an impoverished, undistinguished gentleman wouldn't have a chance with you in a room full of equally impoverished but more socially connected gentlemen.

I simply seized the opportunity presented to me. After she luckily stumbled into my arms in the middle of the night."

"Interesting choice of words, Alistair. An opportunity. Let me see if I understand this correctly: your uncle needs money. So he summons you back from Europe and orders you to court me, the scandalous heiress with an enormous dowry and few marital prospects."

"You are well versed in the ways of the haute ton."

"Tell that to the gossips," she said sharply. "And speaking of the gossips, what happens now?"

"We waltz. And I begin my woefully inadequate attempts to convince you that everything we shared was real, true, and beautiful." He dropped his voice, speaking earnestly, "Because it was, Amelia."

That was the truth. Yes, admittedly, they only enjoyed that day because of a few lies at the outset, but what they had shared that day was something rare, and special and real.

"No, that's not what I mean," she said, impatiently. She looked nervous and sad.

It was clear: he had broken her heart and any feelings for him had died. He could tell, because that sense of laughter and teasing was gone from her eyes and the way she spoke. He could feel her stiff and indifferent in his arms.

It slayed him, that.

He breathed her in, remembering when she was warm and wanting in his arms.

"I mean, do you blackmail me into marriage?" she asked. His heart sank. "You easily could. We could be married by the end of the week. Your uncle could spend my dowry by the end of the month."

Hell, he could say something now and they would be married by morning. Alistair glanced away and his attention happened to land on Wrotham, beaming smugly. It was the closest thing to the approval Alistair had wanted. And damn if he wasn't tempted to play his hand and make Amelia his wife.

But he had memories of when she opened to him, trusted him, let him in. He wanted that again. He wanted her happy and teasing once more. He wanted them happy.

"That is definitely a possibility," he admitted.

"You are so logical. You should meet my sister Claire."

"Please do introduce us," he joked. "Uncle only said I had to marry one of the American girls; he did not specify which one."

She seemed to sense that he was teasing and she scowled at him.

"I am so far from wooed."

"I don't need to woo you. As you pointed out, I have the option of blackmail."

"Be still my beating heart," she retorted.

"Of course I will still try to woo you,

Miss Dish," he murmured, gazing down at her, teasingly gently. "A gentleman must do something to while away the hours. I cannot imagine a more pleasurable way to spend the time."

"I thought you were going to help your uncle with his business affairs." Then she paused as it all made sense. "Ah. I am the business affair. Very clever, Alistair. I see what you did there—you told an impartial truth for exactly this moment. You anticipated I would discover this racket and you wanted to be able to say you never lied."

"We are very greedy in my family. But while Wrotham only wants money, I want something else." He gazed into her eyes. "I want more than one perfect day with you, Amelia."

"Look at you with the devastatingly romantic line. Shall I swoon now or wait for your grand declaration of true love as you attempt to convince me that what we shared was unique and that we belong together forevermore?"

"We have spent but one day together. I might be utterly enchanted by you and gutted to be fighting, but I will not throw around the word *love* so that you might forgive a deception that may well be unforgiveable. When I say it to you, it is because I mean it. Because I cannot *not* say it. And I bet that, at that moment, you'll say it back."

"The problem with your plan is that I've just decided to never speak to you again." And with that, she turned and walked away.

Chapter 17

In which our heroine plots a murder.

The next day

$\mathcal{A}$melia had considered the matter of Alistair's Betrayal all night and decided that the only logical course of action would be to murder him.

It was the least he deserved for the heinous crime of making her fall in love with him, making love to her, while deceiving her the whole damned time about his reasons.

Oh, and then having the nerve to tease her about it.

And then promising to woo her. Within an otherwise polite and routine conversation at a ball, totaling perhaps no more than five minutes, Amelia was made aware that what had felt like love was a lie.

Pistols or poison?

Even worse, she had placed her heart and reputation—and her family's reputation—in the hands of a fortune-hunting scoundrel with nefarious intentions and an ulterior motive (and who lied about it! But was one ever honest about one's nefarious intentions?). She wanted to run away all over again, but that's what got her into this situation, wasn't it?

Knives or venomous snakes?

She had to do something to protect them all, to save them from ruin because of her folly. Never mind that she was only out and able to commit said folly because she had been drugged against her knowledge.

However, she was in no position to *think* at all about how to do away with Mr. Fin-"lying"-Jones due to a few glasses of champagne the previous evening, resulting in a relentlessly pounding head and this stubborn ache in her heart.

It would also help if her stomach ceased threatening to revolt.

"*The London Weekly* is reporting that Amelia was seen quaffing an excess of champagne," Josephine said with a frown at Amelia, who most certainly was. Combined with regret and fury, it was a noxious combination. She was in no position to protest. "When she wasn't quaffing champagne," the duchess read, "she was seen shooting daggers with her eyes at Mr. Alistair

Finlay-Jones, the vaguely disreputable heir to Baron Wrotham."

"I don't know what you are talking about," Amelia muttered. "One cannot shoot daggers with their eyes."

She mourned the impossibility of this. For if it had been possible, the newspapers would instead be reporting on the deaths of Alistair and his uncle and the bloody mess they would have made on the ballroom floor, all thanks to the daggers shot from the eyes of Lady Amelia Cavendish.

"It's not *I* that am talking about it, but rather *The London Weekly* and thus the entire town," the duchess replied. "My only consolation is that they are not speaking about your mysterious illness."

"*The Morning Post* is," Claire said, looking up from yet another newssheet. "The 'Man About Town' says that Lady Amelia appears to have made a remarkable recovery from her grave and sudden illness." Then she read from the column. "In fact, the lady looked as if she had a spent a day out-of-doors rather than a day on her deathbed."

Curses. Hell and damnation. Was that merely idle speculation or had someone seen them? Did she put it past Alistair and his half-wit uncle to plant something in the newspapers, thus forcing her hand? There was a scoundrel out there who had ruined her and the only thing keeping her from a scandal of unfathomable proportions was the word. Of a liar.

Damned curses. Bloody hell and damnation.

"If only they could see you now," Bridget teased. "You really do look incredibly ill."

Anyone would be, if there were a nefarious scoundrel at large, with information that could utterly and irrevocably ruin her. Having had too much to drink had nothing to do with it, though it provided an excellent cover for the real source of her distress.

Amelia halfheartedly swatted at Bridget.

"Sisters," James groaned. He too, seemed to have consumed an inordinate amount of spirits the previous evening. "What did I ever do to deserve *three* sisters?"

Bother her brother's laments about sisters. Bother the dramatic reading of the gossip columns and whatever anyone else was chattering about. Did they not know that everything was wrecked and that ruin might befall them at any second?

In which our hero laments and his valet is impertinent.

Everything was ruined. Alistair wanted to blame Wrotham—the stupid, blathering, scheming, idiotic baron—for ruining his own plan. It was the least the social-climbing, fortune-hunting bounder deserved. To be so close and wrenched away.

But Alistair deserved some blame for the role he played. He was the one who did the old man's bidding; he was the one who swept her away, fell half in love with her, made love to her, ruined all her other prospects.

He didn't even give her a chance. Or a choice. What an irredeemable and unforgiveable scoundrel he was.

He was the one who held the sword over their heads.

And he hated himself for it, almost as much as he hated the choice he had to make.

Alistair could protect Amelia's secret and fail the baron once more. The forgiveness he sought would never be his.

Or it would take just one word with the duke or one well-placed rumor and Amelia would be his wife. He would have a home and family of his own. The baron's approval would be his. It was, oh, everything he had ever wanted.

Neither of these options felt quite *right*. Thus, he brooded, lamenting the state of affairs, while sitting at the small table in his flat and pretending to read the newspaper whilst Jenkins bustled around doing God knows what.

"What are you doing?"

"I am brushing the lint from your jacket."

Alistair glanced over at the navy blue wool coat in his valet's hands.

"You needn't bother," Alistair told him. "I'm not going out. I'm certainly not going out anywhere so fine as that."

Jenkins merely ignored him and carried on with the brushing of the jacket, which was decidedly free of dirt, lint, or anything requiring the valet's attentions. This, clearly, was not about the jacket.

"Where do you think I should be going?" Alistair asked warily, even though he suspected he already knew the answer.

"You're not going anywhere. You just said so."

Jenkins was now turning his attentions to a shirt. Then he started to whistle a merry tune. If there was one thing Alistair was in no mood for, it was someone else's good mood. It interfered with his brooding.

"Why are you so bloody cheerful?" Alistair grumbled.

"Why are you so bloody morose?" Jenkins replied. "It's not as if you have anything to be morose about."

"Of course not."

But that was a lie, was it not? He had been revealed as the worst sort of lying, fortune-hunting scoundrel to the woman he was half in love with. She now despised him, rightfully so. He would lose her *and* his chance at redemption with the baron. So no, there was *nothing* to be morose about. Except for everything.

"You wish to wed Lady Amelia, correct?"

Of course his valet would mention her. Of course he had the valet who, over the years, had become something of a friend and confidant and who had such a sense of security in his position that he would feel at liberty to start such conversations.

Alistair groaned. Jenkins took this as agreement and continued.

"Then just go tell her brother, the duke, that you have thoroughly compromised his sister. You'll be married by sundown."

Jenkins smiled proudly, satisfied with his logic.

Alistair had to concede that was certainly a possibility. He could don that shirt that Jenkins just starched, the jacket his valet had just brushed, and the rest of his finest attire. He could walk to Durham House, confess everything to the new duke, risk being challenged to a duel, and request the hand in marriage of Lady Amelia Cavendish.

He might find himself wed. The baron would be pleased with him for once. He would come home to his beautiful wife, Amelia.

And Alistair would always know that he'd blackmailed her to please the baron, and he suspected that she would be a champion grudge holder.

He would never be truly happy. Neither would she.

No, Alistair did not wish to have her under such circumstances. Because he cared, he could not do that to them both. Damn.

"I cannot do that," Alistair told Jenkins.

"It's because you're a sensitive sort," Jenkins said with a twinge of despair. "You always were."

"You say that as if it were a bad thing."

"That moral compass of yours, too, gets in the way sometimes," Jenkins said, with an emphasis on *sometimes*.

At heart, Alistair was a good person, but he was not a saint. While he did not take advantage of Amelia, he certainly hadn't marched her straight home. He certainly hadn't made much of an effort to stop their lovemaking. His moral compass had certainly taken leave of its responsibilities that day.

For a moment, Jenkins disappeared.

While Alistair was lost in thought and fixated upon lamenting his tragic circumstances (admittedly of his own making), Jenkins reemerged and began bustling around with hot water, soap, towels.

"What are you doing now?"

"I should think it's obvious. I am gathering the accouterments should you wish for a shave."

"Why would I do that?" He had no plans to venture out into polite company.

"In the event that you wish to go out and, say, pay call upon Lady Amelia."

This was the problem with servants who were confident in the security of their positions. They said things about women whom certain gents were trying not to think about.

"I'm not going to blackmail her into marrying me."

He could. Perhaps he even should, if he wanted the baron's forgiveness. But there was a small part of him that rebelled against forcing her hand.

"Did you ever think that perhaps the lady might wish for a marriage proposal?" Jenkins mused. Left unspoken: the words *you idiot*.

"She made it abundantly clear that she would not accept one. My options are to force her hand in marriage by spreading rumors or speaking to her brother, or I can let her go, and live with the baron's eternal disapproval. These are my choices, Jenkins. I find I don't care for either of them."

"I think it's obvious what you must do," Jenkins said simply. "You let the lady decide. You will have to woo her."

Chapter 18

In which siblings interfere with courtship.

Later that afternoon

*I*f it weren't for the odious Mr. Collins, Amelia might never have been at home to Mr. Alistair Fin-"lying"-Jones. She would have refused to see him, being too busy plotting his imminent demise. The future happiness of her entire family was now in jeopardy because Alistair had the sort of charming smile that made a girl forget her wits and he had used it on her.

Swords or a swarm of angry pigeons?

But Mr. Collins—James's heir, a distant relation of the Cavendishes who nevertheless insisted on calling them all "cousin," and an insufferable ass—had come to call upon the family.

The purpose of his visit was to propose to

Bridget, who of course refused him, because he was an insufferable ass.

And because love was what mattered most of all.

Amelia only realized this after Mr. Collins stormed out in a huff and Pendleton was left standing awkwardly with a bottle of champagne, ready to celebrate. Or rather, it was the conversation that happened *after* that made her think differently about that last little shred of *feeling* in her heart. Because, it turned out, a girl couldn't just forget something like love overnight.

"Don't bother to open the champagne, Pendleton," the duchess had said with a disapproving frown after a red-faced Collins left. "It is clear we have nothing to celebrate."

"Did you honestly think that we would?" Bridget asked her incredulously.

"You must marry. You must all marry!"

For once, the duchess actually raised her voice. This intrigued Amelia, so she had paid attention.

"I do not think we are opposed to marriage," James said evenly.

"We are just opposed to pledging our troth to cork-brained men with nothing to recommend them," Bridget said in huff. Wasn't that the truth.

"Well, if you continue to flout society, you may only have the likes of Mr. Collins to choose from!" the duchess cried, and Amelia, a flaunter of society, took note in the form of a small knot of guilt and regret beginning to ache in her stomach.

The duchess continued in a sharp voice, clearly out of patience with the Cavendish siblings: "And he is not the worst possible person. At least the dukedom would stay in the family. You would be provided for. What if your brother dies and you are all unwed? How will you support yourselves? Who will marry you then, when you have no reputations because you have flouted the rules at every turn and when you have no dowries because everything has gone to Mr. Collins?"

"James won't die," Amelia protested weakly. He couldn't die. He couldn't leave them alone, especially not with a potential scandal looming that could ruin them.

"People die, Amelia. Look at our parents," Claire said softly.

Ah, Claire with the logic. As always. Even if it hurt.

"Yes, but people love, too. Look at our parents," Bridget said. "Don't we all want that?"

Everyone fell silent, thinking about true love and happily ever after and maybe, perhaps, even a particular person. She knew Bridget was caught in a love triangle, Claire had a suitor, and James had that distracted look he got when he was infatuated with a woman.

"We want what our mother and father had, Josephine. Love," James said quietly. "The kind of love you throw a dukedom away for."

Amelia may not have that sort of love, ever.

But she would be damned if her one day of adventure and pleasure seeking—an admittedly glorious day—ruined the future happiness of her family and kept them from their true loves.

That was the only reason she was at home to him when he had the audacity to call later that afternoon.

"Mr. Alistair Finlay-Jones," Pendleton announced, presenting his card to the duchess on a silver tray.

"Wrotham's nephew," the duchess said. Then she made A Face. "And a fortune hunter. Though Amelia seemed rather animated whilst waltzing with him."

"Amelia often seems rather animated," Claire said.

"Yes. I am very animated," Amelia said. "It had nothing to do whatsoever with my waltzing partner."

The duchess looked at her with those startling blue eyes, as Amelia wondered if Josephine was, in fact, a witch and could peer into her soul and know exactly what sort of trouble Amelia had gotten into and with whom. But no, that was impossible. Right?

"Another fortune hunter . . ." Bridget sighed. "I had thought we'd met them all by now."

"I'm tempted to give everyone's dowries away to charity if only so we ceased being plagued by them," James said wearily.

"You are the duke. No one would stop you," Claire pointed out. "I wouldn't mind being spared the attentions of such obsequious gentlemen."

They would be spared such attentions if they wed people whom they actually cared for. Which they would not be able to do if Amelia's Escape ruined their prospects. This unfortunate truth was not lost on Amelia.

"Show him in," Amelia said. Everyone turned to look at her in shock. And then everyone turned to the doorway to gawk at Mr. Alistair Finlay-Jones.

He arrived with a posy of violets, which he presented to Amelia.

Her stupid heart skipped a beat.

For a second, everyone was speechless.

Just one merciful second.

Then everyone had something to say about this handsome gentleman with the most unimpressive bouquet of flowers any of them had been presented with.

"An interesting choice of flowers," Bridget mused, eyeing the small violet and white bouquet Amelia now held in her hands.

"It is certainly not ostentatious, which suggests that you are probably not exceedingly wealthy," Claire remarked. She was so logical. And not subtle.

"Which then calls into question your motives toward my sister," James said, adding the Menacing Glare, which he had perfected since coming to England.

Amelia eyed Alistair, watching to see how he handled her siblings, all of them, at once. He didn't say a word; then again they all spoke so quickly that he didn't exactly have a chance to reply to comments about his finances or motives or any other appallingly personal topics that People of Quality did not mention within moments of making a new acquaintance.

She was content to let him fend for himself.

"But it might also suggest a certain confidence; he doesn't need lavish displays of hothouse flowers and such to woo a woman," Claire said thoughtfully. "He just has to strut in here with a modest bouquet—"

"Did I strut?" Alistair interrupted. "I don't think I strut."

"Or is it more of a swagger?" Bridget mused.

Amelia scowled; now they were just teasing him to make *her* squirm uncomfortably. God, he had broken her heart and could destroy them all and they were teasing him about whether he strut or swaggered.

Honestly, it was more of a saunter. Not that

anyone asked her. Not that she would continue this conversation.

"It is a lovely bouquet, with a beautiful meaning," Miss Green said quietly. "The violet symbolizes modesty. The blue violets are said to signify faithfulness and the white ones suggest taking a chance on happiness."

"Which you would all know if you attended to lessons," the duchess said, pointedly. The three Cavendish sisters groaned. Lessons on the secret meaning and symbolism of flowers was exactly the sort of thing Amelia had ran away from.

"Or they are simply flowers," Amelia said crossly, attempting to diffuse speculation about anything between her and Alistair. She failed, magnificently.

"Ah," Bridget said, eyes wide with comprehension.

"I see," Claire murmured, smiling.

Amelia wanted to throw a pillow at them both.

"Interesting," James said, grinning as he looked from Amelia to Alistair and back again. He settled into his chair, comfortably. "Do join us, Mr. Finlay-Jones. I think I speak for all my siblings when I say that we are delighted to make your acquaintance."

"Not all of us," Amelia muttered.

"Is that because you have already made his acquaintance?" Claire inquired in a decidedly put-on oh-so-innocent voice.

"We know she has," Bridget said. "They waltzed at the ball."

"And she was, to quote the papers, shooting daggers at him with her eyes," James added. "One doesn't engage in such ocular violence with a mere stranger."

"Does any self-respecting man really quote the gossip columns?" Amelia grumbled.

"Living with you lot of females has ruined me," James said.

"Never mind the state of James's masculinity," Claire said and Miss Green blushed. "Bridget, if you would stop mooning about Darcy for one second and *think* . . ." Claire said pointedly.

Lord save her from exceedingly smart sisters.

"I'm not mooning about—" Bridget retorted. And then, "Ooooh."

Comprehension had dawned.

As far as anyone knew, Amelia had only met him last night, they'd had an unremarkable conversation, then waltzed, and then she was seen "shooting daggers at him with her eyes" and now he was here with violets.

It was all a bit much for a simple conversation of introduction at a ball full of introductions and simple conversations. Combined with the fact that Amelia had been missing . . . Claire was *very* good at putting two and two together.

Amelia wanted to fling the posy of violets at her.

"Do give our guest a chance to speak," the duchess cut in. "What brings you here with that little posy of violets, Mr. Finlay-Jones?"

Alistair didn't shrink from the duchess's stare. Amelia had to admit, privately, that it was impressive.

"Lady Amelia."

His voice was low and seductive. His gaze was focused and intense.

Longing flared within her. Warred with feelings of betrayal.

Her sisters sighed.

"Oh don't fall for this romantic nonsense," Amelia said, exasperated. And, as much as a reminder for her as the rest of them: "He is only here at the wishes of his uncle."

"Our sister has never been known for her subtlety," James said to Alistair.

"Subtlety is overrated." Amelia and Alistair said this at the exact same moment. Eyebrows arched all around the room.

"I heard you have been traveling, Mr. Finlay-Jones," Josephine said, changing the subject. "Where have you been causing trouble?"

"The usual haunts: France, Italy. India."

"What took you to India?" Josephine asked. "Most gentlemen find enough entertainment closer to home."

"I wanted to see where my parents had met and where I had been born."

"Ah. I see," the duchess said. But Amelia didn't see. She only had more questions. Who was this man, really? Who was this man who had some sort of Secret Pain and little family to speak of, who had spent years traveling and yet had come back from such adventure simply because his uncle wished him to make her acquaintance?

She thought she knew him and it seemed she didn't at all. Now she had a million questions for him, which was in direct conflict with her determination to avoid him forevermore and to Banish Him From Her Heart. Damn.

"You have been gone for some time," the duchess said. "I haven't seen you since the funeral."

"Yes."

It was as if a cloud passed over. His expression darkened. His demeanor changed and Amelia's curiosity flared once more. What funeral? Who had died? And why did Alistair look as if it'd only happened yesterday?

"It is good of you to return, finally, and good of you to call upon us." The duchess's dismissal was clear. Alistair took his leave—but not without one long, heated, lingering look at Amelia. If she were interpreting it correctly, he said, with just his eyes, *I have seen you naked and I want to see you naked again.*

Her body's reaction—the spark of wanting, the slow burn of longing—was another betrayal.

The doors had scarcely shut behind him when everyone turned their attentions to the duchess.

"What funeral?" Amelia asked. She didn't even try to sound like she wasn't that interested. Because she was. Oh, she was. "Who died?"

"It sounds so dramatic and ominous," Bridget said, dramatically and ominously.

"If you wish to know his private, personal business then I suggest that you ask him yourself," Josephine replied and Amelia scowled mightily in frustration.

"I was about to but then you practically pushed him out the door," Amelia said. "And now I cannot because it conflicts with my plan to never speak to him again."

"Why don't you wish to speak to him again?" Bridget asked. Amelia ignored her.

"But now you are keen to see him again, aren't you?" The duchess smiled devilishly. There was no other way to describe it. All Amelia could think was, *Touché*. She was no match for her own curiosity.

An hour or so later, Amelia strolled into the duchess's bedchamber for the first time, unannounced and uninvited to boot. But Amelia had questions and her curiosity demanded satisfaction. She would much rather risk Josephine's ire with a personal visit than swallow her pride and speak to Alistair.

The duchess was sitting at a small writing table, tending to her correspondence. Miss Green sat nearby, assisting.

"You are devious," Amelia declared.

"Thank you." The duchess did not miss a beat in her reply. She did not even look up from her correspondence.

"I'm not certain I meant it as a compliment."

"I am certain that you did."

"Josie, now I cannot stop thinking about him!" Amelia heaved a mighty sigh and took the liberty of collapsing on the duchess's bed in a fit of despair and frustration.

It was true; she could not stop thinking about him. Not since their parting at the theater, not since she saw him at the ball, not since he came to call this very afternoon. The duchess had to go and intimate that there were dark secrets. Amelia wanted to understand him.

Because then she would know whether he was a worthless scoundrel. Yes, that was a perfectly logical reason for wanting to understand him. It had nothing to do with wanting to know him.

Amelia sat up and asked, "Why are you looking at me like that?"

"Because I am not accustomed to young girls entering my chamber unannounced and flinging themselves on my bed in a fit of lovesick despair."

"I'm not lovesick."

"Of course not."

"I merely find my thoughts occupied by a particular gentleman."

"You are the only one of your siblings to be so vexed by his call this afternoon. And you are the only one to storm in here and have a fit about it."

"This is not a fit. You have seen me have a fit."

"Touché. The less said about that, the better," the duchess remarked. "At any rate, it's not that interesting. It was merely the death of his beloved cousin in a tragic accident. I daresay it shaped the young man's life and character irrevocably."

Amelia wanted to scream into a pillow.

"What circumstances? What tragedy? I cannot bear not knowing."

The duchess just smiled—that devilish smile again—and said, "You will have to ask him."

Of course this was not the answer Amelia was looking for. She would be content with nothing less than the whole story, preferably delivered by someone other than Alistair. She feared if she were to speak with him, or be near him, she would lose her resolve to keep him at a polite distance until her siblings were happily married and unruinable by scandal. But she would probably perish from curiosity first.

Amelia scowled at the duchess and quit the room, leaving the door open behind her.

"I daresay you played that girl like a harp," Miss Green remarked.

Amelia shouted back: "I heard that!"

Chapter 19

In which our heroine is determined to behave and our hero is determined to cause trouble.

Yet another ball

Tonight, Lady Amelia Cavendish was determined to behave. There had been a snippet in *The London Weekly*'s gossip column that morning that was rather unnerving.

> *A melee involving Bow Street Runners, innocent bystanders and a young couple was reported at Vauxhall earlier this week. Lady B— thought she recognized the female half of the dashing away duo.*

The duchess had gasped when she read it at the breakfast table. James had raised one eye-

brow and given her The Look. Claire and Amelia
had exchanged nervous glances. Amelia found
herself without an appetite.

They didn't *know* it was her. But they had their
suspicions and Amelia didn't have it in her to lie
and dissuade them.

The newspaper item wasn't mentioned again,
but Amelia knew it was on everyone's minds,
along with a dozen other vexing questions: Had
she been recognized? Who else had seen her?
What other trouble had she gotten into?

The best course of action, Amelia decided, was
to be on her best behavior. She would do her very
best to communicate to one and all that she was
an innocent angel who couldn't possibly be em-
broiled in a scandal.

It was necessary. The more she thought about
her situation with Alistair—and she spent far
more time than she cared to admit engaged in
such thoughts—the more it became clear to her
that her reputation in society was too precarious
to weather such a scandal. Ditto for her siblings.
Much as she hated to admit it, her best behavior
was essential (or someone else's best behavior).
She might also think of marrying *well*. Very well.
Better than Alistair well.

Even if word got out about their escapade,
and they married, they were both too far on the
fringes of society to be fully accepted.

Best. Behavior.

Thus, at the ball tonight, she smiled the appropriate amount—somewhere in the middle of gargoyle and simpering idiot miss. She kept herself fully attired, including satin shoes and the hair ribbon her maid had used to style her hair. And when one Mr. Alistair Finlay-Jones bowed and asked her to dance, she said yes.

Actually, she said, "I suppose," while holding out her hand. The prospect of dancing with him inspired a tumultuous mix of feelings: anger at his deception, but longing to be close to him again; wanting to deliver a devastating setdown, but fear that it would provoke him into blackmailing her; wanting to refuse to make a point, but determination to be on her best behavior.

"Your enthusiasm makes my heart skip a beat," he remarked dryly. "You can always say no."

"Actually I cannot," she confided. She leaned into him so he might hear when she spoke softly. And also so that she might breathe him in. "Tonight I am trying to be on my best behavior."

Alistair chuckled and then swept her into his arms for a waltz.

"Why the devil would you want to do that?" Alistair asked, gazing down at her. She pursed her lips.

"You wouldn't believe it, but there is this threat of a terrific scandal hanging over my head."

"What sort of scoundrel would do such a thing?"

"You tell me." She gazed up into those dark eyes of his.

"I would never."

"Never?" She echoed. But there had been something in the paper that morning . . . "And what of your uncle?"

"My uncle, who believes that he is the one to introduce us?"

She leaned in and lowered her voice. "Are you saying that we are the only ones who know?"

They were the only ones who knew. So many secrets, large and small, just between the two of them. So many little moments of understanding and intimacy.

Alistair smiled at murmured, "Know what?"

She was enchanted for a moment, before she realized he must not have read the newspaper that morning then.

Alistair had persuaded her to dance with him, and it had felt *right* to hold her in his arms. With her, he was surprised to find that he felt like less of an outsider at ton functions. He was reluctant to part from her.

A short while later, they stood off to the side of the ballroom, trying to avoid the crush. A footman passed by with a tray full of glasses.

"Champagne?" Alistair offered.

"No thank you," Amelia demurred. "After the gossips noted that I had been quaffing an excessive quantity of champagne, I'd better restrain myself. If they had said *sipping*, that would have been one thing. But quaffing! I was informed in no uncertain terms that proper young ladies do not quaff anything."

Alistair sipped his champagne and gazed down at her, mildly amused and very impressed. This was the girl who once ran through the rain and danced around his kitchen wearing his breeches.

"You really are determined to behave."

"I am," she said sadly. " 'Tis a mighty struggle that pales in comparison to any challenges Hercules faced."

Alistair leaned down and whispered in her ear. "I love it when you misbehave."

He was rewarded with a blush across her skin.

"I bet you do," she murmured, snapping her fan open to cover her pink cheeks.

"You seem warm," he couldn't resist pointing out, and she scowled. "I suppose I cannot persuade you to join me for air on the terrace?"

"Are you trying to compromise me?"

Subtlety is overrated indeed. How many maidens would have protected their virtue if they'd only just asked such a question?

"Quite the opposite. I'm trying to woo you."

Subtlety indeed.

"You shouldn't have said that," Amelia chided him. "For I do like to be contrary. Just to be contrary."

"How charming."

"Not according to my siblings. I have been told that it is a horrible defect of my character."

"Are you trying to scare me away, Lady Amelia? Because it's not working."

"I'm merely trying to scare you into keeping our secret. After all, who wishes to find themselves saddled with a contrary wife?"

He didn't hear the phrase *contrary wife* so much as *our secret*. Their day together was this thing that hung in the air between them. It had brought them together—just as he had predicted, it did distinguish him from all the other fortune hunters in the room. But he had not anticipated that it would keep them apart. She feared being forced into a marriage to a man who had lied to her. In fact, he had the distinct impression that she was just *making nice* so that he wouldn't reveal the secret.

He hated that.

He could not fault her for that.

But he also could not deny how he ached for her. He'd been all over the world but only she made him feel right, complete, and at home. Even if she was contrary. Maybe he wanted contrary. Maybe he wanted someone who challenged him and tugged him out of the fog he'd been living in the past six years and into the sunlight.

"Your secrets are safe with me," he said softly as he strolled with her in the direction of the terrace.

"Are they?" There was no hiding the skepticism in her voice and in her expression as she peered up at him. She had every reason to doubt him because he had so much to gain from revealing her secret—or threatening to do so. "And what of *your* secrets? I should like to have one. Then we'll be even."

He took her arm and guided her out to the terrace. It was hardly the desolate, romantic spot he hoped for. More than a few guests had escaped the suffocating heat of the ballroom for the cool night air.

"I'll tell you a secret," he confided and her eyes sparkled in anticipation. "I once spent the day gallivanting around London with a runaway heiress."

"I already know that one." She scowled.

"But I want you to know that no one else does."

"Oh, I know that they don't know. For if they did, I would not be at this ball. Instead I would be locked away in a tower, at a monastery, on a remote island. But I want to know about you, Mr. Finlay-Jones. Whose funeral?"

The words blindsided him. One second they were flirting at a ball, like any other young couple. The next, she was casually inquiring about the most devastating incident of his life.

Alistair didn't want to talk about it. He never did. He struggled to remember Elliot, alive. Not the wretched aftermath. And he certainly did not make a habit of trotting out his Secret Pain so that he might elicit sympathy from women.

His instinct was to say nothing. But Alistair thought of soft pale skin and sweet, passionate kisses. He thought of her boundless enthusiasm and the wonderful but maddening excitement of not knowing what would come next with her. Then he thought of losing her. He thought that since she had trusted him with a massive secret, then perhaps he could open up to her and share his.

He found the words.

"My cousin, Elliot. Wrotham's son." As if that explained anything. "I should add that he was nothing like Wrotham."

"Your grief makes more sense then."

His grief still made it hard to breathe and made it hard to get the words out. But for her . . .

For Amelia he would try.

"He was my cousin. My best friend. My only true family—I lost my parents at a young age. And then Elliot died too. It was a carriage race. We were racing. There was an accident and I survived and he didn't. So you see, Amelia, I'm all alone in the world. Except for Wrotham."

"That is the saddest thing I have ever heard," she said softly. She reached out to touch his arm affectionately, consolingly. He wanted to say something about how opening the door to see her in his home was the happiest moment, how he longed to wake up beside her. But then . . .

"Oh God, it's working!" she lamented. "It turns out I am one of those females whose hearts are softened by stories of tragic pasts and secret pain." She glanced up at him. "I'm sorry, that is a horribly insensitive thing to say."

For a moment, he was not sure how to respond.

"I lost my cat when I was a young boy of eight," Alistair said, finally. "A young orphan boy alone in a foreign county. Tip Toes was just a kitten. I sobbed for days."

"Stop." Amelia made a choking sound. Was it laughter? Or was she crying? She was holding on to him now, leaning in close. He felt her breasts brush against his arm. Relating tales of woe was indeed a promising way to woo reluctant females. Damn if he had only known it sooner.

"And my dog—" He added.

"Oh, don't say anything tragic about a dog!" She wailed and then she was pounding against his chest with her little fists. He caught her wrists. Gazes locked.

They burst into laughter, drawing looks from other guests on the terrace.

When no one was looking, he stepped back and tugged her with him. They slipped around the corner, into an alcove, where it was quiet and dim. There were things he wanted to say to her with the hopes that she might understand him and forgive him.

"I have known pain. And loss. And grief. And then there is you . . ."

"It was just one day." She tried to sound flippant.

"The best day," he said earnestly.

"I'm so mad at you for your deception, Alistair. And I'm so angry with myself for believing in you. And I'm so distressed because it ruins the memory of that one perfect day."

"I'm so sorry," he whispered. "But I am not sorry for what we did that day."

And then, after a long moment of silence, she said, "I can't say I'm sorry either."

It wasn't clear whose lips found whose. One moment they were whispering and gazing into each other's eyes and the next . . . sparks gave way to a slow smolder. He tasted, she yielded, and then they switched, a delicate back and forth of wanting, having, craving, knowing. Always, always that feeling of connection and belonging he had sought for so long. It was here, in her arms, his lips against hers. It was a sensation so intoxicating it could make a man forget everything.

Except . . .

"Wait. Stop." He jerked back. He whispered an explanation: "I don't want us to get caught."

He braced himself, waiting for a well-deserved, mocking comment: *Are you sure about that?* But there was none forthcoming from her lips, reddened from his kiss.

"When I marry you, I want it to be because you choose me," Alistair added. He still wanted the baron's approval. But he also wanted a life with Amelia. He wanted Amelia to choose him, flaws and all. He wanted to have it all.

"Then we had better return to the ballroom before anyone notices we are missing."

No one noticed they were missing. This time.

In which siblings are exasperating.

Later that evening

Whether in America or in England, the Cavendish siblings had a habit of congregating in Claire's bedroom late at night just to talk. Bridget, Amelia, and Claire snuggled up in her large, four-poster bed. James pulled up a chair.

They had all survived another ball, in which, miraculously, nothing of note happened. There were no faux pas or scandals. Amelia had been on her best behavior. There had been no removal of shoes or other attire. She had not quaffed, sipped, or imbibed champagne. She had danced and conversed amiably about the weather. She'd been perfect.

Except for that one stolen kiss that had her reconsidering the virtues of being virtuous (she decided that, like subtlety, it was overrated). It was a kiss that had ended too soon.

She'd been left breathless and wanting more.

No one had noticed. The kiss, that is. Not that she was left breathless and wanting.

This was for the best. She couldn't help but marvel that Alistair *had* her in a perfect trap. He had lured her away, kissed her senseless, and anyone could have seen. He could have easily arranged for them to be discovered.

But he didn't.

It almost made her think that she could trust him after all.

"So, Amelia, did you enjoy the ball this evening?" Claire asked. It was an innocent question, but one look at her sister and she saw the sly insinuation in her eyes. *What had Claire seen?*

"Of course not," Amelia grumbled, lying. "I never do. Social affairs bore me to tears."

"How funny," Claire mused. "Because you seemed to have a lovely time. I saw you dancing, and conversing and taking air on the terrace . . ."

Amelia took a moment to grumble over perspicacious older sisters.

"You mean that she didn't cause a scandal," Bridget said. "For which I am so glad."

"Yes, I kept my dress on and everything," Amelia retorted.

"No, I mean that she spent most of the evening in the company of Mr. Alistair Finlay-Jones," Claire said.

Another moment lamenting perspicacious sisters was had.

"Was he the one you spent the day with?" Bridget asked, nudging her.

"I told you a thousand times, I'm not talking about That Day."

That Day was hers and hers alone. She cherished those memories of following her whims, roaming all over the city and finally feeling fully alive. And then there were the intimate, quiet moments in Alistair's flat where she lost herself but found him. No, these weren't things she wished to talk about with people who weren't there. Who weren't Alistair.

But that didn't stop her siblings from pestering her for details. Amelia didn't blame them for it; she would have done the same.

"At any rate, he is clearly in love with her," Claire said with such assurance.

"Not exactly," Amelia said. "He is only courting me for my dowry at the behest of his uncle, who is an old toad."

"To hell with fortune hunters," James grumbled. Amelia concurred.

"I met the uncle and he is an old toad," Bridget concurred. "His wife—his *young*—wife is quite nice though."

"We are not talking about some toady old baron and the young lady with the misfortune to be wed to him," Claire said. "We are talking about the young, handsome nephew who is in love with our sister. It's so very clear from the way he looks at you . . ."

"Can we not discuss men looking lustily at my sisters?" James said, pulling a face.

"I'm not betting my entire future on the way a man looks at me," Amelia said.

And that was the crux of it. She thought she and Alistair had shared something like love, something true and genuine and beautiful. But he'd had an ulterior motive with her from the beginning and had lied about it. So how was she supposed to trust him now? How were they even to have a happy life together if they wed only because of a looming scandal?

Every day that details of their exploits did not appear in the papers made her trust him a little more. Yes, there had been that vague mention, but it had clearly been reported by Lady B, whoever she was, and there wasn't enough information to compromise her.

He had stopped the kiss.

He had kept their secret.

He courted her, like a proper gentleman.

Every day that he courted her anyway, every kiss that wasn't discovered, made her fall for him a little more.

"But you admit he looks at you like he loves you?" Claire persisted.

Amelia mumbled something, again, about nagging older sisters.

Because yes, he looked at her like he was undressing her, pulling away one layer after another to reveal the woman underneath. And yes, he gazed at her with love and lust so plain she felt it warming her from the inside out.

"Why don't you just marry him already?" James asked, a bit exasperated with the conversation. "That'll be one sister off my hands."

Amelia had to laugh a little. Her sisters would spend an hour at midnight dissecting how a man might look at her, but James cut right to the heart of the matter.

"I'm not certain I trust his motives," Amelia said. And the sword of scandal hanging over her head did put a damper on romance. "I need someone to love me, for me, and not just my dowry. Because, you know, I can be difficult sometimes."

"Oh no," Claire said. But her lips were twitching with the effort to hide a smile.

"Occasionally I can be contrary."

"Never say," James deadpanned.

"And I sulk if I don't get my way."

"Whatever are you talking about?" Bridget asked, giving in to giggles.

"What if I am too hard to love?" Amelia cried. Ugh, she hadn't meant to say that! She didn't even know where the words had come from. It wasn't a conscious thought but just a feeling that had been lurking inside. But now that she gave voice to it, everything made sense.

She couldn't believe that Alistair could really truly love her. Because she was contrary, difficult, sulky, trouble . . . all those things. *And* she had a fortune that his uncle wanted. This was not a recipe for happy ever after.

But as soon as she said the words, her siblings dispelled the notion.

"Never that, Amelia," Bridget said sweetly, as Claire pulled her into her arms for a hug.

"If you were so hard to love," James pointed out, "would we really have put up with you all these years?" He lifted his brow, questioning.

"We could have left you in America," Bridget said, clasping her hand. "But we didn't."

"We were never going to leave you," Claire said. "Don't listen to her."

"We love you, Amelia, even though you cause trouble," James said. "And we Cavendishes stick together, even when it's hard to do so."

And that was the other thing: For all that her siblings vexed her, she was dismayed at the prospect of being separated from them, dismayed at losing *this*. If she married—if they married—there wouldn't be any more of this.

Chapter 20

In which our hero resorts to bribery.

This time, when he called on the Cavendish family, Alistair was ready. It had become clear to him that in order to win Amelia's heart, he would have to gain the approval of her family.

Having grown up without much family to speak of, he longed to join the ranks of the Cavendish clan, and yet they terrified him all the same. James said little but missed nothing. Claire was reputed to be more intelligent than half the ton. Bridget was known to speak her mind freely. And Amelia was unpredictable. And then there was the duchess of Durham, who had been terrifying the haute ton for decades.

Not being above bribery, Alistair arrived with gifts for the ladies.

For Lady Bridget, he brought a fine pen, saying, "Lady Amelia tells me that you love to write."

Reading her sister's diary was one of those things Amelia had chattered away about as they walked through the gardens at Vauxhall.

But Bridget's brows arched up high. "Does she now?"

Amelia just laughed; her sister clearly did not share her amusement.

For Lady Claire, he brought a new book on mathematics.

"I hope you haven't read it already. I also hope it isn't too simple. I had a look at it and was completely confounded, but that isn't saying much."

"No. This is wonderful, thank you," Lady Claire said. If he wasn't mistaken she seemed genuinely touched. He wondered if, as a lady, perhaps she wasn't encouraged in such pursuits?

For the duchess, he brought flowers: elegant hothouse blooms that had cost a small fortune, which he'd won off Lord Burbrooke in a card game at White's.

"Aren't you a charmer, Mr. Finlay-Jones," she murmured. "I am appreciative of the gesture but not at all fooled."

"It's really just bribery," he said honestly.

For Amelia, he brought one orange. He grinned as he tossed it to her. She caught it easily and smiled.

"I don't suppose that has some significance,"

Claire said. "Some secret, romantic significance known only to the two of you."

"I don't suppose I would tell you if it did," Amelia replied.

"I don't suppose that I would read about it in your diary," Bridget said. "Oh wait, you are too busy reading mine to write your own."

"Dear Diary, Lord Darcy and I—"

"Amelia!"

Alistair watched the back and forth—teasing comments, sly grins, a spark of amusement to reveal that it was really all in good fun and there was no love lost.

"Hush, you two," Claire chided her sisters. "We have a guest. A gentleman guest whom I'm guessing Amelia does not wish to be embarrassed in front of."

"It is actually heartwarming to see such familiar banter," he said. "It wasn't something I had much experience with growing up."

"Wrotham isn't known for being lighthearted, kind, or humorous," the duchess said.

Alistair did not correct her. But it felt wrong to completely malign the man.

"He has his faults. But he has also done right by me. Wrotham took me in when I had nowhere else to go."

Even though Wrotham had made it clear it was only some notion of duty and appearances, not because he actually wished to do so.

"How good of him," Claire said. Then, grinning, she added, "We were just speaking the other night about leaving Amelia behind because she is such trouble."

"Claire!"

"He should know what he is getting into with you," Claire said with a loving smile.

"I already have an idea," Alistair added.

"Is that so?" the duchess arched one brow. *Shit.* He should not have said that. He glanced at the duke, who was *not* pleased.

"And yet here you are," Bridget said, eyeing him.

Aye, he knew about Amelia, for better or for worse, and here he was trying to bribe and charm and court his way into her heart.

"And here I am, listening to the lot of you talk about me as if I weren't here," Amelia said crossly.

"What did I tell you about ladies being seen and not heard?" the duchess said flatly . . . though . . . was that a glimmer in her eye? Was she teasing?

"I have no idea, Josie," Amelia replied flippantly. "I'm sure I wasn't paying attention that day."

By some miracle, they found themselves alone in the foyer as he was taking his leave. The tension, the something between them was real. He could feel it. The look in her eyes said she could too.

With no one looking, he tugged her close for

a kiss. Lips colliding, a sharp intake of breath, the soft murmur of surrendering. The quick, passionate sort that is not nearly enough but everything all at once.

Alistair stopped, reluctantly.

His heart was pounding.

Amelia pressed her fingertips to her lips and smiled.

A short while later, Alistair left Durham House feeling . . . happy. Like he'd found the place in the world where he wanted to belong and where he had a chance of doing so. He felt happy, like he'd found love. Like everything might work out after all.

This, of course, foretold doom.

Later that afternoon

Amelia had been on her way to her bedchamber to change her dress *again* in preparation for their evening out when Bridget cornered her. She was still tingly and daydreaming from that all-too-quick kiss from Alistair and was not exactly thrilled with an interruption from her sister about an orange.

"He brought you an orange," she said, stating the obvious.

"Yes. It looked delicious, did it not?" Amelia eyed it, appraising it. "I can assure you that it was."

"It must have some significance," Bridget pressed.

"It does," Amelia said gravely. Just to vex her sister more. Sometimes there was nothing more enjoyable than that. Except, maybe, making love to Alistair, which is something she tried not to think about.

She thought about it frequently. Her cheeks were often pink.

"You really aren't going to tell me, your dearest beloved sister?" Bridget smiled and put her arm around her.

Amelia took a moment to pretend to consider it. Then she grinned. "Annoying you with a secret is just so much more fun for me."

"But you don't deny that I am your dearest beloved sister," Bridget pointed out.

"You are one of them," Amelia called out as she walked away. "Top two, certainly."

First the posy of violets and then the orange did indeed have significance. Both were reminders of their one special day when she could just be Miss Amy Dish, finishing-school escapee, and he could just be Mr. Finlay-Jones, man about town with a pretty girl. Before she knew that he had been assigned to follow her, woo her, wed her. Before her guard had gone up (though perhaps it ought to have gone up sooner).

Either way, here she was with an orange and a posy of violets pressed between her tattered copy of *Burton's Guide to London*. Perhaps, most important of all, Alistair had been here as well, courting her properly and charming her family. He kissed her and stopped before anyone could catch them and demand a wedding.

Her grudge began to falter.

In which everything goes wrong.

A few days later

Everything was going so well. His efforts to woo Amelia were being met with some success— there was that waltz, that kiss, the way they couldn't help but banter.

And *he* was falling for her more and more.

There was that waltz when he was all too aware of her and was reminded of what it felt like to make love to her. There was that kiss; it took all of his self-restraint to end it. There was the way they laughed and teased and she always said what she was thinking. The way he could not stop thinking about her.

When he saw her at the Marleton ball, Alistair knew he had to marry her. It was no longer about orders or wants, but an aching need to have her in his bed, in his life, as his wife.

The entire Cavendish clan greeted him warmly. He was not certain if it was because

they genuinely liked him or because they genuinely liked teasing Amelia about him. Probably
a bit of both.

But he was especially glad of the kind recep-
tion; he started thinking about speaking to the
duke of his intentions to wed Amelia.

He had some notion of doing so without giving
away their secret. Alistair dared to hope that
perhaps he could have his cake and eat it too—a
love match with Lady Amelia and earning the
baron's approval and forgiveness. He could save
the Wrotham estate and make love to Amelia. It
was almost too good to be true.

That should have been his first clue.

His second clue was Wrotham. The baron was
also in attendance this evening. Alistair waited
until Wrotham was engaged in conversation
with someone before he went over to say hello—
one must keep up appearances by conversing at
public functions. But one might also choose a
moment when an acquaintance was present to
prevent overly familiar conversation.

Wrotham gave Alistair a snide smile. Alistair
felt a knot of despair. They were family. And
yet, they were not. Not like Cavendishes were
family—Alistair glanced over and saw them
standing in a pack, chattering and laughing happily amongst themselves. He promised a waltz
to Lady Amelia and couldn't wait for it to begin.

But first, familial duty.

He exchanged pleasantries with Wrotham, who then introduced him to one Lord Shrewsbury, who was a tall, gray-haired dandy. He had a monocle.

"This is Mr. Finlay-Jones. My"—the baron coughed as he said—"heir."

"Ah, the nephew who has been traveling," Shrewsbury said, surprising Alistair. He couldn't imagine that he had any knowledge of Alistair's existence, let alone interest in his activities. And yet: "And where have you traveled, young man?"

"Paris, Vienna, Rome. India." Alistair rattled off places.

"Ah. I see." Lord Shrewsbury peered at him through the monocle. Alistair was not quite sure what he saw, but had the distinct impression it was not good."

"But he's back now, ready to resume his place in society," Wrotham said.

"Ah. I see," Lord Shrewsbury said again. "You have been courting one of the Cavendish sisters, have you not? There has been gossip."

And now it was Alistair's turn to see: this Lord Shrewsbury was the rare breed of male gossip who trucked in the goings-on of all and anybody but himself.

"It was my idea," Wrotham said.

Alistair hated that his romantic status was being discussed so casually, as if a mere tidbit of information to be traded. As if it wasn't his future happiness. More than that, Alistair *hated* that that was true. The courtship had been Wrotham's idea. And Alistair couldn't lie and say that potentially earning the baron's approval by wedding a woman Alistair happened to love wasn't a fact.

"Given all the gossip about the Cavendish family, I daresay those girls will need to make splendid matches. Yes, their brother is a duke, but . . ."

Lord Shrewsbury did not need to finish his sentence to make himself understood. Not even a lofty title could make one forget that James Cavendish spent most of his life mucking around in horseshit. Hardly dignified.

Alistair was tremendously relieved when he heard the orchestra start to play a new song, providing him an excellent excuse to quit this conversation.

"Excuse me. I promised this waltz to Lady Amelia."

"And she's the most scandalous one of them all," Shrewsbury murmured.

Something happened as Alistair crossed the ballroom. Something terrible and tragic. Something called *logic* and *reason* took hold of his brain.

Truth: *The Cavendishes were scandalous.*

Truth: *Alistair was hardly good ton.*

Truth: *Together they would only drag each other down socially.*

When Alistair thought of Amelia's kiss, or the way she always seemed to be smiling, her enthusiasm, the way her body felt against his, then there was no choice—he had to marry her. It was a driving need.

But when he considered the truth of their situation, he realized that in spite of her kiss, or her sense of humor and delight in the world and the way her body felt against his, they might never be truly happy.

He wanted her to be truly happy.

Alistair looked back over his shoulder at Wrotham; that was a mistake.

The baron was smiling. Like he'd already won.

Another truth hit Alistair between the ribs.

If he married Amelia now, it would be so he could settle his debts with Wrotham. Hell, he would be forever settling debts. The baron would press upon Alistair the need for some of her dowry. A repair here, a tradesmen's debt there. Repayment for years of schooling, etc. Would the baron lord it over them that their match had been his idea? He was the kind of man who would expect their eternal gratitude and their firstborn son named in his honor. What snide and stupid remarks would the baron make at family suppers that would forever cause strife between husband and wife?

All because of Elliot's death, which had been Alistair's fault.

In an effort to repay one debt, would Alistair then incur another, to Amelia for saving him with her hand in marriage and fat dowry? Would he owe her, too?

She deserved better than all that, better than him. He loved her, yes, but how could he move forward to his future when his past had such a tight grip around his present? Could a social outcast like himself make a woman on the edge of scandal happy?

"Alistair, there you are!"

He took her hand. *He shouldn't take her hand.*

They started toward the space allotted for dancing.

He glanced around. It seemed everyone was staring and whispering. It would always be like this, would it not? She was prone to scandal and he would never have the clout to make everyone overlook it. They would be miserable outcasts.

He could not do that to her. Alistair would not ruin the rest of her life. Instead, he would ruin her evening.

"I'm sorry, Amelia, I cannot. I must go."

Alistair was accosted by Darcy on his way out.

"Alistair—" Darcy's voice echoed in the foyer. Darcy also happened to have the voice that one physically could not disobey.

He turned around, even though he was anxious to loosen his cravat and get the hell out of this ballroom, this house, the high society that he did not belong in.

"What was hell was that?" Darcy asked.

"Nothing."

Darcy disregarded that.

"You abandoned Lady Amelia before a dance. You left her stranded in the middle of the ballroom. It is not the done thing. I'm given to understand that women do not care for it."

"I have to go. I don't belong here, Darcy."

"Alistair—"

But he had already turned on his heel and stepped out into the night.

Chapter 21

In which our hero finally understands.

There was a letter from the baron the next morning. It was, predictably, another sparsely worded note demanding Alistair dropped everything and come pay a visit for what would certainly be a setdown after what had happened last night.

Even though he was a grown man.

One who ditched women in crowded ballrooms and fled from parties.

No, he was a grown man who recognized the truth of the situation and placed long-term happiness over short-term satisfaction. For once.

The truth, as he saw it, was that he didn't deserve her. He couldn't ruin her life by marrying her and bringing along an insufficient social status to allow her to be herself, and an uncle who would sponge off them until the day he died.

This was for the best.

Even if it felt like the worst.

But it was about to get worse, he thought, knocking on the door at number seventeen Curzon Street. Then staring into the butler's blank expression. Then demanding an audience with Wrotham.

When the butler disappeared to check with the baron, Alistair cooled his heels in the foyer. It was there that he encountered the baroness as she descended the stairs. There was no hiding the fact that she had been crying.

When she saw him, she said, "If he hated you less, this might be easier for me."

"What do you mean?"

He honestly didn't know.

"Never mind," she said dismissively. Alistair eyed her, perplexed, as she took a deep breath and forced a smile.

"Calling hours," she explained. And with that, a footman opened the doors to the drawing room and she swooped in, ready or rather "ready" to receive visitors. What had just happened? What was she about?

The butler returned then, leading Alistair to the baron's study. He grew up visiting this house and knew the way by heart. He would one day be lord and master of this house. And yet, he was still treated like a guest.

No wonder he never settled anywhere, or knew what *home* truly felt like.

Knowing that the baron, seated behind the desk, would not acknowledge him—not where there were missives to peruse and opportunities to make Alistair feel small and insignificant, Alistair spoke first.

"Your wife seems upset."

Not that Alistair was one to speak about upset females. He had left Amelia standing alone in the ballroom. He had walked away without a word. And why?

"She has failed me again," the baron said witheringly. He turned his attentions back to the paper in his hand. A second later he crumpled it in his fist and slammed it down on the desk. "An heir. All I need is an heir! She has one task. One task. And every month she fails me again."

Ah. And now Alistair understood the tears in the foyer.

"It might not be her fault."

"Well it certainly isn't mine."

Of course it wasn't. How *dare* Alistair make such a suggestion. But while he was making unwelcome observations, he made one more.

"You have an heir, Wrotham."

Look at me. See me. Be family to me. Love me. Hell, just try to like me.

The baron laughed. "I have *you*." He laughed again. "A half-breed wastrel who does nothing but gallivant around the continent. You're useless. You don't fit into society. You don't know anything about managing an estate. You can't even make a match with the laughingstock of London society. You can't even get through a waltz with the girl."

The baron laughed again. Alistair just stood there, barely managing the basic functions of survival, like breathing, or having a heartbeat. He wanted to protest, but he could not, for every accusation was true. He was a half-breed wastrel who had spent his adult life traveling from here to there with no purpose or destination. He did not fit into society. He did not know anything about estate management; it had never been in his course of study. And no, he could not make a match with Lady Amelia, he hadn't been able to muddle through a waltz and he raged at the way the baron spoke of her.

He raged at all of it. The laughter. The smugness. The refusal to recognize they were *family* for better or for worse. The refusal to recognize that he too was grieving. The refusal to see him as a human, worthy of consideration.

"So yes, Alistair. I need an heir."

"But you haven't much to leave to an heir now do you? Just a mess of debts and a tangle of entailed estates. And what will it matter to you, anyway? You'll be dead."

The baron paled. It was the first time Alistair had even spoken sharply to him.

And then Alistair understood. Finally, he understood.

"You don't want an heir," he said softly. "You want Elliot back."

The baron, tellingly, looked away.

"You will never forgive me for my role in his death. And I deserve that. I will never forgive myself either."

The baron said nothing, yet still managed to speak volumes. Alistair wasn't ordered to stop, or get out. There was no laughter. Finally, Wrotham was listening. Finally, Alistair knew what to say. He kept talking.

"And nothing I can do will ever bring him back, or ease the pain or repay that debt."

Alistair spoke now for himself more than anything. He hadn't realized these truths until this moment, when he spoke the words.

Elliot's death had been a terrible, tragic accident.

Could it have been prevented? Possibly. But if it wasn't that carriage race, it might have been another. Could Alistair go back and change anything? No. He had to find a way to live with the way things were.

He could continue to blame himself—and take the baron's blame—but to what end? There was no point in trying to win the baron's favor. He'd never ever had it. And the baron would never bestow it, for reasons that were simply beyond Alistair's control.

"I won't do it anymore. I won't even try."

Already he felt lighter. Freer. Sad, but no longer strangled by an impossible task hanging around his neck.

"But we *need* you to marry. The estate needs the money . . ." Wrotham continued in a hollow voice, as if Alistair had never spoken, as if such truths and revelations had not been revealed, as if nothing had changed. And nothing *would* ever change if Alistair carried on in the same way; the baroness would still be distraught, the baron would still be fixated on his absent heir, and his increasing debts, and Alistair would still be some traumatized good-for-nothing failure. No, things could not stay the same. They had to change, starting now. This moment. With this choice.

He would no longer live his life, making every effort to earn Wrotham's favor. Even if it meant he would not marry Lady Amelia.

Chapter 22

In which something changes everything.

$\mathcal{A}$melia had not seen Alistair in days. Her last glimpse of him had been his back as he walked away, leaving her by herself in the middle of the ballroom, even as she called out to him.

That was awkward, as was returning to her family and explaining that Alistair had simply left her without explanation.

That was embarrassing.

No one knew what to say.

That was humiliating.

Then the days went by without word from him. Not one. He simply vanished.

That was heartbreaking.

Every time she thought of him leaving her in the lurch, she felt sick. In fact, she felt sick and tired more often than not these days. This she attributed to relief; she had nearly fallen in love and wed a scoundrel who had used her, tempted her, and then left her without explanation.

She was *lucky* to be free of him. Or so she tried to tell herself. In his absence—during which she didn't receive one letter, or read a mention of him in the gossip columns or see him across a crowded ballroom—she missed him so much that she wondered that maybe it wasn't the most unforgiveable thing if he had seized an opportunity to spend the day with her.

He was gone. Just as suddenly as he'd arrived in her life, he was gone. He charmed her, seduced her, *made her believe* and then left.

Scoundrel.

Jackanape. Bounder. Cur. Rogue. Wanker. Amelia muttered all the unladylike swear words she had learned back home, from sailors on the ship during the crossing, and from the stable hands and even James when he was angry. None of them made her feel better.

She knew why Wrotham wanted Alistair to marry her—money was always an easy motive to understand. But what she didn't know was why Alistair would even try to honor such a request.

Had she been feeling more like herself, she might have plotted ways to find him and compel him to tell her everything. But instead, she languished. And cast up her accounts.

Josephine found her in her room, being sick. When

Amelia hadn't come down to breakfast, the duchess herself came to check on her personally. This was significant. As far as Amelia knew, the duchess was not in the habit of strolling into other people's bedchambers, uninvited and unannounced. That was something done only by ill-bred people, prone to informal behavior. It was something Amelia did, when she was feeling more like herself.

Amelia warily glanced up, expecting pursed lips or a frown. She had tried to hide and had been caught. Surely, she was in big trouble now.

"Either last night's supper doesn't agree with you, or you snuck out for a night of debauchery," Josephine said. She sat on the bed and smoothed out her crimson skirts.

At the mention of food or debauchery, Amelia heaved again.

"Although," the duchess said thoughtfully, "no one else is ill."

Amelia shifted her position. She had her suspicions about what had happened and when and how; she just didn't know how to say it.

Out loud.

To someone like the Duchess of Durham.

She really missed her mother right now.

"You have been quite subdued lately," the duchess continued. By subdued she meant too exhausted to cause much trouble.

"I think we both know what is happening," Amelia said. Thanks to a maid back home who believed that young ladies should be informed, Amelia knew.

"You are with child."

"I think so," Amelia mumbled. She bowed her head. Unwed ladies were not supposed to get with child. It was the worst thing that could happen. This would certainly cast the family in shame and ruin them all. She would have a child and bring it up in shame, all because Amelia had fancied a spot of fun one day.

It had been just a lark of a day!

How was she to know it would alter her life permanently, forever? The enormity of the consequences of it made her sick all over again.

"I know I am being punished for running away. And . . ." Well, she couldn't quite bring herself to say what, though it was clearly apparent what she had done. "I made a mistake. And now I'm paying for it."

There was a rustle and swish of skirts as the duchess dropped to her knees on the floor beside Amelia. She smoothed Amelia's hair back and pulled her close.

"It is not a mistake," she whispered fiercely. "Don't ever say that."

That was not what Amelia expected her to say. It might have been the last thing she expected to hear. But it was welcome. So very, very welcome. "Sometimes," the duchess continued, "a family comes to you when it's time, not when you

planned it. And it may seem like a disaster"—
Amelia suspected the duchess was talking about
her and her siblings now. "But it isn't. It's just . . .
right."

"There will be a scandal."

"Shh . . ." The duchess—Josie, she could certainly call her Josie now—just held her. She
wasn't the maternal sort, and the hug was a bit
stiff and awkward, but she was trying. And that
was everything, because Amelia needed some
mothering at a moment like this.

"And Alistair left."

Her voice cracked. She tried to hold back a sob.
He left! And she was crying over him!

"You are lucky, Amelia, and don't you forget
it."

Amelia peered up at the duchess and didn't
see the fearsome Duchess of Durham who terrified half the ton. There was just a woman, on
the floor beside her in her hour of need, doing
her best to comfort her. Amelia couldn't entirely
see how she was lucky right now—a baby without a wedding ring was an unprecedented level
of trouble for her—but there was something in
Josie's eyes and voice that made her believe that
this little thing inside of her was a good thing
and not just something making her heartsick
and just plain sick.

"What am I going to do, Josie?" Amelia asked,
leaning against her.

She stiffened a bit, presumably not quite used to moments like these. Then she softened.

"Well, as I see it, there are three options," she began. "First, you can marry the father."

"Who has left me. And disappeared. What is the next option?"

"You can quickly bamboozle another man into marriage and hopefully convince him that the babe is his," Josie said. "It's done all the time."

Amelia heaved once more.

"Or you can go live at one of our country estates with your child. You won't be able to return to society, though. Your brother and sisters and I can come to visit."

This would be her way out.

No more shoes that pinched, frilly dresses, or late nights spent waltzing. No more calling hours or endless conversations about the weather. She could wear breeches and ride astride and do whatever she pleased. She and the child could have adventures, play games, and enjoy life together away from the judging eyes of society.

But there would also be no more teasing with her siblings or kissing Alistair or the hum of city activity. She wouldn't have someone to marvel over the child with, except, perhaps a stern old housekeeper and straight-faced butler (it seemed all housekeepers were stern and all butlers were straight-faced). She may not have loved the social whirl, but she was a person who thrived on company and activity.

And *family.*

"And perhaps, in time, your child will be able to make his or her debut," Josie said. "We could certainly manage some sort of match."

Amelia could just imagine what it would be like for the bastard child of the scandalous American hoyden who became a recluse and was known to wear breeches, ride astride, and otherwise buck convention. It would be a mighty challenge for a child who should have every advantage and yet would spend its life at a disadvantage because its mother decided to have a spot of fun one day with a scoundrel.

She already wanted more than "some sort of match" for her child.

She did not want "some sort of match" for herself, either.

What did she want?

"You do not have to decide this now," Josie said. Indeed, it was not a decision to be made whilst casting up one's accounts. But it was a decision that would have to be made *soon.*

But she did not feel old enough to decide people's fates on her own.

Amelia found herself longing for Alistair.

Who had not come to call in days, after mysteriously leaving her for reasons he did not deign to explain.

Men.

She did not understand them.

Fortunately, she had a brother who did.

In which our heroine questions
her brother about men.

Later that afternoon

Amelia found James in the stable, even though he was told time and again that dukes were not to muck about in stables. They were above all that and had Important Ducal Matters (whatever those were) that required their attentions. That was just one of the things about being a duke that James disregarded. He knew what he loved, what he was good at, and he stuck with it. That was one of the things she admired about him.

She found him in a stall, brushing one of the mares, Cassandra. She came with the title. Amelia joined them both.

"I need you to explain men to me," she said, apropos of nothing.

James looked heavenward and did that thing he did where he muttered about the injustice of having to be responsible for three sisters, one of whom who thought nothing of joining him in a small confined space with a large, powerful animal to ask him the simple question of explaining half of humanity.

"I'm a simple man," he said, pausing in his work and turning to face her. "I like horses. Women. A good whiskey. And yet I constantly find myself besieged by sisters. And female problems."

He resumed brushing the mare.

"My heart bleeds for you. But I came to discuss *my* problems. My problems with men."

"When I look at you, I see a girl of eight who fell out of a tree trying to rescue a kitten. That she had placed there in the first place." Ah, Millie. Turns out she was not a climber. "She is too young to have men problems."

"Be that as it may," Amelia said, using a lovely, polite way of saying, *I hear what you are saying and it is completely irrelevant to my agenda*. She had learned it from the duchess. "I am a grown woman of two and twenty years and I have men problems. Well, a man problem."

"Thank God it's singular," James said. Then he set down the brush and sat on an overturned bucket—hardly ducal, that—and asked, "What is it?"

"Alistair has vanished. Without word or explanation. Why?"

She had considered the matter extensively, between sleeping and being sick, and decided that if she knew *why* he'd disappeared she could determine *how* to proceed with deciding their collective fates.

But asking Alistair himself was complicated. Because he had vanished without word or explanation.

"Well, as I see it, there are two possible reasons," James said. "No, three."

"Do tell."

"The first is that he is a horrible, irredeemable scoundrel who uses young women and abandons them to dire fates," James said. "It's been known to happen."

"What are the other reasons?"

"Another is that he is dead in a ditch somewhere." James paused. "It has probably happened, though not as frequently as it has been cited as a reason for a man's disappearance."

"And the third?"

"You'll have to ask him." James picked up the brush and carried on with tending to the mare.

"That is all!? Dead, scoundrel, or I have to ask him myself? *Those are the reasons?*"

Outraged. She was Just. Plain. Outraged. She'd half a mind to kick that bucket in frustration, but she didn't want to startle the horse. James just shrugged and said, "That's men for you."

"I am disappointed. Or infuriated. I'm not certain which, but it is one of the two."

"At least we're simple. Unlike women . . ."

Pfft. If she weren't in the throes of a romantic

crisis that would determine the fate of her entire life, she would argue that point. Priorities. She had them.

But . . . she couldn't resist needling her brother.

"Having women troubles, are you James?"

"I thought we were discussing your problems with a man," he replied. She took that as a *yes*. "Look, Amelia. You're young. You have time to let things happen. There is no need to rush."

"But there is a reason to rush . . ." she whispered.

That got his attention. He looked at her closely.

"Are you saying what I think that you are saying?"

She nodded yes. She could chatter for hours with a brick wall, but this was one hard word to say to her beloved older brother.

"What should I do, James?"

And then he said something that surprised her. "I have no idea, Amelia." Then he pulled her into his arms for a hug and said something that was muffled by her hair but that sounded a lot like, "But it should be something that makes you happy."

Chapter 23

In which our hero finally (and reluctantly) confronts his demons.

White's

So you see, I cannot marry Amelia because it will just be to repay my debt to Wrotham," Alistair explained to an audience consisting of Darcy, Fox, and Rupert. They were at White's, idly playing cards and drinking brandy. He might have been talking for some time now, judging by the bored expressions on his companions' faces. "It was his idea, his order. And that won't change anything! What kind of man am I if I just do another man's bidding and drag an innocent woman into it? Not a man who should marry."

Fox knit his brow and spoke slowly.

"I know I'm not the sharpest tool in the shed,

but you're going to need to explain this once more."

"No, he doesn't." Rupert cut him off. "Because what he's saying is absolute rubbish. If he actually believes this, then Lady Amelia is better off without him."

"I don't think that Lady Amelia is better off without him," Darcy stated. "In fact, I think Lady Amelia is deserving of a marriage proposal from you, immediately, regardless of what *feelings*, which you attempt to disguise as logic, that you profess."

This was punctuated by a pointed look that said: You Compromised Her. Propose. That Is All.

No one at the table disagreed with Darcy.

Alistair blinked once, twice, taking it all in. The brutal honesty was breathtaking and it was a moment before he was even able to form words. Given the lack of air to his brainbox, Alistair didn't even have a good reply.

"Are you calling me a coward?"

"It would seem so," Darcy said evenly.

How dare he call him a coward! Scared, foolish, stupid . . . his blood went from a simmer to a boil. He was *not* a coward. He was a rational man explaining his logical decisions. Darcy was such a know-it-all and it was time someone put him in his place.

"I should call you out for that," Alistair said

hotly. Rupert raised a brow. Fox looked intrigued at the prospect of a fight.

Darcy wasn't the slightest bit ruffled. "Are you calling me out for a slight to your honor, as a gentleman? A gentleman who will not propose to a lady when a proposal is in order?"

Alistair lunged for his friend. Fox was quick to hold him back.

"What is your meaning with all this?"

"I am trying to get you to see that you are throwing away true love for some stupid, cowardly reasons," Darcy said.

"If someone as reserved as Darcy is talking about true love and whatnot . . ." Fox said.

"Darcy is beginning to get soft," Rupert added. "The American influence . . ."

Darcy gave his brother an annoyed glance.

"See, even the Darcys of the world can fall in love and think of wedding one of those American Cavendishes."

"If I had Darcy's status and reputation . . ." Alistair muttered, settling back into his seat.

"Ah, and now we get to the heart of the matter," Rupert said.

"Lady Amelia is a scandal. I haven't the reputation to protect her. I am not enough of a gentleman."

"But you went to Eton. And Oxford," Fox said. "You know how to fence and can hold your brandy."

As if that was all it took to be an English gentleman.

"You count among your friends an earl, a marquis, and a baron, among others. You are to inherit an English title yourself," Darcy said.

"You are drinking and wagering and brooding at White's, for Lord's sake. Why do you think you don't belong?" Rupert asked.

"I am only *half* English," Alistair said. That other half Wrotham wouldn't let him forget—and he didn't want to forget it. But he didn't want the circumstances of his birth to be an impediment to love and acceptance.

"One's ancestry doesn't matter to people who matter," Darcy said softly.

Coming from Darcy, that was something. Hearing it spoken so plainly made him realize the truth. Alistair felt a swell of love for his friends—who loved and accepted him as he was. He even felt a surge of hope for his future with Amelia—who might love and accept him after all. He was a gentleman. And gentlemen proposed. And if she didn't accept, it was because of mistakes he'd made, not because of who he was.

And if the whole haute ton didn't accept them? To hell with them—he knew an earl, a marquis, and a duke who would stand by them.

"Is this the moment where we, uh, say something, professing, uh fondness for one's friends?" Alistair asked, happy, but also uncomfortable with the feeling that he should profess some emotion.

"God no, we're English gentlemen," Fox said. "We'll raise a glass instead."

Alistair returned to his flat as a new man. One with a purpose.

"Jenkins. We need to make me into a gentleman. I'll need a new suit of clothes and some books on estate management. I shall probably need a betrothal ring as well."

Chapter 24

In which disaster strikes.

*I*t is a truth universally acknowledged that a scandal will break at precisely the worst possible moment.

Amelia was with child and without husband when Bridget's diary went missing, which would not have been a problem if Bridget hadn't faithfully detailed the family's time in London, including, among other things, Amelia's great adventure.

Fortunately, Bridget didn't know the worst of it—Amelia's pregnancy was known only to her and the duchess and James. But nevertheless, Amelia saw her sister's anguish at her actions potentially causing the social downfall of the entire family. She herself felt it deeply.

It wasn't just the social standing that was at stake, but the Cavendishes' opportunity to marry

well, or to marry for love. Rumors and scandal
had a way of wrecking one's options.

It made Amelia think long and hard about her
own situation. She would have to decide, soon,
whether she should track down Alistair and
demand that he wed her, or dupe some unsuspecting gentleman into a quick trip down the
aisle. Or perhaps she should just give up and
rusticate in the country.

She didn't know what to do. But she did know
what she wanted: the best for her family, including the baby. She did *not* want to be the reason
for anyone's unhappiness.

Little did she know, that ship might already
have sailed.

**In which there is gossip. Delicious,
scandalous, outrageous gossip.**

Lady Esterhazy's Ball
Later that evening

Lady Esterhazy's ball was a crush. And in that
crush were members of the haute ton who had
just witnessed Lady Bridget make quite a scene,
as the Cavendishes were wont to do. Everyone was talking about her grand declaration of
affection—how embarrassing, how *American*—
for a certain English lord. They had also wit-

nessed something else . . . and they were also
talking about that something else . . .

"Those Cavendishes . . . it's just one scene and
scandal after another with them," Miss Randolph said to the *two* eligible gentlemen standing
with her. She was going on her third season now,
and *really* needed to snare a husband.

"That was quite the display tonight from Lady
Bridget," Lord Fraser agreed. It should be noted
that he was handsome, though deeply in debt.

"Usually it's Lady Amelia causing the embarrassing scene," Miss Randolph added. "Remember the night she was discovered without her
shoes? At a ball!"

They all shared a laugh over that.

"Why, just that coiffure alone is a scandal,"
Fraser added.

"Short hair on a woman. It's insupportable!"
Algernon added. He wasn't as handsome or as
smart. Or sober. But he was second in line for an
earldom, so he was not to be ignored.

Miss Randolph leaned in close to Fraser, with
the smile of one about to divulge a secret. "My
maid saw her getting it cut."

"When? And where?"

"Oh it was . . . a fortnight ago, or so. Something
like that. My maid saw her down near St. James's
Park."

"Wasn't that when she was ill?" Fraser asked.
His brain did that thing where it synthesized

disparate pieces of information to arrive at con-
clusions. Hard work, that.

"I haven't the slightest," Miss Randolph said.
"Perhaps."

"Then it makes more sense . . ." Fraser said.
Then he smacked Algernon on the arm and said,
"Remember that morning we were in St. James's
park and saw someone who we thought looked
like Lady Amelia?"

"No."

"You were still drunk, most likely," Fraser
said. "Wastrel, this one. Not like me. I thought
nothing of it at the time, but now that you mention it, that must have been her."

"But why would she be getting her hair cut off
down at St. James's Park?" Algernon asked.

"I beg your pardon, but I couldn't help but
overhear you discussing Lady Amelia Cavendish and the date she became ill." The conversation widened to include Lady Carsington. "The
date was June third. I know this because the
entire Cavendish family failed to attend the ball
I was hosting that night, owing to Lady Amelia's
mysterious illness."

Lady Carsington was clearly still bitter about this.

The group conferred and concluded these
events had all taken place on the same day.

There were gasps and murmurs as the implications of this were considered. Lady Amelia
Cavendish was in big trouble. Ruinous trouble.

"Now that I think about it, it was shortly after that day that my neighbor, Lady Boswell, came to tea with Lady Somerset and told me about the most curious thing," Lady Carsington continued. "There had been a brawl at Vauxhall, where she had taken her granddaughter, and she could have sworn that she saw someone looking like Lady Amelia running away from it. But the duchess would never allow that, so we thought it must be nothing."

"That brawl was mentioned in *The London Weekly*, just the other day!" Miss Randolph exclaimed. Everyone already knew this. But now *three* people had seen Lady Amelia out on the same day that she was supposed to be at home, ill. One person could be dismissed, two could be ignored. But three . . . then Miss Randolph spied someone she knew: "Oh, Lady Francesca! There you are. We were just talking about Lady Amelia Cavendish."

"I'm not in the mood for any more Cavendishes this evening."

"I don't understand," Algernon said. Francesca rolled her eyes and started to walk away, but doubled back when she heard Fraser's explanation:

"So it seems that a woman matching Lady Amelia's description was seen around town on the very day that she was supposed to be at home, ill."

"I daresay you have the right of it," Lady Francesca said with a malicious smile.

"And she was seen with a gentleman," Miss Randolph added.

That got everyone's attention.

"Why are you only telling me this *now?*" Lady Francesca grumbled. "Who was it?"

"My maid didn't know—he was of slightly above average height. Dark hair."

"Well that could be anybody," Algernon said, thoroughly exasperated by the whole conversation now.

Fraser, who was also of above-average height, with dark hair and debts in need of a bride's dowry, agreed.

It could be anyone.

Even him.

In which gentlemen are idiots. Or are they?

Even later that evening
White's

Fraser and Algernon followed the crowd of gentlemen from the ball, onward to White's, where the evening would continue with more drinking, gaming, and wagering—this time without young ladies and their chaperones around to ruin the fun.

Fraser leaned against the wall in White's, sipped his brandy.

"Why are you so quiet?" Algernon asked.

"I've been thinking."

"Lord help us."

"Lady Amelia is unwed."

"Last I heard."

"If what we learned about Lady Amelia is true—that she was out, unchaperoned, with a gentleman who has not wed her—then she is in *desperate* need of a husband."

"Yes but she's American," Algernon said skeptically. "She doesn't wear shoes to parties."

"Yes but she's a *rich* American. And now that Darcy is connected with the family . . ." Darcy had recently attached himself to the family, via Lady Bridget. *Darcy* was the living embodiment of a perfect English gentleman who was probably born wearing a perfectly starched cravat. Respectability for the scandalous Cavendish clan was sure to follow.

"So you have your eye on her do you?" Algernon asked, taking a sip of his brandy.

They were interrupted by Lord Burbrooke.

"Who do you have your eye on, Fraser?"

"No one."

"Lady Amelia Cavendish," Algernon said loudly. Heads turned. Other people listened.

"The American?"

"*Shut the hell up, Algernon.*"

Fraser's idiot friend did not listen. His insistence on silence only intrigued more people.

"The American who was seen out a fortnight earlier with a gentleman of above average height and dark hair," Algernon explained.

"Well that could be anyone," Burbrooke said.

Fraser groaned as comprehension dawned around the room. An heiress. Potentially ruined by a man who could have been anyone in this room. Except for Burbrooke, who was ginger. And Lord Patton, who was short.

Suddenly, things like a lack of shoes or a grating American accent seemed to matter less to the group of men who saw an easily attainable fortune.

Fraser quit the club immediately. He would have to be the first one to call the next day.

Chapter 25

In which our hero is too late.

The next day

Alistair was wearing his finest coat. His finest everything. He climbed into a curricle and picked up the reins. His heart was pounding. He was nervous, plain and simple. It wasn't every day that a man proposed to a woman.

Especially one whom he had left in the lurch.

There was a good chance that she would be angry, or refuse him. But that was a chance Alistair would have to take.

He loved her. He wanted to spend his life with her. Make a family with her. Just . . . love her. And that was the reason why he was going to propose. This time, neither Wrotham nor the past had anything to do with it. Alistair was ready for the future and he wanted a future with Miss Amy Dish or Lady Amelia Cavendish or whomever she chose to be.

With a snap of the reins he urged the horses to walk. A few minutes later, having given the matter extensive consideration, they acquiesced and started plodding their way toward Durham House.

Upon arrival, Alistair saw he was too late.

There was a pack of carriages parked before the house. He had to leave his own curricle and horses halfway down the block.

A visibly exasperated butler answered his knock—the merest sliver of emotion on a butler's face was *never* a good sign.

Alistair was shown into the drawing room. Amelia was there, along with her family. The room was packed with just about every known fortune-hunting rake in London.

And flowers. Good God, the flower arrangements. They were outrageous and numerous. And Alistair held a mere posy of violets.

It was, Alistair noted ironically, exactly the situation he had hoped to avoid: he was just another undistinguished man in a room full of fortune-hunting scoundrels. Only now it was worse: he had deceived Amelia and broken her heart and publicly humiliated her.

In which our heroine receives a proposal. Or four. Or more.

Meanwhile, in the basement

Amelia and her family were celebrating Bridget's recent betrothal to Darcy in the kitchens, because that is where the Cavendish siblings were often to be found—because that is where the cake was.

They were just toasting to the future happiness of Bridget and Darcy when Pendleton interrupted.

"There is a caller for Lady Amelia." He cleared his throat. "In fact, there are several."

"Define several," the duchess requested.

"A half dozen, at least."

Amelia exchanged confused looks with her siblings. She shrugged her shoulders as if to say, *I have no idea*, because truly she had no idea why on earth more than one gentleman had decided to come calling.

There were more than a dozen by the time she made herself presentable and found her way to the drawing room.

"What have you done now, Amelia?" the duchess murmured.

"I honestly have no idea," she replied.

"Do you want me to get rid of them all?" James asked. He flexed his fists, ready to throw punches. Brothers.

Before she could answer, a gentleman she didn't recall ever having met flung himself at her feet.

"Lady Amelia, ever since we spent that magical day together in St. James's park, I have been dying to make our love official. Marry me."

Oh. My. God.

"Oh my God," her sisters gasped.

"Oh dear God," the duchess said.

Amelia had been seen. Her secrets had been discovered. The scandal had broken. She glanced at the duchess, who had her I-don't-care-for-this-behavior expression. As if it were a mere lapse in etiquette and not the entire world crashing down around Amelia.

Amelia was jilted, with child, and about to be so thoroughly ruined she'd have to return to America.

Unless one of these men—she looked around the room warily at all these men—was her salvation.

"Oh get up, Fraser. It wasn't you," another gentleman said. "'Twas I who enjoyed an enchanting excursion with Lady Amelia and 'tis I would like nothing more than to make an honest woman out of her."

What the devil?

"I don't know what you're talking about," she told the men before her on bended knee. "I don't even know who you are."

"Darling . . ." one of them murmured as he reached for her hand.

"It was me . . ." another one said.

"It was me!" some other corkbrain yelled out.

Amelia glanced around the room, from one shouting gentleman to another. Many were strangers to her; quite a few she remembered as having snubbed her.

One of them was Alistair.

Her heart leapt upon seeing him among the crowd. And her heart leapt again when she remembered something he once told her: he seized the opportunity to spend the day with her because otherwise he would just be one of a dozen or more fortune hunters seeking her hand. He would have been indistinguishable from the rest. He wouldn't have stood a chance otherwise.

She had dismissed his concerns then, but now she saw what he had feared. Here he was in a room with a dozen or more fortune hunters, all of above-average height with brown hair, seeking her hand. He was taking a chance anyway.

"It was me," he said, loud and clear. Half the men ignored him and insisted *they* were the one to have squired her around all day.

She smiled, recognizing the truth of this farcical situation. With all these proposals, Amelia had a choice in her future. She had options.

She could marry any of one these dolts and salvage her reputation and that of her family.

There was surely an earl or impoverished marquis in the bunch. Maybe even a duke's brother. What they lacked in funds, they would certainly make up for in social connections.

Or she could, as the duchess suggested, live in a castle in the country.

Or she could marry Alistair because he was *here* and her heart skipped a beat when she saw him.

"It was me," he said again, eyes gazing deeply into hers.

"Finlay-Jones, you hadn't even returned from the Continent then," one of them retorted, before she could reply.

It was then that the brawl broke out. Fists flying, punches thrown, glass things shattering. The duchess immediately ushered the girls out of the room—alas!—and James and the footmen set out to stop the brawl.

Later, as Amelia toured the drawing room—which had been left in shambles—she found the violets Alistair had left behind. But where had he gone?

Chapter 26

$\mathcal{S}$trolling through Mayfair singing bawdy songs was far less embarrassing when one did it in a state of intoxication at a late hour. This Alistair learned later that afternoon as he strolled through Mayfair singing a certain bawdy song.

By "strolling through Mayfair" it should be noted that he really was pacing outside one particular house. Singing.

A country John in a village of late,
Courted young Dorothy, Bridget, and Kate,
He went up to London to pick up a lass,
To show what a wriggle he had in his a . . .

People passing by looked at him oddly. This was not typical behavior for a gentleman of the ton, which usually involved dressing up to stand around and complain about being bored. Alistair was done trying to fit in. He had a gentleman's education, gentlemen friends, and a gentleman's sense of honor. They would accept him or they would not, for reasons beyond his control. Only one woman's opinion mattered.

He looked up at all the windows of Durham House and wondered which was hers. Singing outside a woman's window may have been crazy, but it was also a standard course of action for a man in love.

Amelia pushed open the window and leaned out, wanting a spot of fresh air before the night ahead. She was supposed to be resting before the ball tonight—one which was sure to be a doozy after the events of the afternoon.

She heard singing. A man's low baritone.

She shivered. Memories.

Amelia leaned out, straining to hear more. She gasped and smiled when she heard the words. They were horribly inappropriate but held a certain significance.

A country John in a village of late,
Courted young Dorothy, Bridget, and Kate,
He went up to London to pick up a lass,
To show what a wriggle he had in his a . . .

A flash of memory: his voice, a warm summer night, leaning out the window, wanting. Feeling lured by his siren's song, calling out to her.

She didn't think twice about dashing down the corridor—another memory came back to her. Down the servants' stairs. Yes, it was coming back to her now. Outside, into the garden. Another memory.

He turned when he heard her approach. Seeing his face, seeing her—that was a memory to treasure forever. It was love and hope and everything she was feeling in her heart.

"Amelia."

"Alistair."

"I have come to ask you a question," he said.

"And I have a question for you," she replied, a slight smile. "Ladies first."

"Anything," he whispered.

"Why?" She waved her hand at the world at large. "Why did you travel so long? I know why you returned, but why did you even agree to try to wed a girl, sight unseen? Why did you still try to woo me after our day together? And why did you leave me on the dance floor that evening?"

"This is the part where I tell you about my secret pain," he said, with a half smile. "I was planning on this."

Amelia put her hand in his.

"Amelia, I am half English, half Indian. I am an orphan, raised by a man who never wanted me in his life. As such I have never felt like I quite belonged anywhere—not here, not India, not any of the places I visited on the continent."

"That is a feeling I can relate to," she said softly.

"I came to England at the age of eight. Wrotham's ward. I had a cousin, Elliot, who was the brother I never had and the strangely kind, generous, intelligent spawn of Wrotham. He died in a carriage accident. A race that I had challenged him to."

"Oh, Alistair . . ."

"Because *we were bored*, Amelia."

She thought of all the silly, stupid, foolish things she had done because she was bored. The list was long. She bored easily. But nothing had ever really come of it. No one had ever *died*.

For a moment, she imagined it. Felt it. Her heart ached for him.

"I left for the Continent shortly thereafter. There was nothing for me here. No one for me here."

"Oh Alistair," she sighed, full of empathy and heartache. How lonely he must have been. She squeezed his hand to let him know that she was still holding on to him.

"I felt I owed Wrotham anything. Everything. And if all he asked was that I court a pretty girl whom I quite liked . . ." He shrugged. "I couldn't say no. I was too desperate to belong, too desperate to earn his approval. But what kind of man did that make me? One who didn't deserve you. I love you, Amelia. I want you to be happy. And if it so happens that I do not deserve you, I want it to be your choice."

What was plain to see: he had conquered these demons for her. There was no greater romantic gesture than standing in the garden, speaking honestly, of what it took for him to arrive at this moment.

She held on to his hand, a little gesture that she hope conveyed everything in her heart: I love you. I am with you. I am yours.

It was so simple. So bloody simple to explain himself now that he *knew*. It only took some brutal honesty from friends, some reflection, some forgiveness.

Hours in quiet reflection.

Excruciating minutes in conversation with Wrotham, saying hard things that had needed to be said.

For this moment: Alistair could tell these truths to Amelia as an important formality to moving forward happily. It was no longer a painful wrenching of the truth from his soul. That had already happened.

He had suffered through it and persevered so at this moment, he could explain himself to the woman he loved, so that they had more moments after this one.

Now he was free to just love.

"I am now Wrotham's heir, a state of things he despises, which is completely understandable."

That was the thing: Alistair did understand. He couldn't paint his uncle as a villain and dismiss him. The man had suffered unimaginable pain. Though Wrotham would never admit it, he was a man with feelings.

"He is lucky to have you," Amelia said.

And that was why he loved her. Anyone else would see someone of questionable heritage, someone lacking the education to run an estate, the connections to make his way in society, and the money to make everyone forget all that.

And she thought Wrotham was lucky to have him.

He would be lucky to be with her.

"The other thing I have learned—confirmed, concluded, what have you—is that I love you, Amelia. Amy. Whatever your name is, I love you."

"I love you, too."

Alistair pulled her close, savoring the sweetness of her lips, the warmth of her body against his, the sensation of her in his arms. He never wanted to let go.

"I love you," he had to say it again. "You are home to me. I want to be your husband and have adventures with you. I want to have a family with you. I want—"

"That might happen sooner than you think," Amelia whispered.

It took a long moment before he fully understood. She was expecting. *They* were expecting.

The other day he had almost walked away from her, and their child, and his family because of his old fears, his old pain. The realization was chilling.

But then Amelia was warm in his arms, with their baby in her belly, and he wasn't too late after all. Then he laughed, a sound of joy. Because he had found love, earned love, and would treasure this love forever.

Then he pulled her close and held her tight. He felt her melt into him, so he wrapped his arms around her and held her close and whispered the words he'd wanted to say since the day they'd met: "I want to be with you, Amelia. Forever. Will you be with me?"

"Yes," she whispered happily. "Always. Forever."

Epilogue

White's
St. James's Street, London
A few years later

Of all the things that Alistair Finlay-Jones never expected, this was high atop the list: a conversation about which carriages best accommodated a growing brood of brats, with his friend and brother-in-law, James Cavendish, otherwise known as the Duke of Durham.

"Your curricle days are over, my friend," James said.

"I am glad of it," Alistair said.

"Shh. We are not supposed to admit to such aloud. Our manhood will be called into question."

"Well, speaking of my—" Alistair began, just to taunt him.

"Say no more," James said, holding up a hand. He was *still* an overprotective older brother.

Also, they were interrupted, by a not-unwelcome guest who stepped close cautiously and interrupted the conversation nervously.

"Alistair, hello."

He turned. "Hello, Wrotham."

"I was wondering if you received my missive."

"Yes. I just haven't had a chance to reply." Amelia kept him busy, along with their twins, who absolutely took after their mother, given their propensity to cause trouble. "But I am looking into the matter. Of course, I will have to confer with Lady Amelia."

"Right."

The three gentlemen exchanged an uneasy look, harkening back to the unconventional terms of the marriage contract. To put it simply: Amelia was to have a say in the spending of her dowry, right down to every last farthing. Wrotham didn't have the complete, unfettered access he had anticipated when he hatched his match-making scheme. But the Wrotham estate wasn't in a state beyond repair, either.

"The baroness has been badgering me about it," the baron said. He almost sounded *proud* to be badgered by his baroness. Quite a turn of events.

"Congratulations, again," Alistair said, meaning it completely. He'd been as happy as anyone when the baroness was safely delivered of a baby.

"It was just a girl . . ." Wrotham said, but there was no hiding his pride and joy. She wasn't his new heir, but she was his child and his chance to begin anew. "But make no mistake, the baroness assured me she has a strong kick. And you wouldn't believe the lungs on the girl. And . . ." The baron coughed. "She has Elliot's eyes."

Elliot, who was now a portrait. A memory. A link. And the name of Alistair's own son. He wasn't a ghost or a shadow, as he used to be.

"We will come visit soon," he promised.

"Please do," Wrotham said, clearly meaning it. Then he tipped his hat and nodded good day. They would speak later, and dine together regularly, and they would join the Cavendishes on the holidays, and Alistair would have more family than he had ever imagined.

"Now, what was I saying?" James asked. "Oh right, Mackle's new landau design is quite good. It can comfortably accommodate more than a few people."

"Ah, there you are, Finlay-Jones. Have you heard? Your wife . . ."

There was always a long pause after the words *your wife*. It was typically a long pause, owing to the person struggling to find the words to convey just what trouble Amelia was engaged in now.

"What has she done?" Alistair asked.

The man mumbled something about unconventional attire whilst riding at quite a clip in Hyde Park at an unfashionable hour. Alistair pushed his fingers through his hair. This was not *news* exactly. She had mentioned something about it this morning, but he had been preoccupied by the way her dressing gown kept slipping down her shoulder and then *she* had been preoccupied by him for the better part of a very pleasurable hour.

Alistair sipped the drink, thanked the man for telling him, and turned back to James, who just gave him a look.

"She's your responsibility now . . ."

She was *his* and she practically leapt into his arms when he arrived home a short while later.

"Alistair! You'll never guess what!"

"You wore breeches while riding hell-for-leather in Hyde Park at an unfashionable hour."

"How did you know?" She was disappointed not to be the first tell him.

"I heard a rumor . . ."

"I swore no one saw me . . ." She pursed her lips. "I shall have to practice the tricks we saw at Astley's during a weekend in the country then."

"You are hard not to notice, lady wife."

"Oh hush," she treated him to a quick flash of a smile and a spark in her brown eyes. "Do you know who is hard not to notice?"

"One or both of our children?"

"Yes. Both. They are such trouble. They must get it from you . . ."

"No, you . . ."

"This argument again?"

And so they teased and sparred on their way up the stairs to see their children in the nursery. But not without a little detour on the way, in which Alistair pulled Amelia in for a kiss; the kind he knew would leave her breathless and a little bit dizzy. Or maybe that was him. All he knew was that this was happiness: a kiss on the stairs, regardless of who might see. One stolen moment of many.

Keep reading for an exclusive sneak peek
at the third enchanting tale in
USA Today bestselling author
Maya Rodale's
Keeping Up with the Cavendishes series,

LADY CLAIRE IS ALL THAT

In which the mighty hath fallen

Lord and Lady Chesham's ballroom
London, 1824

It was a truth universally acknowledged that Maximilian Frederick DeVere, Lord Fox, was God's gift to the ladies of London. He was taller and brawnier than his peers, and in possession of the sort of dark and chiseled good looks that were more often found in works of classical art.

Everything about him induced sighs.

Fox strolled through the Chelsham's ballroom as if he owned it. He nodded at friends and acquaintances—Ashbrooke, with whom he fenced, and Fitzwalter, who he had soundly thrashed at boxing last week, and Willoughby, who was always game for a curricle race.

Fox flashed his famous grin as he heard the ladies comment when he strolled past.

"I think he just smiled at me."

"I think I'm going to swoon."

"God, Arabella Vaughn is one lucky woman."

"*Was*," someone corrected.

Fox's grin faltered.

That was when his friends Mr. Rupert Wright and Mr. Hugh Mowbray found him.

"We heard the news, Fox," Rupert said grimly, clapping a hand on his shoulder.

"I daresay everyone has heard the news," Fox replied dryly.

It didn't escape his notice that the guests nearby had fallen silent. They were watching him to see how he would react, what he would say.

"Who would have thought we'd see this day?" Hugh mused. "Miss Arabella Vaughn, darling of the haute ton, running off with an actor."

"That alone would be scandalous," Rupert said, adding, "Never mind that she has ditched *Fox*. Who is, apparently, considered a catch. What with his lofty title, wealth, and not hideous face."

Fox's Male Pride bristled. It'd been bristling and seething and enraged ever since the news broke that his beautiful, popular betrothed had eloped with some plebian *actor*. To lose a woman to any other man was insupportable—and until recently, not something that ever happened to him—but to lose her to someone who made his living prancing around on stage in tights? It was intolerable.

"Just who does she think she is?" Fox wondered aloud.

"She's *Arabella Vaughn*. Beautiful. Popular. Enviable. Every young lady here aspires to be her. Every man here would like a shot with her," Rupert answered.

"She's you, but in petticoats," Hugh said, laughing.

It was true. He and Arabella were perfect together.

Like most men, he'd fallen for her at first sight, catching a glimpse of her tall figure and golden hair from across a crowded ballroom. His breath had caught in this throat.

Fox remembered his heart racing—nerves!—when he proposed. He remembered the pride he felt as they strolled through a ballroom arm in arm and the feeling of everyone's eyes on them as they waltzed so elegantly. They were *great* together. They *belonged* together.

Fox also remembered the more private moments—stolen kisses, the intimacy of gently pushing aside a wayward strand of her golden hair, promises for their future as man and wife.

And she had eloped. With an actor.

It burned, that. Ever since he'd heard the news, Fox had stormed around in a high dudgeon.

"Take away her flattering gowns and face paint and she's just like any other woman here," Fox said, wanting it to be true. "Look at her, for example."

Rupert and Hugh both glanced at the woman he pointed out—a short, frumpy young lady nervously sipping lemonade. She spilled some down the front of her bodice when she caught three men staring at her.

"If one were to offer her guidance on supportive undergarments and current fashions and get a maid to properly style her coiffure, why, she could be the reigning queen of the haute ton," Fox pointed out.

Both men stared at him, slack jawed.

"You've never been known for being the sharpest tool in the shed, Fox, but now I think you're really cracked," Hugh said. "You cannot just give a girl a new dress and make her popular."

"Well, Hugh, maybe you couldn't. But I could."

"Gentlemen . . ." Rupert cut in. "I don't care for the direction of this conversation."

"You honestly think you can do it," Hugh said, awed.

Fox's Male Pride and competitive spirit flared. He turned to face Hugh and drew himself up to his full height.

"I know I can," Fox said with the confidence of a man who won pretty much everything he put his mind to—as long as it involved sport, or women. Arabella had been his first, his only loss.

"Well, that calls for a wager," Hugh said.

The two gentlemen stood eye to eye, the tension thick. Rupert groaned.

"Name your terms."

"I pick the girl."

"Fine."

"This is a terrible idea," Rupert said. He was probably right, but he was definitely ignored.

"Let me see . . . who shall I pick?" Hugh made a dramatic show of looking around the ballroom at all the women nearby. There were at least a dozen, of varying degrees of pretty and pretty hopeless.

Then Hugh's attentions fixed on one particular woman. Fox followed his gaze, when he saw who Hugh had in mind, his stomach dropped.

"No."

"Yes," Hugh's said, a cocky grin stretching across his features.

"Unfortunately dressed I can handle. Shy, stuttering English miss? Sure. But *one of the Americans*?"

Fox let the question hang there. The Cavendish family had A Reputation the minute the news broke that the new Duke of Durham was none other than a horse trainer from the former colonies. He and his sisters were scandalous before they even set foot in London. Since their debut in society, they hadn't exactly managed to win over the haute ton, either, to put it politely.

"Now, they're not all bad," Rupert said. "I quite like Lady Bridget . . ."

But Fox was still in shock and Hugh was enjoying it too much to pay any mind to Rupert, coming to the defense of the Americans.

The bluestocking?

That was the thing: Hugh hadn't picked just any American, but the one who was insufferably intelligent and seemed destined to be spinster.

Lady Claire had already earned a reputation of her own—for boring the gentlemen of the ton to tears by discussing not the weather, or hair ribbons, or gossip of mutual acquaintances, but *math*.

Even the legendary Duchess of Durham, aunt to the new duke and his sisters, hadn't yet been able to successfully launch them into society. And she'd already had weeks to prepare them. It seemed insane that Fox should succeed where the duchess failed.

But Fox and his Male Pride had never, not once, backed away from a challenge. It was an impossible task, but one that Fox would simply have to win.

"Her family is hosting a ball in a fortnight," Hugh said. "I expect you to be there—with Lady Claire on your arm as the most desirable and popular woman in London."